The Peacemaker's Patch

The Peacemaker's Patch

Shauna Leigh Richter

ISBN # 978-1-7778688-0-2
ISBN # 978-1-7778688-1-9 (e-book)

For everyone with a dream.
May you find what you need to bring it to life,
and have no regrets.

My name is Mona Lisa Brown. Yes, that's my actual name. A cruel joke my late parents played on me when I was born–probably trying to spice up our lackluster last name. Instead, it caused me no end of problems in grade school and aggravation anywhere my full name is required. As if the name Mona wasn't bad enough, they had to layer on 'Lisa,' eternally connecting me with a 16th-century oil painting that frankly, isn't that impressive. That pretty much sums me up–not that impressive. Five-foot-four inches tall, brown hair, brown eyes, one hundred and thirty-five pounds, give or take the week; average build, average intelligence. I blend in everywhere I go; there is nothing notable or memorable about me. And worse still: I can't stand conflict, so it's not like I am known for anything at all because I never have the courage to take a risk. It is far easier to change direction. This is me–nothing remarkable about my life. At least, this was true until I arrived in Buckley Brook, heralded as the home of Charles Theodore Baker Buckley, founder of the prestigious Buckley University in 1893. Buckley Brook: where my ordinary life became extraordinary.

CHAPTER 1

I rushed down the sidewalk, quickly scanning for the house numbers on the brick century homes that lined the street. This would be the eighteenth apartment I had seen over the last four days. They were all blurred together in my mind now. This had to work out, but showing up late was not going to help my chances. "Where is this place?" I muttered to myself, adjusting my backpack, which was still damp from the torrential rain the day before. My shoes were still damp, too. For half the day yesterday, there was a splorching noise with each step I took. I am sure showing up like a drowned rat in the rain with splorching shoes did not help my chances of renting any of those apartments. "Rent me the apartment. Of course I have enough money to pay the rent. I really do dry up nicely." I took a big breath and sighed to myself, "Thank goodness it has stopped raining today. It's a fresh start."

Finally, I saw number 26. The house was a red brick heritage home with an addition on the right side, making it very large. "I wonder how many apartments are in this house?" I said aloud, as I stared at the large building. A round face popped up out of the garden into my view, a bit too close for my liking.

"Five to be exact, well four–plus ours at the back. You must be Mona. I'm Ethyl Findler," she said in an all-business tone. She had been gardening. She dusted the earth from her hands by clapping them together aggressively and stuck out a chubby hand at me in greeting. We shook hello. She was certainly stronger than she looked. Ethyl was a short, compact woman, stocky in stature, about five feet tall. She looked like a short version of one of those shot put throwers you see every four years in the Olympics on TV; always looking surprisingly limber for their size. Her feet were small, like her hands and covered in black ankle boots that zipped up the middle and she had a well-worn brown leather bag slung across her left shoulder.

"Alright then, you are late, so let's get to it," she said.

"Yes, I am sorry, it . . ." I started to explain, but she was determined to keep things moving.

"As I said, this is a five-unit house. We are looking at the main floor unit today. Lovely unit really, just lovely. Shall we?" she asked. As I listened to Ethyl, I noticed that she had the most piercing green eyes. They were striking, next to her straight black hair, cut chin-length.

I followed Ethyl along a stone path through the garden toward the front door. A beautiful, wide staircase of six steps extended from the front porch that covered the entire front of the house. "Wow," I thought, imagining myself sitting on the porch on a warm sunny day. "What a great spot. It really expands the size of the apartment having this outdoor area."

Ethyl ascended the stairs a bit faster than I expected her to move in her floral dress. I hurried to keep up with her, but I realized as she stopped on the stairs that I hadn't been listening to the conversation. I stopped daydreaming and quickly snapped back to the present, trying to catch up and not look foolish. "We have owned this house for 38 years now. A lot of people have lived here, some real characters. I don't have time for funny business, you know, so you better not be bringing any funny business," she said, disapprovingly. She paused and looked at me over the top of her glasses. "What brings you to Buckley Brook?" she asked.

I paused to consider before answering. Buckley Brook . . . Buckley Brook. Is "Mona Lisa" actually going to move to Buckley Brook? If 28 years of being Mona Lisa Brown doesn't get you, just add 'of Buckley Brook' to the mix. I paused for another second to figure out how to respond to Ethyl's question.

"I'm tired of the pace in the city. My aunt used to live here and I would visit when I was young. I think it will be a nice change. I'm a bookkeeper. I think this town could give me the added option to continue my education part-time at the university."

She turned down her mouth and gave me a skeptical look. "And how are you funding this move from the city?" she asked, judgmentally.

Before I could answer, the storm door flew open and a massive man stumbled out of the door with a thud, clearly winded by whatever he had been doing. He was tall and lanky, well over six feet, wearing grey pants, a brown leather belt, and a collared plaid shirt. I could see a bit of white undershirt peeking out of his button-up. From the bottom of the steps, I noticed his extremely large brown loafers. They must have been size 14 or more. Noticing me, he adjusted his disheveled clothing and greeted me with a warm smile.

In a deep, warm voice, he said, "Well, hello, you must be here to view the unit. She's all fixed up and ready to move into. This apartment has seen a lot of miles. I remember when we first bought this place . . ."

"Now, now, Randy, let's not get sentimental," Ethyl cut in, giving him a look that conveyed she would take it from here. As we passed on the stairs, Randy gave me a mischievous smile and a wink. My eyes followed Randy as he headed down the stairs and lumbered along the path to the right side of the house. As I watched him, I couldn't help but smile. I turned to face

Ethyl and took notice of the garden. It was still early spring, but I could see little plants peeking through the ground. "I can see your garden is starting to come to life. I bet this is quite something to see in full bloom."

Ethyl smiled at me for the first time. "Yes, I love this time of year. This is my pride and joy. I spend hours here planting, weeding, and moving things around."

"My Aunt Audry had a beautiful garden. That's my best memory of Buckley Brook as a kid. We used to spend hours in the garden with Aunt Audry when we would visit."

Ethyl's grin widened and something changed in her demeanor. It's like her guard came down just a little as she said in surprise, "You are Audry's niece? She was a dear friend of mine. She owned a property up on Morgan's Way. We spent hours and hours playing cards and drinking her homemade lemonade in that garden. Oh, those lemons were so sour, but somehow Audry worked magic with them to make her famous lemonade. Do you know she started them from tiny plants inside in her solarium at the back of the house? What a labor of love. She was always fussing over those things, pruning and fertilizing. They really weren't suitable for our climate, but she was a miracle gardener. I was so sad when she had to sell that place and move away."

As quickly as it had come, the smile faded from Ethyl's face as she returned to the present and the task at hand. "All right then, let's take a look at this apartment," she continued, reverting to the businesslike tone of voice she had met me with earlier.

I paused at the top of the stairs to admire the covered porch that spanned the front of the house. This alone topped my shoebox apartment with no balcony in the city. The large front door was impressive. This must have been the front of the house at one time before it was segmented into apartments. What a house this must have been. As I walked inside, I was struck by the light pouring in through the large windows, the tall ceilings, gorgeous wood floors, and ornate wood trim still preserved after so many years. The house had a feeling of comfort and warmth, so different from my place in the city.

To the right of the front entrance was a very comfortable-looking sitting room. A huge window to the right of the door overlooked the porch. I could imagine spending a lot of time in this room, especially when winter came and the porch area was less inviting. The kitchen was on the far side of the room. I was surprised by such a modern layout in an older home. All the other apartments I had looked at in older homes were a series of small rooms. I could envision myself preparing dinner at the counter facing the sitting area and looking out into the garden. It would be a wonderful view while cooking. Maybe the surroundings would help my cooking abilities; doubtful, but at least I could wreck food in style.

To the left of the door, separated by a hallway, were two large bedrooms. Just inside the hallway to the left was a bathroom, which looked like it had been recently redone. There was a one-piece acrylic tub and shower on the outside wall. Since the ceilings in the house were so high, above it was a long narrow frosted window, which lit up the bathroom. The vanity looked new too, and had great storage with shelves inside and three stacked drawers.

At the end of the hall on the right was the door to what I presumed was the main bedroom. I was amazed that there would be room in the bedroom for a small sofa. The whole apartment felt huge compared to the city apartments. On top of that, there was something special about this place. "The house is in beautiful condition," I said, smiling at Ethyl.

"Yes, it is all Randy. He is a stickler for detail. Loves the old wood," she said, shaking her head.

"I can see myself living here. It is a wonderful apartment."

We spent the next few minutes talking details about the apartment–heat, water, electricity, and all the costs per month. "I didn't notice the parking. Where do residents and visitors park?" I asked.

Ethyl didn't miss a beat, "Around the left side of the house is a narrow driveway leading to a large parking lot. There is plenty of parking there for everyone. Randy and I park there, too. Our entrance door is at the back of the building. Shall we take a walk over there? Do you have a vehicle? I noticed you arrived on foot today."

"I don't have a need for one in the city right now with public transit being so convenient and parking is terribly expensive, but I can see it would be very handy to have a vehicle in Buckley Brook," I answered.

We walked out of the unit and Ethyl pulled the door closed behind us. I paused at the bottom of the stairs to let Ethyl lead the way around the building. We walked along a stone pathway that snaked around what I imagined would be a stunning spring garden in just a few weeks. As we rounded the corner, a man in his early thirties stopped to avoid crashing into us. He stepped off the path into the surrounding gravel to allow us to pass by. "Oh, hello, Mrs. Findler," he said with a smile. "Hard at work renting that main floor apartment today?"

"Always hard at work, Max. That's what keeps this place running, you know; hard work," Ethyl said, with a stern and serious face that broke into a warm smile.

"True enough!" he replied.

"And I told you to call me Ethyl!"

"Sure thing, Mrs. Findler, err . . . Ethyl." As he dashed off, he flashed a wide grin at me. "Welcome to the building!"

"That's Max," Ethyl said, as she continued down the path

toward the parking area.

I turned and followed Ethyl in a bit of a daze. "Where is he heading off to so quickly?" I asked.

"He's a Ph.D. student, studying computer engineering at the university. Not just a pretty face, that one. Works hard, too," Ethyl said proudly. I sensed a deep respect for hard work with Ethyl and made a mental note of that.

Suddenly, a huge black and white Maine Coon cat ran from the back of the building toward us at breakneck speed. As it approached me, I could see a huge fish in its mouth. Hot on its tail was Randy–screaming as he chased it. With his left hand waving in the air and the right waving what looked like a shotgun, he yelled with his big booming voice, "Thief! Get back here, you thief!"

Randy's long legs allowed him to close the distance in only a few strides. I took a step back toward the house to let the commotion through, but just as the huge sticky-pawed feline and its red-hot fish slid past, Ethyl stepped in front of Randy, and he was forced to end his pursuit.

"Not today, Randy. As angry as that cat makes you, we don't need more trouble from the city by-law officer for shooting cats with bean bags. Do you remember the last time?" Ethyl asked tersely. I couldn't help but open my eyes wide in surprise. Randy, clearly annoyed and defeated, succumbed to Ethyl's strong argument and stomped through the parking area to the back of the house, gun in hand, head hung low. "Damn cats. Out to get me and my fish. No good. No good comes from a cat!" I heard him sputtering as he rounded the corner.

"As you might have determined, this is a no-cat house," Ethyl noted with great seriousness as she continued walking.

"That's fine with me. I am very allergic to cats," I said, trying to hint that I was a good choice for the apartment, but using a tone aimed to lighten the mood. "Where did that big cat come from?" I wondered to myself. "And what on earth had Randy done to the neighbors?" This house was definitely shaping up to be far more interesting than my dull little apartment in the city.

The parking area in front of us was a large gravel lot at the side of the house with ample room for residents and guests to park. Halfway along the house on the edge of the lot to the left was another entrance. At the top of five wide concrete steps was a landing. This entrance had a large wooden door with a small glass window in it. The area looked different from the front of the house; an addition had been made to convert the house into separate apartments, I assumed.

As if reading my mind, Ethyl ambled up the stairs and opened the entrance door for us. "This is the entrance for three of the apartments. There is one unit in the basement where Max lives. Then there are two twin units upstairs. Inside this doorway are all the mailboxes for the house. There is a spot for large parcels, too." I took a quick glance inside and noticed a set of stairs on the left heading downstairs and another larger set on the right leading upstairs with five keyed mailboxes inset into the wall just inside the door on our right.

After she closed the door, we walked back toward the front of the house. "It certainly is a well-kept house both inside and outside," I thought to myself. Besides their idiosyncrasies, the landlords seemed to genuinely care about maintaining a nice place to live. This town had its quirks, but perhaps this was just what I needed in my life right now.

Lost in contemplation, I missed Ethyl's question. I could tell by her impatient look that this was frustrating to her, "I'm sorry, I was deep in thought processing the fabulous tour you just gave me. Can you repeat your question, please?"

"I asked if you are interested in taking the apartment," she said quickly.

Without hesitating, I confirmed. "Yes, I would love to rent the apartment."

We discussed the details around the application process and I wrote Ethyl a cheque to hold my spot. I agreed to email the application documents over to her later that day. We said goodbye and I walked back down the street with a newfound spring in my step. With the beginning of the next month rapidly approaching, I was relieved to have found an apartment. I started thinking about moving arrangements and a smile crossed my face for the first time in a long time. I actually felt a glimmer of excitement, eager to begin this new adventure.

CHAPTER 2

Spring had arrived in full force. Finally, I felt settled into my new place in Buckley Brook. Even though in the city I only had a small apartment and not much furniture, I had hired a moving company to do the heavy lifting. I ordered some additional furniture to fill the other spaces too, including a brand new Queen-sized bed. Although the movers had delivered my furniture, I was left with the daunting task of unpacking all the boxes.

I had set myself a goal to try to finish as quickly as possible so that I could turn to building my bookkeeping business in my new town. It wasn't financial pressure as much as getting back to my routine. Both of my parents had passed away within a few years of each other. My mother struggled with cancer for many years. After we lost her, my father seemed to give up. He had never taken very good care of himself and after Mom died, he really let things slip. His heart finally gave out a few years later. As the only child, I inherited enough money to keep me going with a moderate lifestyle, but it was no substitute for my family.

I had started doing tax returns when I was in school to make some extra money. I am not sure why everyone is so afraid of doing their taxes. It's just numbers. Maybe it's fear of the bottom line at the end that scares people. After losing my parents, bookkeeping became a safe distraction from the sadness of life. I thought it would be a perfect way to transition into a new town. People are always excited to meet a good bookkeeper. As much as keeping the books is undesirable for most business owners, it is even harder to trust someone else with your books.

I stopped to take a rest from unpacking and walked out onto the front porch. As I carefully sat down on my new swing in front of the window, Max appeared on the sidewalk in front of the house. He sauntered through the garden up the path toward the house. When he noticed me on the porch, he stopped and said enthusiastically, "Hello! You took the apartment. I knew you would. I could tell the other day that Ethyl liked you. She tries to be all-business, you know, but she is a softie at heart. How are you enjoying the apartment so far?"

"Great! I am so lucky to have found it. I can't believe the little shoebox I left in the city compared to this amazing place. I have the second bedroom set up as an office and a view of this gorgeous garden from both the kitchen and my desk," I said.

"What do you do for a living?" he asked.

I hesitated. Here was my chance. I could make up something wildly fantastic. A sports agent for a pro-tennis star, an epidemiologist here to work at the university researching a rare disease, or a novelist finishing the movie script to turn my blockbuster novel into a Hollywood picture. Instead, I did what I always do, opting for the truth, and sheepishly admitted, "I'm a bookkeeper."

"I have to spice up my life," I thought to myself. "Mona the bookkeeper; dependable, reliable, boring. Mona, the bookkeeper."

He smiled warmly, "Well, I am sure you will have no end of work here in Buckley Brook. I'm Max, by the way. I don't think I introduced myself the other day. I live in the unit below you. I teach and study at the university. I have been living here for almost four years now."

"Great to meet you, Max. My name is Mona," I replied.

He looked around the garden and down at the little smiling garden gnome at his feet. "There is something special about this place. It is almost magical. I know that sounds crazy. I can't put my finger on exactly what it is." He paused, looking around and shook his head. "Just a feeling, I guess." He gave me a big smile and said, "Nice to meet you, Mona; welcome to the house." He patted the little gnome on the head and walked away, following the path along the side of the building.

Out of the corner of my eye, I am sure I saw the little gnome wink at me. I looked back to see him frozen in the same spot with the same mischievous grin as before. I paused for a moment and gave him a long stare, but he didn't move.

"Get a grip, Mona."

CHAPTER 3

I decided to take another break from unpacking and walked around the property to look at the beautiful gardens that were growing quickly in the warm spring weather. I closed the front door and paused on the porch to lean against the tall wooden supporting post at the top of the stairs. Looking down from the porch offered a different perspective on the garden. The flagstone paths wound around creating lovely sections, which Ethyl had organized into groupings of plants clustered together. Each section was carefully planned out to enjoy blooming flowers all season. I could only imagine what she had created in her back garden.

My eyes wandered to the right of the house, over to the neighboring property. The house was set back farther from the street with a large yard around it. It was a similar, old Victorian style, but preserved without any additions to it. The brick was more of a yellow color with a small front porch covering only one section of house to the right of the front door. I was surprised when I noticed Randy stomp out of the house waving a wrench in his hand. He was spitting-feathers mad, cursing, and muttering under his breath as he walked toward me. He looked up at me mid-stride. I waved and smiled, trying to pretend that I hadn't been watching him. "Morning, Randy."

He paused, and visibly tried to change his demeanor, "Oh, hi there, are you making out okay in that apartment? Did you find the thermostat and figure out how to use the washing machine in the kitchen?"

"Oh yes, thank you, everything is wonderful. How are you doing? I noticed you next door," I said, trying to make conversation.

"Bah, deadbeat brother-in-law plugged the toilet again. This is the second time in three months. I should make him pay for a plumber this time, but they'll just muck it up and clean out my wallet. I'll end up fixing it myself anyway, so I might as well fix it right myself, now. Did you know that I found a comb stuck in the toilet last time? Yes, a comb. Who flushes a comb down the toilet, anyway? Just downright disrespectful, if you ask me. No respect. If you do drop something down the toilet, 'cuz stuff happens,' put your big boy pants on and put your darn hand in the toilet and pull it out. I better grab my tools and go back before he decides to play handyman and 'fix it' himself. You have a good day now."

Randy stomped off behind the house and I was left staring across the garden at the neighboring house wondering what the backstory was with the brother-in-law. Why was Randy doing maintenance over there? The brother-in-law can't be that incompetent.

I decided against the walk and wandered back inside. Time to tackle the last set of boxes. I was about to head into the bedroom when I heard voices from above. "Oh, don't think you can get away with it this time, Nathan Laine. I have had enough of your whistling kettle at five a.m. I tossed and turned all night long and when I was finally sound asleep this morning, I heard it through the wall–the sound of your incessant kettle screeching away like nails on a chalkboard–waking me out of a deep sleep. You are downright disrespectful. I am starting to think you are doing this on purpose to bother me," a shrill voice said.

A man laughed and responded, "You old bat, you can barely hear anything on a good day. I'm shocked you can even hear that kettle through the wall. If the sound of a little kettle through a wall is waking you up, you have bigger issues to deal with. Maybe if you spent less time attacking my kettle and more time taking care of those deep psychological issues causing you not to sleep, your life might be a whole lot better."

"How dare you say such things? We are through here." The woman yelled, then slammed the door so hard that the walls shook in my apartment.

I dropped down on the sofa with a sickening feeling in my stomach. What had I done? I came to this town for peace and quiet. Now, I had to live underneath these two? The house had seemed so perfect and quiet when I viewed this apartment. No wonder it was vacant. I couldn't bear to live in a war zone. This wasn't going to work at all. Regret flooded me as I realized I had not checked out the neighbors. "That's house hunting 101, Mona. How could you have been so stupid?"

I decided to make myself a cup of tea and sit on the porch to think about my dilemma. Maybe staring at the garden would give me some inspiration.

I carried my steaming cup of mint tea outside and settled on the swing. As the swing gently rocked, and I inhaled the fragrant mint, I started to relax a little. I was captivated by a tall group of scarlet red poppies at the side of the garden. They must have just opened. Swaying in the light breeze, their fragile petals were mesmerizing.

I was so taken by the beauty of the flowers that I didn't even notice a man walking into the garden. "I am sorry to interrupt. You look deep in thought," said a deep, warm voice.

I jumped in my seat, spilling tea all over my hand. I casually wiped up the tea with my other hand, trying not to look as embarrassed as I felt at that moment. Standing in the garden next to the poppies was a man I would guess to be in his late sixties. He was tall, and fit-looking, with dark skin and eyes. His black hair was mixed with grey. He smiled at me and said confidently, "I am Nathan. I live upstairs. We haven't met yet. I am sorry that I startled you."

I returned the smile and introduced myself. "How could this be the same person that I heard upstairs having a war of words with the woman living above me?"

"Oh, hello. I am Mona. How long have you lived here?"

"About seven years now. It's a good house. Each apartment is in great condition and just look at Ethyl's garden. It is a remarkable work of art. I can see it from upstairs. It is something to behold, especially at this time of year," he said.

"Yes, I noticed the garden right away when I was first looking at the apartment. Even then before things had started to bloom, I could imagine that it was going to be something special. I never imagined all of this, though. It is easy to see how much care Ethyl has taken to plan it out and nurture each plant. As you noticed, I can get lost staring at the plants," I replied, as a warm blush of embarrassment spread across my cheeks.

"Have you figured out where everything is located yet? How about the grocery store?" he asked.

I paused to reflect and realized I had no idea where anything was located. I smiled. "I am so used to being surrounded by everything in the city. I actually didn't stop to figure out how far the grocery store is from the house. I guess it is looking more like I am going to have to buy a car."

"While that might be true as it will give you some freedom to move around, in this case, the grocery store is only two blocks away. It's not the only one in town, but it's mighty fine. I think you will find a lot of what you need only a walk away. I am heading there now. Why don't you come along to see it? It will give you an opportunity to look at what is available there," he suggested.

"That would be lovely. Thank you. I'll go get my wallet and shoes from inside. I'll be right back." I dashed inside and slid into my shoes. My wallet was on the end of the kitchen island on the counter. I picked it up with my apartment keys, turned the lock on the handle, pulled the door closed and skipped down the stairs to meet Nathan, who was waiting on the sidewalk.

We walked down the street toward the house where Randy's brother-in-law lived with the cat who stole Randy's fish. "What do you think of the neighborhood so far? Have you met everyone yet?" Nathan asked.

"I am slowly meeting everyone in the building. I haven't met any neighbors, but I did meet the wily cat who lives here," I said, gesturing to my right at the neighbor's house.

Nathan laughed, "Oh, that cat does try Randy's patience. It is almost like he lies in wait waiting for an opportunity to foil Randy's best-laid plans."

"Yes! I know just what you mean. I witnessed his removal of a large bass that Randy was preparing to grill," I noted.

"Woooweeee, that must have been something to see," he said.

"I don't know if I was more stunned to watch such a massive cat tear off across the lawn with a whole fish in its mouth or Randy running behind it with the shotgun. If it had not been for Ethyl shutting things down, I'm pretty sure that cat would have stolen its last fish."

"Nah, Randy is more bluster than action. I'm sure he would have come to his senses by the time he reached the front garden," Nathan speculated.

I laughed, remembering the event. We walked in silence for a few minutes, taking in the spring blossoms on the trees that lined the street. It was so different from where I lived in the city–quieter, more peaceful. There was something about Nathan, too, that was different. He was relaxed and comfortable; easy to be around. I surprised myself by summoning a newfound sense of confidence and tentatively asked, "Earlier today, I heard yelling upstairs. There was a woman's voice. Who was that?" Nathan bristled with irritation and I instantly regretted asking my question, "Oh, I'm sorry, I should not be so nosy."

"No, please don't apologize. I let that tyrant upstairs push my buttons today. It doesn't happen often, but every once in a while I let her get under my skin. Her name is Margaritta Merchante. She is a professor of English with tenure, at the university. She won't let anyone forget that point. The old bat should have retired years ago. I can only imagine how horrible she is to have as a teacher. Poor kids are just waiting for her to retire and open up the spot for a younger, more reasonable professor. Must be nice to slide into a job that is guaranteed for life regardless of how terrible you are at it," Nathan grumbled.

I waited in the uncomfortable silence, not sure what to say. Dread from the animosity crept back over me. The sickening feeling in my stomach worsened when I thought about living below that terrible woman. I was kicking myself for not investigating this part of the house more thoroughly.

Nathan's words stopped me from spiraling further down my rabbit hole of anxiety, though. "I hope you don't think less of the house. It's not as bad as it may have sounded today," he said, as if reading my thoughts. "Today wasn't typical by any means. Something must have been gnawing at the old crow to set her off. She was particularly tyrannical today." His use of the word 'tyrannical' did not help my disposition in the least.

Before I could sink further, Nathan exclaimed, "Here we are!" I looked up to see a small store, not much bigger than what I would call a corner store in the city. There was an entrance door in the middle of the building with windows across the front on both sides of the door. The sign across the top of the building read, 'Paul's Gourmet Grocery,' in large black block letters. There was a small sitting area outside to the left of the door with three bistro-style table sets. To the right were buckets with cut flowers in them for sale.

"Don't get turned off by the size. The prices are really reasonable and he manages to stock one of everything I need in here, with a few gourmet extras that you might fancy," Nathan enthused. I smiled, taking in the whole picture as we walked toward the door.

CHAPTER 4

The store wasn't a disappointment. I had intended to accompany Nathan just for the walk and to see where the store was located, but as I followed him through the aisles, I could not help picking up a few items. Before I knew it, I had a bag full of salami, special cheese, and some basics that I was running low on. Nathan had been right; somehow within the little space, it had everything I needed and more.

Back at the apartment, I put my wallet and keys on the end of the kitchen counter and started to unpack my bags. As I sorted through the items, there was a knock on the storm door. I had left the main door open when I came in, so I could see through the window of the storm door onto the porch. No hiding from whoever it was, as the person was staring straight at me. I walked across the sitting room toward the door. I could see a woman's face with shoulder-length, fine, straight white blond hair. She was wearing a light blue, short-sleeved women's collared dress shirt, tailored to fit her perfectly. When I opened the door, I noticed it was light blue linen, layered over a navy linen pencil skirt to her knees. She had flat, leather, open-toed dress sandals on her feet with bare legs. She looked amazing. How do some women manage to make linen look so elegant? When I put it on, it's just a rumpled mess.

"Can I help you?" I asked tentatively, standing in the doorway, as I already had an idea who was standing in front of me.

"Mona! I just had to come and say hello and welcome you to the building! Ethyl told me all about you. I hear you have come from the big city to Buckley Brook. How lovely. Forgive me, I am Margaritta Merchante. I live upstairs," she said, finally pausing to take a breath.

"Nice to meet you," I answered quietly, holding the edge of the door with both hands, not sure where this conversation was heading.

"Mona. A quaint, but posh name, all at the same time," she chuckled. I grimaced, now I knew where this was going. "I didn't catch your full name, dear."

Here we go. "Mona Lisa Brown," I answered.

"Oh, how perfectly fantastic. Mona Lisa, just like the painting; exquisite, yet homely at the same time. Pairs just perfectly with your last name–Brown," she said, rolling the 'r.' "Mona Lisa Brown, that is just a perfect pairing indeed. How very whimsical," she laughed.

Was that a compliment or a punch in the face? I couldn't tell. How was I to respond to that?

"Thank you," I said, trying to hide my immediate disdain for this woman.

"Now, you are familiar with the rules of the house," she said as a statement, emphasizing the 'r' again on rules.

I hesitated, not sure what I was getting myself into with this part of the conversation, "Which rules are you referring to?"

" 'To which,' dear," she replied, looking at me impatiently. I returned a puzzled blank stare. "To which rules are you referring? You cannot leave a preposition just dangling in the air at the end of a sentence. Pair it up, my dear." Noticing my stunned expression in response to the correction of my sentence structure, Margaritta laughed. "Oh dear, you do know I am a Professor of Literature at the university. I know all the rules of the English language. Such a shame what has come of it." She stared dramatically down the porch, appearing to be in a moment of mourning.

She returned her gaze and fixed it squarely on me, "As I was saying, the rules of the house." Before launching into her soliloquy on rules, she whipped out a white laminated card and proudly handed it to me. I looked down at the black text as she launched into the rules, which she seemed to have committed to memory.

Noise is to be kept to a minimum. This is a quiet house. Laundry hours are between 8 a.m. and 8 p.m. There are to be no large house parties; and no excessive noise after 9 p.m. and that includes loud laughing. Noise travels, you know, and this is a shared space.

Garbage must be removed promptly from your unit and placed in your garbage bin inside the shed at the side of the house. Garbage day is on Wednesday and your bin must be placed there before 7 a.m. or you risk missing the pick-up.

Tidiness is essential. Leaving belongings on the porch is strictly forbidden, including shoes outside your door or dishes on the porch. This is the gateway to our house and must be treated with the utmost respect.

"I think that covers everything. I really think these are quite reasonable to follow. Don't you, dear?" she paused to ask.

I stood there, frozen. Dozens of things I wanted to say back to her in response rolled through my mind, but I couldn't muster the courage, so I just stammered like a fool, "Uh, yes, of course."

She gave me a sickly sweet smile and said, "Good, then. I will be off." She turned and walked down the stairs, pausing on the last step to say in a shrill voice, "Welcome to the building, Mona Lisa Brown."

I gave her a weak smile, mad at myself for not being stronger and standing up to Margaritta. Who did she think she was, coming downstairs like that, telling me how to behave in my own apartment like I am a child? This apartment, this house, it had seemed so perfect. How could I have been so stupid to not even think of checking out the tenants?

I closed both doors this time and leaned my head up against the door for a moment. "What have I done?" I sighed, the sick feeling in my stomach deepening. I took a deep breath and slowly returned to the kitchen to put away the rest of my items from my shopping trip, hoping to calm my nerves at the same time. I don't know if I was more frustrated with Margaritta trying to boss me around or at myself for letting her. There were so many things I could have said in that conversation, but I could not find the nerve to say them.

I walked over to the kitchen and stood at the counter, staring through the window at the garden. Perhaps a nice cup of tea on the porch would help alter my sour mood. If I pulled the sun curtains across, I might get a few moments of peace without talking to anyone. I imagined nestling in the soft outdoor papas-an chair next to the swing with my tea and a good book and I was instantly happier.

After the kettle boiled, I carefully took my mint tea outside to the porch. I pulled the sun shades across to make my little cocoon. The shades were made of a patterned beige fabric that blocked the sun in the afternoon. They were translucent, so I could still see beyond the porch, but they provided a small break from the comings and goings in the front garden. I could imagine these would be handy in the hot summer sun in a few months. I settled into my cozy spot, listening to the peaceful trickling sound of the garden's water feature. I had not paused long enough yet to hear that captivating sound. I took a deep breath and settled into my little piece of tranquility with a smile on my face.

Just as I drifted off into my afternoon siesta, I awoke to screaming coming from the backyard, heading toward me. My eyes popped open. It took a second to process the noise, then I jumped up to find out what was going on. I held onto the post at the top of the stairs and peered around it into the garden to see what was happening. At the same time, Randy rounded the corner from the back of the house, screaming, "They got me, they got me." He was wearing a netted jacket that was tented over his face and attached to a big hat. That was when I saw the cloud of bees around him. "They got me, they got me," he screamed, as he reached the water feature.

With what looked like a feat of superhuman strength, Randy picked up the basin of the stone bird bath from the top of the water feature and proceeded to douse himself with all the water in it. He put it back down with a clunk and paused, collecting himself for a moment. I stood helpless, staring from the top step with my mouth wide open in shock, not sure what to do.

Unfortunately, the water appeared to aggravate the bees and they came back in full force. Randy looked up at me with panic on his face and yelled, "Mona, the shed; run and open the shed. Go fast!" I hesitated for a moment until I realized he was talking about the garbage shed beside the house. I had no idea what he was planning, but I ran down the stairs in my bare feet around the side of the house, past the side entrance and the parking area toward the shed.

When I got there, I quickly pulled the door wide open and turned back to look for Randy. He ran through the garden to the sidewalk and then ran down the driveway wildly toward me, hollering at the top of his lungs. His speed had put some distance between him and the bees, but he and the bees were still headed straight for me. He ran directly into the shed and bellowed, "Shut it, shut it, shut the damn door!" I looked up and froze, watching the bees coming right for me. Then I jumped inside, slamming the door at the same time.

The shed went pitch-black and the smell of hot garbage hit me like a wave. Randy pulled a chain hanging from the ceiling and light filled the space. I choked on the smell of the garbage as my stomach churned. "You have no shoes on!" Randy exclaimed, pointing at my feet.

"I didn't have time. I just ran. Where did those bees come from?" I said, still in shock, trying to breathe through my mouth.

"They are mine," he admitted sheepishly. "I was gifted a hive from a friend in the country, but I don't think his bees like me, for some reason."

"I wonder why," I thought to myself.

"How are we going to get out of this stinky shed if they are waiting for us out there?" I asked.

"I have my cell phone in my pocket. I will call Ethyl to bring the smoker," Randy said.

"The smoker? Seriously, is this a regular occurrence?" I tried to hide my annoyance.

As Randy pulled out his cell phone, we heard Ethyl's big voice yelling, "Randy, where are you? I heard you yelling, but I can't find you. You're tangled up with those bees again, aren't you?"

"In here, Ethyl," I yelled with joy, banging on the inside of the door so she would hear us. At this point, I was desperate to get away from the horrible smell of garbage.

The door opened quickly, and there stood Ethyl in the doorway with a beekeeper's mesh hat on and a large smoking device. I looked around her to confirm that the bees were definitely gone.

"Mona! How did you get caught up in Randy's bee shenanigans? What are you two doing in here, anyway?" she asked, visibly confused. She stepped back quickly. "Ugh, that smell . . . . get out! Out! That smell is atrocious. We have to do something about this shed, Randy."

We quickly stepped out onto the pavement of the parking lot;

both of us urgently scanning the area around us to ensure the bees were gone. When we were sure they had all vacated, seeking other unsuspecting victims, Randy removed his bee hat. I recounted the story to Ethyl–the part I witnessed, that is–and how we ended up in the garbage shed. Randy filled in the beginning and how the bees had become so angry with him. Apparently, the bees resided at the very back of the property.

I looked up at Randy and noticed his face. The bees must have gotten him through the bee hat because his eye has started to swell closed. As he turned to look at Ethyl, I noticed his right ear. It was bright red and had swollen up to double the size of his left ear. I tried to hide my reaction, but I couldn't stop looking at his enormous ear.

Ethyl shook her head, "Randy, I will never understand why you agreed to take those bees from Martin," she said. "As much as I appreciate supporting the honey bee population, those bees are more trouble than they are worth. They don't like you. One of these days they are going to finish you off. We will find you dead in the yard from honey bee stings." She looked at Randy's face and shook her head. "You better go inside and take care of those bites before your eye swells completely shut. I just bought a fresh box of baking soda. It's in the back cupboard on the middle shelf. I think you are going to need a good dose of antihistamines. Those are in the medicine cabinet. Make sure you take two."

Randy unzipped the jacket of his bee suit and trudged off towards the back of the house, bee hat in hand. I turned to face Ethyl, not sure what to think. "I hope he is okay," I said, sympathetically.

"Oh, Randy will be fine. He is a tough old bird. He'll get a nice peaceful sleep after he takes those antihistamines, too," Ethyl said with a smile as she pulled off her mesh hat and set the smoking contraption down just to the side of the shed. She looked at my feet as she stood. "Oh dear, I hope you did not hurt your feet in that ordeal. Are you okay to walk back without your shoes?"

I looked down, wiggled my toes and said, "I think I am okay. I will be careful walking back."

Ethyl quickly ducked into the shed and picked up a small bag of gardening tools. Slinging the handle over her left elbow, she fell into step behind me as I started walking back toward the house. There was a moment of silence as we walked across the parking lot toward the front of the house. Looking down to avoid stepping on anything sharp with my bare feet, I heard a familiar, piercing voice, "Oh, hello Ethyl. Nice to see you again, Mona," Margaritta said in her patronizing tone. I froze in the walkway. As I looked up, Margaritta barreled past me, causing me to step into the garden beside the house to avoid a collision with her. "Do look up now, Mona, you never know what might be coming your way around here." She laughed.

Margaritta looked at Ethyl, who stood firmly in place, a few feet behind me at the edge of the garden path where it widened to meet the parking lot. Margaritta walked by Ethyl toward the concrete stairs and looked over her shoulder and said, "I introduced Mona to the house rules earlier today."

As Margaritta started up the steps, Ethyl responded in the most calm, but firm voice, "Oh, really? Were those your rules, or mine?"

Margaritta halted on the first step like someone had grabbed her shoulder. She paused for only a moment and turned to look at Ethyl with a huge smile and said in the most saccharine tone, "Your rules, of course, Ethyl."

"Good to hear. I am sure you extended the warmest of welcomes to our new resident," Ethyl said with a voice that conveyed far more than her words. It was only an instant, but something passed over Margaritta's face, possibly fear, for a fraction of a second.

I bit my lower lip to stifle a smile. Score one for Ethyl. How did she do that? One simple interaction and Ethyl managed to neutralize the person who had dominated me at my own front door. I was impressed.

I snapped out of my awestruck moment to realize that Margaritta had disappeared into the entrance. Ethyl was smiling warmly at me. "Shall we get you some shoes?" Her tone was friendly, as if the previous interaction with Margaritta had never taken place.

"Yes, of course," I said, stepping back onto the path and heading toward the front of the house.

"She isn't as tough as she seems."

I hesitated, not wanting to go where this conversation was taking us, deciding that feigning ignorance was my safest route, "What do you mean?"

"Margaritta. Don't let her push you around, Mona. She really is more bark than bite."

I sighed. "I don't know; the bark was pretty intimidating at my front door earlier today."

Ethyl smiled, "Margaritta likes rules and order, but she has no power to enforce them here. Don't let her get to you."

Before I could protest, we reached the bottom of the stairs to my unit and Ethyl changed the subject, "How are you finding things in your apartment? Everything working okay? If you find anything that needs repair, just let me know. He might not be the best beekeeper, but Randy is quite a wizard with his tools."

"Everything is fantastic, Ethyl. I really love the apartment. It feels enormous compared to my apartment in the city. I absolutely love this front porch," I replied enthusiastically, relieved by the subject change.

"Wonderful to hear. I will leave you to enjoy the remainder of this beautiful afternoon. I see you found the blinds to shade the porch from the afternoon sun. It is quite a hot spot, but the best place in the house for an afternoon nap, next to my hammock in the back," she said, grinning with a wink as she headed into the garden on a mission to inspect her flower patches.

I was smiling as I watched Ethyl pull out hand clippers and go about the business of pruning deadheads and other imperfections in her garden. I was happy to have found an ally who had mastered handling Margaritta. Perhaps this journey to Buckley Brook could turn out okay, after all. I walked up the stairs and took a look at my cozy spot. The late afternoon sun was still warming the porch, even through the blinds. I couldn't resist sitting down. I was tired from the events of the day. My tea, now cold, was still waiting for me on the small table by the chair. The beauty of mint tea is that it is soothing hot and refreshing cold; enjoyable at both temperatures. I snuggled into my chair feeling tired, but content. I yawned, stretched out, closed my eyes and drifted off again in my little porch refuge.

* * *

I awoke from my slumber, shivering. I had no idea what time it was. I must have been asleep for several hours as my cozy spot had given me a kink in my neck and the warm afternoon sun had been replaced with a cool evening chill. I stood up and stretched a bit, shaking off the contorted position I had fallen asleep in, picked up my tea mug and ducked inside.

It was well past my usual dinner hour, but if I skipped eating, I would be hungry by the middle of the night. I decided to break into the salami and cheese I had purchased earlier in the day, and opened the bottle of wine I had picked up to celebrate my move. Tonight was as good a time to celebrate as any, especially if I was opening the special salami and ancient cheddar.

I enjoyed my late evening snack and took my wine to soak in a hot bath before snuggling into my bed. Drifting off to sleep, I thought about all the things that had happened throughout the day. This house certainly had character and a lot of characters to go with it.

CHAPTER 5

The next morning I was dozing in and out of sleep, wanting to enjoy my extra-comfortable new bed for as long as possible when my ears were assaulted by the clatter of what sounded like a pot being banged with a metal object. My eyes opened and I sat up to register whether the terrible noise was actually real. I jumped up, still in my pajama pants and t-shirt and ran out to the kitchen to figure out what was going on.

"Get! Get out of here! You have had your last round of fun in this garden, you poop machine. This is not your toilet!"

I opened my front door and peered through the storm door window. It was Randy. Outside, walking on the garden paths, he was furiously banging on a metal cooking pot over and over with his hammer. In front of him, snaking through the path, just out of Randy's reach was the Maine Coon cat from next door. If cats could snicker, this one would have had a big grin on its face.

I opened the door and stepped out on the porch. This seemed to break Randy out of his cat-chasing mission long enough for the Maine Coon to dart back into the neighbor's yard. Randy lowered the pot and hammer in defeat, looked at me and in a completely serious tone said, "That cat is going to be the end of me."

'Why?" I couldn't help but ask.

"I think it is channeling the spirit of my mother-in-law. I am sure of it. She tortured me in life and now she is driving me mad from six feet under. Figures she would come back as the largest cat I have ever seen. It's quite fitting that her weapon of choice would be to crap all over the garden path, too."

I looked down at the path and while I was suspicious of Randy's theory about his mother-in-law being reincarnated as the cat next door, he was accurate about the weapon of choice. The cat had left some landmines for Randy all over the garden path.

I wasn't sure how to respond to this situation, so I tried the soft approach. "Maybe the cat just wants your attention."

This comment didn't land well. Randy's eyes grew wide. Drawing up into a battle stance, he brandished the hammer and declared, "Never! This is war! War, I tell you!"

A voice floated from around the side of the house. "Who are you at war with now, Randy?" When she saw him, she stopped and shook her head. "Put down that hammer. There will be no war today. Hey, is that our good cooking pot? That's what all that racket was earlier? You better not have been banging that pot with your hammer!"

"Look what that cat has left on the pathway!" Randy exclaimed.

Ethyl looked down and noticed the landmines and chuckled, "My, that cat does have it in for you. I am coming out to work in the garden anyway. I'll scoop the poop. Just go put back the good pot in the kitchen please, will you?"

While this calmed Randy down considerably, he was still visibly angry at the situation, but appeared to accept Ethyl's offer and stomped around the side of the house, pot and hammer in hand. Ethyl continued to chuckle and looked up at me on the porch. "Well, that must have been an eventful wakeup. You look like you were trying to enjoy a relaxing morning before Randy's antics pulled you out here. I hope he did not wake you up."

"No, I was just dozing. I needed to get up anyway." Noticing her basket of gardening tools, I asked, "What garden projects do you have on the go today?"

"Well, I guess first I have to scoop some poop," she said, frowning. "After that, I need to tend to the peonies. Most of them are just about finished and will start looking ratty soon. I need to cut them back for the season. Such a short time that they bloom, but they are gorgeous."

"Yes, I have had the pleasure of watching them bloom from the porch. They are stunning. Would you like some help trimming?" I asked.

"That would be lovely. Please don't feel obligated, though. If you have other things to do this morning, it's okay. I have all the time in the world to putter in the garden." Ethyl smiled at me.

"It's okay, I am happy to help. It is a beautiful morning. I just need to change and put on some shoes. I'll be right back."

I quickly changed into some gardening clothes, grabbed a hat and my shoes and returned to the garden. I noticed Ethyl cutting a cluster of withering flowers. I walked over to see what she was doing.

"I have been gathering these plants over the years. We watch in anticipation as they grow each spring waiting for them to bloom. They are magnificent and then they turn into this," she said, gesturing to one of the shrivelled flowers. "Oh well, perhaps it makes us appreciate them more." She sighed and continued clipping the deadheads, putting them in a basket. "Do you know that peonies bloom with the assistance of ants? The ants eat the green shell-like covering encasing the peony bud and that is what allows the plants to bloom. Someone who didn't know better might be tempted to brush the ants off in an effort to protect the plant, not realizing that this is the only way for the plant to reach its beautiful blooming state. I used to love to bring peonies into the house to enjoy, until the year our house was infested with ants," she recalled, grimacing a bit.

I listened intently to Ethyl, mentally noting not to bring peonies into the house. "May I help you?" I asked.

"Of course, that would be great. Just clip the deadheads off and put them in the basket. I have a compost pile at the very back by the trees where I will throw everything to decompose."

I started on the other side of the patch Ethyl was working on. We clipped away in silence for a few minutes, enjoying the warm spring day. I asked Ethyl a few questions to make conversation, "You mentioned that you have owned this house for 38 years. Have you always lived here?"

"No, we used to own a farm just on the edge of Buckley Brook. We sold that about 10 years ago. We couldn't find quite the right place to move to at the time and the unit at the back opened up. Randy wanted to renovate it, so we thought it was the perfect opportunity to move in and renovate while we were looking for another house. Once we moved in and started making it our own, I got into the gardens and well, here we are still living here 10 years later," she said, shaking her head and smiling as she remembered the past.

"How did your brother end up living next door?" I asked, surprising myself with my boldness. I quickly added, "Randy told me that his brother-in-law lives next door."

Ethyl laughed, "Oh, I can see how you would make that connection. No, Merl is brother-in-law to both of us. He was married to Marise, Randy's sister, who passed away about five years ago. Marise got very sick at the end of her life. We had just purchased the house next door, planning to rent it or move in ourselves when we realized that Marise and Merl needed help. We invited them to live next door so that we could help them, more specifically help Marise.

After Marise passed, Merl stayed. Merl always had great intentions for his life, but nothing really materialized for one reason or another. We have always been friendly with Merl, but we were closer to Marise. She was a special woman, always concerned for everyone else's wellbeing. Do you know she was still volunteering at the food bank right up until a few months before she died? She had a big heart and was determined to help the world."

Ethyl paused to wipe a tear with her sleeve and looked up with a smile.

"I'm sorry to upset you," I said, feeling badly about opening an old wound.

"Oh, Mona, don't apologize. I love thinking about Marise. As painful as it is to think about how we lost someone so lovely, I love getting a chance to remember how fantastic she was. It really brings me joy; thank you."

I smiled in understanding, thinking about my own parents.

We clipped away for another 45 minutes in the warm spring sun. The conversation moved to lighter topics, ranging from past tenants to interesting things to do in Buckley Brook, but mostly we talked about gardening. While I knew how much work it required, I had no idea how much knowledge was needed to create a garden like Ethyl's. Each patch had been planned out based on grouping the plants so that they work together effectively, but also so that the garden had something in bloom all season long. I knew Ethyl had a vegetable patch behind the house. We didn't even get into the details of successful vegetable gardening.

We finished up and parted ways to go on with the day. I went back inside to make some breakfast and get ready for what more the day had to bring. As I sat down on the porch swing with a fresh cup of mint tea, Max walked around the corner of the building.

"Good morning, Mona. How are you today?" he said happily.

"Hi Max, I am doing really well thank you. Where are you off to this morning?" I responded, excited to see him.

"I have to run over to the university to pick up some documents that were sent by courier. I have no idea why they could not have emailed them to me. All this tech and we are still moving documents around to each other with couriers. I also have a novel to pick up from the library. I placed a hold on it weeks ago and it finally arrived!" he said enthusiastically. "Everyone makes fun of me for still reading paper books. While my whole life may be surrounded by tech, there is something satisfying about turning the pages of a good book."

I smiled at this, being able to relate. "I couldn't agree more with you on that!" I said emphatically.

"Hey, have you been to the university yet? Do you want to come along? It's about a 15-minute walk from here, but it's a nice walk and it's a great day today!" he said, looking up at the clear blue sky.

Excited to have a destination to visit and to see somewhere new, I answered quickly with a big smile. "I would love to walk over to the university. Can you give me two minutes to put on my running shoes?" I asked.

"Of course, take your time," Max responded.

I lifted myself carefully off the swing, carried my tea inside and sat it on the kitchen counter. I found socks and running shoes; grabbed my wallet and keys off the counter, locked the door and pulled it tight. Max was sitting on the bottom step looking at his phone while he waited for me. I sat down on the top step to put on my socks and shoes. Max looked up at me with a slightly annoyed look on his face. Confused by the change in his demeanor, I gave him a puzzled look. "Is everything alright?"

Max sighed. "I don't know. I just got a message from my girlfriend Tish."

"Girlfriend?" For some reason, I was disappointed by this new piece of information. I shook it off, curious about where that feeling came from and focused on listening to what Max was saying.

"We were supposed to drive into the city later this afternoon, visit the art gallery and have dinner at a restaurant that we both love. There is a show at the gallery featuring one of the painters she has been studying and I reserved tickets for us tonight. I have been planning this for weeks. I messaged her this morning to arrange the details of when I would pick her up this afternoon and she just messaged me back telling me that she had completely forgotten about our plan and that she is reviewing for an exam." Max explained. He sighed and looked off across the garden, visibly disappointed. He looked back with a sad smile, "I'm sorry, we were going for a nice walk to the university and I laid this on you," he said, defeated.

"That doesn't have to change," I said optimistically, trying to cheer Max up. "It's a beautiful day, let's not waste it. Let's go walk. It will help get your mind off things. Shall we?" I offered a big smile as I stood up, ready to go.

Max broke into a smile and looked happier. "You're right, let's go."

Max and I walked over to the library through the winding streets of Buckley Brook. He was surprisingly familiar with the history of the town, which was really fascinating to hear as a new arrival. When we reached the university, I was struck by the size of it; a mixture of very old and new buildings all fitting together like an old quilt that had been repaired with fresh new modern patches of fabric. With roads, trails and greenspace winding around everywhere, it was like a small town inside the town. The library was just inside the entrance and we decided to head straight there to pick up Max's book.

"This is the library," Max declared proudly, standing in the courtyard outside the double glass doors.

"I imagine you have spent a lot of hours here." I said, smiling warmly.

"You are correct there!" He laughed and nodded his head. "The thing is, this is more of a library for the arts students. There is a whole other library on the other side of campus for Science and Engineering students," he said, gesturing across the green-space to our left. "There is something about this library that I really like, though. I have a great spot on the third floor that is quiet and near a large window. There is a small desk and even a sofa near it where I find I am the most productive. It gets me away from home where there are distractions that can pull me away from what I need to get done. If I am on a deadline, you will find me up here on the third floor," he explained.

As we looked up toward the third floor, we heard a familiar female voice coming out of the entrance, "Dear, you must understand how this works. I assign a grade to your work and you accept it. This is the system we are in," she said condescendingly.

A small, soft voice responded, "But, Professor Merchante, I worked really hard on this paper. I truly thought it would be worthy of an A."

Max and I looked at each other and frowned, recognizing the voice, coming from outside the doorway to the library.

Margaritta laughed and continued, "Dear, everyone always thinks their work is worthy of an A. I have to tell you, very few pieces of work are rewarded with an A in my class and unfortunately, this latest piece of yours is no better. It certainly does not sit in the category of 'A' material."

The young woman recoiled at this hurtful comment, visibly offended and clearly speechless. She put her hand to her chest and took a step back. I was not sure if she was going to cry or scream at Margaritta.

Margaritta, unaffected by the woman's reaction, continued,

"I took the time to add comments to your work. Do go back and read these as they will help you when creating your next piece," she said in her sugary tone. And with that, she left the distraught young woman and walked away, heading right toward us.

There was no time to duck out of her path. Margaritta looked directly at us and closed the gap in five determined steps. As she walked, she greeted us in the same syrupy tone, "Max! Mona Lisa Brown, how lovely to run into you today!" she said, as if we were long-lost friends.

She turned and homed in on me; looking down over her glasses, but saying nothing. I felt like a specimen under a microscope of an unpredictable scientist. Finally she said confidently, "Good to see you getting away from the house and exploring Buckley Brook, Mona Lisa Brown. If you find this library too complex to navigate, there is a community library down the road, too," she said, laughing at herself.

I contained my disdain and tried to hide the sick feeling in my stomach from showing on my face. "Why did I ever tell her my full name? She is going to use it every time I see her now. I should have made up a different, really cool name. Darn it. And how dare she infer that I can't handle a university library?"

As I mentally anguished over this interaction with Margaritta and how terrible she was to her student and to me, another voice from behind us cut in, "Margaritta, continuing your reign of terror across campus, are we?" asked a deep, smooth voice.

Surprised, Max and I turned to see Nathan smiling, holding an armful of books. To say the least, I was relieved and excited to see him.

"You never cease to amaze me with your own rudeness, Nathan Laine," Margaritta said.

"Ah, we have something in common, then," he replied without missing a beat.

I couldn't help but jump for joy inside at this interaction. It was all I could do to keep a straight face.

"Well, I know where I am not wanted. Max, a pleasure to run into you today. I do hope you find what you are looking for at the library," she said. "Mona Lisa Brown, best of luck at this academic library." In a huff, she walked away toward another building.

The three of us watched Margaritta in silence for a moment and then turned to face each other, not sure what to say. I let out a frustrated sigh that broke the stillness. Nathan looked at me with a smile and quizzically said, "Mona Lisa Brown?"

I growled in frustration and responded, "Yes, that is my name: Mona Lisa Brown. Why I ever told that woman this detail about me, I will never know! Her maniacal ways squeezed it out of me at my front door while my defences were down. She won't let it go, and now, she insists on toying with me and using my full name everytime we meet. Pure evil, she is."

Nathan laughed, "As much as I agree that she is pure evil, I disagree with your assessment of your name. I like it, but if you aren't that fond of it, we will just keep calling you Mona or whatever name you prefer."

I jokingly replied, "I have always wanted to be a 'Melanie.' There was the most beautiful girl in my class in grade school named Melanie. I wished I was just like her."

"Melanie? No, no, Mona Lisa is much more unique. It is a dazzling name. Also, we all pick up our mail in the same space. Your true identity was bound to come out to the whole building at some point," he said, tilting his head with a smile and a quick wink.

I smiled and nodded self-consciously, acknowledging he was right, embarrassed at this attention over my name. Recognizing this, he turned to look at Max and changed the subject.

"And how are you today, Max? What brings you to campus

on this fine spring day?"

"I need to pick up some paperwork that was couriered to my office and I have a novel I had on hold here for ages that is finally ready," he said, gesturing toward the library. "Mona and I ran into each other this morning at the house and I suggested she come for the walk to see the university." Max looked at his watch and scrunched his face, thinking. "I wonder if I should run over to my office now and then come back to the library. Nathan, I assume you are going in to return those books. Do you mind giving Mona a tour of the main floor? I should be back in 10 minutes and then I will catch up with you both inside."

Nathan smiled and said, "Of course, I would be delighted to be the official tour guide of this esteemed university library."

"Perfect. I will see you both in a few minutes," Max responded and took off across campus in a light jog.

As we watched him leave, I smiled at Nathan, "Thank you for agreeing to give me a tour. That is really nice of you. If you don't have time though, I am happy to just poke around the stacks on my own," I offered.

"Not at all, I am happy to show you around. Shall we, Mona Lisa?" Nathan extended his bent elbow toward me.

I laughed and happily linked arms with him, "Yes, we shall," I responded with a smile and we set off, arm in arm, toward the library entrance.

CHAPTER 6

All in all, the visit to the university library was really enjoyable. Nathan gave me a great tour and even got me set up with a library card to borrow books. Max caught up with us shortly after he returned from his office. He picked up his book and then showed us his secret study spot on the third floor. Once we had our fill of the library, we left and took a different route home so that Nathan and Max could show me more of Buckley Brook as proud tour guides. I couldn't help but notice how much they loved living in this town. It was nice to come to a place like this where people were here for the love of the place and the people. It wasn't like that in the city. The people I met were there for a purpose, either work or school generally, and they moved on when that purpose ended.

The route home took us past Paul's Grocery. We were all famished, so we stopped to visit the delicious deli. At a bistro table outside the grocery, we were enjoying thick deli meat sandwiches in the exceptionally warm spring afternoon. After the most scrumptious bite I declared, "I could really get used to this." Mouths full, Nathan and Max nodded emphatically in agreement as they enjoyed their huge sandwiches. We ate in silence for a few minutes, all of us thoroughly enjoying every bite. Max finally leaned back and said, "I am stuffed! I don't know what their secret ingredient is, but this place makes unbelievable sandwiches. I don't think I am going to need dinner tonight."

Nathan put the rest of his sandwich down and chuckled, "I have a ribeye defrosting on my kitchen counter that I have been drooling over in my mind all day. I picked it up here a few weeks ago actually. The butcher is exceptionally talented at selecting cuts of meat. Every once in a while they have a little sale, too. If I catch it, I take advantage and stock my freezer." Nathan's eyes twinkled. I was not sure which delighted him more, imagining eating the meat or the fact that he got it on sale.

Max laughed, then sighed and looked at me sincerely. "Well, thank you, this day hasn't been the total loss that I feared it was going to be. He looked at Nathan and then me. "Thank you both for cheering me up."

Nathan, unaware of the events that had unfolded earlier on my front porch, tilted his head and gave Max a quizzical look.

"Sorry, Nathan, you missed the drama earlier. I had this amazing night planned for Tish and I in the city–art gallery show and dinner reservations."

"Let me guess. She bailed again?" Nathan gave me a knowing look.

"You got it."

"Honestly, my young friend, when are you going to see the writing on the wall with this girl? This is not the first time she has let you down and it's not going to be the last. I have told you before; you deserve better. Take a stand or she is going to keep walking all over you," Nathan said firmly.

Max sighed. "I know you are probably right, but there is something about her. She isn't all bad. To be fair about tonight, she is preparing for an exam."

Nathan shook his head and said, "This time, but what about the last five times? She is no good for you. She is going to break your heart, slowly, into tiny pieces."

"Yikes," I thought, wondering what had happened to Nathan for him to take such a stance on Max's situation.

Max sighed again. "I hope not, but I will do some hard thinking about what you said."

Out of the corner of my eye, I saw a large striped cat walking toward us down the sidewalk with a slow, confident stride like it was king of the jungle or at least king of the sidewalk. Surprised, I pointed toward it and said, "Hey, look! Isn't that the cat from next door that Randy is at war with?"

Nathan and Max looked over and nodded, not in the least bit surprised to see the cat. Nathan explained, "Oh yeah, it wanders the neighborhood on its own all the time."

Still stunned, I persisted, "But that's not safe. What if something happened to it? What if it gets hit by a car?"

They both laughed and Nathan responded, "Listen, city slicker, you are in the small town of Buckley Brook now. Nothing is going to happen to that cat. Besides, from what I have seen, it has about 200 lives."

"Better not let Randy see your concern for that cat!" Max added.

Both Nathan and Max laughed again, agreeing on these points. They looked away. Just beside the entrance to the store, a newspaper box featuring a baseball player making a catch over his head grabbed their attention and they started talking about the game from the previous night.

Fascinated by the cat, I watched it stride down the sidewalk. I was mesmerized. How did it project such confidence? As if it knew I was watching, it turned to look at me, holding my gaze while continuing to slink down the sidewalk and just as it was about to pass out of sight, I was sure it gave me a wink.

I shook my head and pulled myself together. "First winking garden gnomes, now cats. Mona, you are losing it." I scolded myself silently. "It is a cat! A cat!"

I turned back to face Nathan and Max as Max checked his watch, "I better get back home. I have some phone calls to make to unravel my plans for tonight, " he said.

Nathan agreed. "Yes, time to head back. It has been a pleasure to run into you two today. We must do this again!"

We all smiled, nodding in agreement with Nathan's idea. Then we tidied up our mess from the sandwiches, stood up and pushed in the iron bistro chairs before we headed back to the house. I smiled inwardly, thinking of my newfound friends; warmed by how they seemed to genuinely care about each other, even me, the newcomer. I had never found this in the city. Everyone I met there was so busy and focused on themselves. There never seemed to be any time available for building real relationships. "The whole thing is bizarre really, because they are all missing out on something amazing."

The walk back was quick. We recounted our earlier run-in with Margaritta; all of us contributing our opinions on what we wished we had said to her.

"I don't know, I think it's kind of sad," Max said as Nathan and I looked at him in disbelief. "Her cruel treatment of other people means she misses out. It must be lonely going through life that way."

Nathan shook his head and grumbled, "You see, it's this stuff that gets you into trouble with women, my friend. That woman is pure evil, in my opinion. If she is missing out on life, it's one hundred percent her own doing."

Max and I laughed at Nathan's passion for the subject as we arrived back at the house, neither of us wishing to dive any deeper into the topic with him though. We said our goodbyes in the garden, at the foot of the stairs to my apartment. I realized as I climbed the stairs that I was feeling tired from my adventure. I opened the doors to my apartment, leaving the main door open, walked over to drop my keys and wallet on the end of the counter, and set down my bag with the novels from the library in it.

I spotted my cold tea on the counter from that morning. Rather than waste it, I filled a tall glass with ice and poured the tea over the ice to make iced tea. I couldn't resist opening the bag and selecting a novel. Then I carried it with my glass of tea outside. Setting my tea and novel on the table, I dropped into the papasan chair in my cozy corner of the porch. I leaned over to unlace my running shoes and took off my socks, setting them aside on the deck. I stretched my legs and arms out wide, wiggling my toes, feeling the warmth of the afternoon sun streaming onto the porch. "This is what total contentment feels like," I thought, smiling happily to myself as I took a long sip of my iced tea.

My moment of contentment was rapidly broken by a scream above me, followed by frantic footsteps running around. I sat up and listened to the commotion. Something had happened upstairs. Not very eager to get involved, I continued to listen, snickering to myself, until Margaritta ran outside onto the balcony above me yelling in desperation, "Mona, Mona, help, there is water everywhere. Call Randy!"

That's when I connected the dots. Water everywhere above my apartment equaled water inside my apartment soon! My pulse spiked and a wave of panic flooded me. "Randy! We need Randy!" In a panic, I ran inside and grabbed my phone, praying Ethyl would answer. In just a few rings she picked up, "Hi Mona, how are you today?" she answered calmly.

"Hi Ethyl, I was fantastic until just now when Margaritta ran onto her deck screaming that there is water everywhere in her apartment. I am really hoping Randy is home. I am worried the water will come down into my apartment soon," I said quickly.

"Oh, no, this does not sound good at all. Randy is in the backyard. Give me two minutes to get him over there with his toolbox," said Ethyl. "Thank you for letting us know so quickly," she added and we both hung up.

By this time, Margaritta was beside herself, running around upstairs and screaming, "Everything will be ruined, just ruined!" If it weren't for the fact that the problem was water-related and I was directly below her, I would have been loving the moment. My better nature took over and I walked back out onto the porch and down the stairs into the garden to see if I could call up to Margaritta to tell her Randy was on his way.

By the time I got out into the garden, I heard Randy's voice upstairs in Margaritta's apartment, "Margaritta, I need you to settle down and give me some space to work, please," he said, with more patience than she deserved, in my opinion.

"Are you sure you are qualified to handle this? Should we call a professional?" Margaritta continued.

Randy replied slowly in a calm, but seething voice, "Step back and let me work, Margaritta, or I am going to have to ask you to leave."

"Leave? Leave my own apartment? How dare you talk to me that way?" she shrieked. I heard stomping coming toward me, so she must have decided Randy was serious about having her removed. My stomach dropped as I imagined having to talk to Margaritta in this state. In a panic, I dashed gingerly around the house toward the parking area, forgetting my shoes again.

Unfortunately, there were witnesses to my odd escape from Margaritta. Nathan, Max and Ethyl were standing in the parking lot just outside the side entrance to the building. When I rounded the corner, they stopped talking and looked at me running toward them. I stopped at the edge where the path and the parking lot meet and stared back at them, not sure how to explain my cowardly escape.

Ethyl asked, "Mona, where are you going? You don't have any shoes on–again. You are going to hurt your feet." Ethyl's face changed to concern and she asked, "You aren't getting water in your apartment, are you?"

"Oh no, the apartment is fine. I just . . ." My voice trailed off as I searched for how to explain why I was tiptoe running–shoeless–through the garden.

Thankfully, I was saved by Randy, whose voice we could hear booming down the stairs through the open side entrance door as he walked down the stairs carrying an armful of soggy rags. As he emerged, we all looked at him expectantly, waiting to hear what had happened.

"Well . . ." Ethyl prompted him as he got to the bottom of the stairs. "What's happened?" she asked

"It looks to be a clogged toilet. I don't understand why there is so much water, though. It's like that cow upstairs just kept flushing it, hoping it would magically unclog with every subsequent flush," he said, obviously annoyed.

We were all snickering by now at the thought of the perfect Margaritta clogging her toilet.

"I'm not sure what she put down that toilet yet. I need to go get more rags. There is still water up there. I need to dry it up before I can get in there and take a closer look. Thankfully, I turned off the water to the toilet, so if little-miss-know-it-all decides to play plumber while I am gone, she won't keep flooding the place," Randy said confidently.

"Where is Margaritta now?" I tried to act casually.

"She's outside pouting on her deck. I told her she needed to back off and let me work or I was going to have her removed," Randy answered.

We watched him stomp off behind the house grumbling to himself, "Plumbing. The issue is always plumbing. I hate plumbing!"

We all stood staring at each other after Randy turned the corner. A few seconds later we heard footsteps descending the stairs. We looked over at the side exit to see a very flustered Margaritta. Her usual perfect appearance seemed askew, with her leather bag teetering, barely balanced on her right shoulder. Her keys were dangling from her long index finger on her left hand. Her face flushed from the excitement, she halted on the stairs when she saw all of us in the parking lot staring back at her. The look on her face conveyed that she was not happy to have an audience at this moment.

With his usual timing, Nathan didn't miss a beat, "Margaritta, I hear you have some trouble with your toilet. Were you trying to hide the evidence? You know, a standard toilet only has so much capacity."

We stifled our laughter in the uncomfortable moment that followed, but Margaritta took the bait and screamed back, "Nathan Laine, I have had just about enough from you! Take your smart mouth elsewhere. I have no patience for it today!"

I am pretty sure all our mouths dropped open. We all stood in shocked silence, staring at the disheveled Margaritta who seemed to be unravelling in front of us. Ignoring us, she marched down the stairs to her late-model BMW, got in and slammed the large driver's door. Then she peeled out of the parking lot like a Formula 1 racer.

Randy rounded the corner of the house and stopped in front of the group, asking, "What on earth was that racket?"

"The one and only Margaritta," Ethyl grumbled.

"You sure you can't get rid of her?"

Ethyl sighed, "Now Randy, we could do a lot worse than Margaritta. She may be rude, but she is tidy, pays her rent early, and for the most part, keeps to herself."

Randy shook his head, grumbling, "Well, she sure can plug a toilet. I better go back up and sort it out."

As Randy turned to leave, Max jumped in, "Randy, I'll go give you a hand." Randy hesitated uncomfortably, considering how to respond. Before he could find the words, Max added, "Oh, I know you like to work alone. I won't get in the way. I'll just be there in case you need a second pair of hands."

Randy's demeanor changed and he responded, "I guess it might not hurt to have some help up there to sort out that mess.

Come on, then."

Randy turned and walked over to the side entrance, carrying his tools and another bag of rags. Before climbing the stairs, Max subtly scooped the rag bag from him and followed Randy up the stairs with Nathan close behind them.

I looked over at Ethyl and smiled uncomfortably, saying, "There really is never a dull day around here, is there?"

Amused, she laughed, nodding her head, "You are correct there, although there has been far more action since you moved into the house. Keeps us young, I suppose. We really should check your apartment to make sure none of that water from above has made its way down, and we need to get you some shoes!" she exclaimed, looking at my feet and shaking her head.

After making our way back to my apartment and thoroughly inspecting the unit for water, we confirmed that thankfully, the water was contained upstairs. Ethyl shared some flood stories with me. Lost in the moment, we almost forgot about poor Randy upstairs until the banging of pipes was followed by screaming.

I looked at Ethyl, concerned. "Oh, that does not sound good at all."

Sighing, she said, "I guess I better go check things out to see if he needs help."

"I'll come, too."

"Oh, Mona, you really don't have to. This is one of those perks of renting; we are here to fix things for you," she responded, smiling.

"It's okay. I don't mind at all."

I slid on a pair of shoes at the door and we dashed down the stairs and around the corner. By the time we got there, Randy and Max were coming down the stairs and out the side entrance onto the landing, awkwardly carrying the toilet between them. I'm not sure how I sensed this was not going to turn out well, but suddenly the toilet was not being carried by Max or Randy any longer. The toilet had picked up momentum and had slid out of poor Max's hands. The transfer of speed was too much for Randy; suddenly, we watched the toilet launch itself off the landing. In a last-ditch effort, Randy reached behind himself in a lunge trying to grasp the toilet, but all he managed to do was set it into a spin causing toilet water and other foreign material to slop all over him and the stairs. The toilet bounced down the concrete stairs, each crash shattering the porcelain a bit more until it lay at the bottom of the stairs in pieces.

While we stood frozen in the shock of the moment, not sure what to do, defeated and covered in toilet matter, Randy sank down onto the top step and put his head in his hands, sighing, "Plumbing. I hate plumbing."

It was Max who spoke first. Staring down at Randy from the landing, with a horribly guilty look, he said, "I tried to hold on, but I think the toilet was wet from the pipe breaking upstairs when we were lifting it out. It just slipped right out of my hands as we got through the door."

Ethyl didn't wait for Randy to speak. She jumped into the conversation and walked toward him.

"Oh Max, don't you apologize at all. You were only trying to help. Everyone knows that. Thank you so much for helping to carry that heavy old toilet down the stairs with Randy." She paused for a moment, staring down at the wreckage of the toilet scattered across the parking area and continued, looking at Randy, "You know, we keep saying we should change that toilet. The consumption of water by that old thing was horrendous."

Randy slowly nodded his head, acknowledging that Ethyl was correct. Nathan piped up from the doorway, asking, "Randy, did you ever figure out what clogged the toilet in the first place?"

"No," he said, looking at the shattered mess below him, "I guess we will never know now."

"What is that?" asked Max, pointing at the bottom of the

stairs.

"What do you see?" Randy asked, standing up as Max and Nathan walked out.

"It's something shiny." Nathan pointed.

We moved closer to take a look. Being the only one with gloves on, Randy bent down and put his hands into the toilet rubble and fished out a thin, shiny, rectangular metal box, half the size of his palm. We crowded around him trying to get a look as he opened the top of the box. The top was fastened to the bottom along the one side with old metal hinges and inside, we could see a gold necklace with an old-fashioned locket in it. As we started to examine the necklace, a car came speeding down the driveway and pulled into a parking space.

"Uh oh, here she comes, back to reign terror on us all," Nathan commented under his breath, as we looked at the car.

Margaritta paused as she noticed us staring at her, but only for a moment, before she grabbed her belongings from the passenger seat, flung her door open and got out, slamming it behind her. She strutted toward us, clearly ready for battle, "What on earth is this mess, Randy? I hope this is not the toilet from my apartment!"

Randy growled under his breath and started to say something, but wisely, Ethyl cut in first. "It's been quite an afternoon, Margaritta. I know you can appreciate this," Ethyl said with a tone that conveyed she was not going to put up with anything Margaritta might be preparing to dish out.

Spotting what was in Randy's hands, Margaritta's whole demeanor changed in an instant. Tears were in her eyes as she said with a break in her voice, "My locket . . . you found my locket. I thought it was lost forever. You don't know how happy you have made me, Randy. Where did you find it?"

Flustered by the total change in Margaritta's behavior, Randy stammered and finally pointed down at the disaster at his feet. Looking down, he said, "It was in the toilet." Randy looked up at

Margaritta, gently placed the locket back in the metal box and gave it to Margaritta.

Lost in the moment, Margaritta stared down at it in her hand and managed to whisper, "Thank you, Randy. I thought I would never see my locket again."

As fast as this other side of Margaritta appeared, it was gone. She stashed the metal box in the front pocket of her leather bag and composed herself by standing tall, with her chin in the air. "Well, I better go inside and see the mess in my apartment." With that, she resumed her customary strut and walked across the parking area, then went up the side stairs.

When she reached the landing, Randy turned and called up to her. "Margaritta, I'm not finished in your apartment. It's still quite a mess and you, uh . . ." he paused, looking at the chaos around his feet. "You have no toilet. I happen to have a replacement toilet in the back storage shed, though."

Realizing he was right, Margaritta stood on the landing, appearing to think through her options as we watched, waiting for more fireworks. Instead, Ethyl spoke first. "Margaritta, I am sure this has been an unsettling day for you. How about you go up and put your things away and then come to the back garden for a cup of tea? I have a great new herbal blend that is very refreshing. Come try it with me while Randy fixes your toilet."

Margaritta responded quietly, "Thank you, Ethyl, that is very kind of you. Give me a moment to go upstairs and I will meet you in a few minutes." With that, Margaritta turned, went inside and walked up the stairs.

Randy shook his head and gave Ethyl a look. "You want to have tea with that creature? You are crazy." He shrugged and headed toward the back of the building muttering to himself as he walked away, "Back to work. It never ends around here."

As Randy disappeared around the corner, Nathan, Max and I turned to face Ethyl. "What just happened?" I asked, amazed.

"You invited her for tea?"

Ethyl smiled and laughed, "It won't be so bad. It will buy Randy some quiet time to get the apartment sorted out without anyone hovering over him. I better go make the tea," she said and walked toward the back of the house.

Nathan called out to Ethyl, "But what about this mess?"

Over her shoulder, she responded, "Don't worry; leave it for Randy. The porcelain is sharp. He has thick gloves and will use his big metal shovel to clean it all up."

Nathan continued, "That box of Margaritta's was the cause of this whole thing, though. She should be paying for the repairs."

Ethyl stopped and turned to look back at us, hands on her hips. "While you are correct, Nathan, we really were intending to replace that old toilet. Sometimes, we have to choose our battles," she said calmly. With this comment lingering in the air, she gave us a smile and a wink, then turned and walked around the corner.

Nathan looked at us and shook his head, "They are too kind, sometimes. Well, I guess the show's over, then. I, my friends, have a steak to cook!" He laughed and practically skipped over to the stairs of the side entrance and ran two at a time up into the doorway.

"I still feel terrible for dropping the toilet. Look at this mess." Max said, eyeing the debris. "I should at least try to clean it up."

"I don't know, Ethyl was pretty insistent that we leave it for Randy. We definitely shouldn't be touching this without gloves. I am sure he will just shovel it into a garbage bucket like Ethyl said. I would love to help, but if we end up injured, that's not helping anyone, is it?"

Resigned to the fact that I was right and probably imagining a nasty injury, Max nodded slowly and said quietly, "This day definitely turned out differently than I thought it was going to. Do you know–I was going to propose to Tish tonight?"

"What? You did not tell me that part of the story, Max!" I said, stunned to learn this missing detail. "Does she know?"

"No, I don't think so."

"Have you talked to her since this morning?"

"No, I was so frustrated and disappointed. I needed time to cool off. She won't get it, either. The next time I talk to her, she will be all happy and sweet, oblivious to what she did," Max said.

Treading carefully to avoid saying anything offensive to Max about his idiot girlfriend who obviously was a total fool to treat him this way, I tried to be sympathetic. "I am really sorry she upset you so much today."

Max paused for a moment and stared at me, "Thanks. I just wish it was only today."

I nodded supportively, still questioning in my mind why Max stayed with someone who caused him such grief.

"I can smell Nathan's steak. He must be barbecuing it on the balcony. He is quite a chef! We will have to figure out how to get him to cook for us one day," Max said, changing the subject.

"That's a great idea. If we go buy all the best ingredients for one of his favorite recipes, I bet he would make it for us," I suggested excitedly.

My excitement burst as Margaritta exited the building, heading to Ethyl's apartment. "Mona dear, glad you could find some shoes with which to come outside this time," she said, walking past us, laughing. "Always a pleasure, Max." She smiled and disappeared behind the house.

"Argh! I always freeze up when that woman is near me. One of these days I am going to give her a piece of my mind," I said in frustration.

Max laughed, "Don't let her get to you. It's not worth it."

"Fine," I murmured in response. Continuing with this approach and despite my better judgment I made a suggestion to

Max, "I think you should go call Tish. Tell her how you are really feeling."

"I don't know, Mona. I think I need to sleep on all this and give it some thought first," he said as we walked toward the house. "Thanks for listening today. I appreciate it," he said with a weak smile.

"Any time, Max. Thanks for the tour of the town and the university library."

We said our goodbyes and I walked back to my apartment. My stomach was rumbling for some food. I walked into the kitchen to concoct something to eat, contemmplating whether Max would actually tell Tish how he was feeling. "I will never understand why fantastic guys hook up with women who treat them like garbage," I grumbled, shaking my head.

As I finished preparing a plate of cold cuts and veggies and dip, the smell of Nathan's barbecue wafted through my window again. The smell was heavenly. Max and I definitely had to figure out how to get him to cook for us. I made a mental note of this as I carried my food outside to the small table and chairs under Nathan's balcony on the right of the stairs.

As I nibbled at my plate of food, I stared off into the garden, taking in all the colors. I thought about all the things that had happened since I had arrived. I was pulled from my daydream when I noticed movement in the garden. I looked more closely and spotted the large cat from next door. Slinking around the garden, he settled down onto the ground, curled around the gnome.

Knowing how Randy felt about the cat and that he was still running around dealing with the toilet situation upstairs, I decided to encourage it to go home. The last thing Randy needed today was to be taunted in the garden by his nemesis. I could only imagine–in his current state–what might result and no one needed that today.

I got up and walked over to the stairs and whispered to the cat,

"Psst, psst, you better go home," I said quietly. But, the cat just put its head down and sprawled out. "Come on now, Randy is going to see you and there will be big trouble," I continued, but the cat just stretched out even more, rolling onto his back.

I moved to the bottom of the stairs to get closer and try again, "Psst, you really need to go now," I said, more urgently this time. The cat rolled back over, before getting up to slowly walk toward me. Weaving in and out, rubbing against my legs, it began to purr. I couldn't resist its soft fur and sat down on the stairs, smiling. I reached down to rub behind its ears and it leaned into my hand for more. Then it looked up at me, moved onto the bottom step and hopped onto my lap. The friendly animal barely fit, but somehow managed to balance across my legs. I stroked its back, admiring its striking black and white stripes. Its purring was so soothing, too.

After a few minutes, the cat stepped back down, brushed against my legs one last time, and slinked away, heading next door. I smiled after it, wondering how Randy could possibly dislike such a lovely creature. My eyes wandered back into the garden, settling on the peculiar garden gnome for a minute. Such a quirky little creature, sun-beaten with its paint peeling in spots. I chuckled to myself, wondering what the backstory was on the gnome. As my eyes moved away, I was sure I saw it wink at me. My gaze jumped back again, trying to catch it in the act, but I only saw the same little smirk it always had. I stood up, deciding that I had better get out of the garden, back to reality and to my dinner.

I sat back down at the table, smiling to myself and tried to enjoy the magic of this peaceful moment. That's when my nose started to prickle and my eyes began to itch. I let out a huge sneeze, which reminded me how terribly allergic I am to cats.

CHAPTER 7

Over the weeks that followed, the lazy summer days settled in and things at the house became a lot quieter. Max and Tish left for several weeks to visit her family. While we never discussed it again, I am sure Max never gathered the courage to talk to Tish about their relationship. I suspected they would continue the same cycle, Tish doing whatever she wanted, oblivious to the impact, leaving Max perpetually disappointed by her behavior.

Margaritta's washroom was repaired and things seemed to settle down for Randy at the house. Margaritta went to a beach house for the summer to work on a book, which really made the house peaceful. I dreaded her return and the cloud of doom that would inevitably follow her back.

Nathan played tour guide, introducing me to various parts of Buckley Brook. One day we walked to the river that runs along the edge of town to an old mill, no longer in operation. It was fascinating to visit such a historic feature of the original town.

Between touring around with Nathan and helping Ethyl with her stunning summer garden, I should have been in a perpetual state of glee. Yet, against all logic, my thoughts continually stirred around my interactions with Margaritta. My mind replayed our conversations over and over, every time imagining all the things I should have said to her with the same level of venom she spewed out to the world. It became a vicious cycle I couldn't escape. Despite the beautiful summer weather, my mind kept wandering to this dialogue, day and night.

Looking for ammunition, I began poking around online to find out more about Margaritta Merchante. I invested hours scouring articles for nuggets of dirt I could use against her. Being a tenured professor, a lot had been written about her and her work. To my disappointment, all of the articles were glowing. She had built a strong reputation in the field of literary studies. Reading the accolades only served to deepen my distaste for the neighbor upstairs and fueled my pursuit to find anything to knock her off the pedestal from which she loved to look down upon the rest of the world.

I needed to go deeper, farther back. I moved my search to the library, hoping to tap into more obscure resources, but as I continued to spend hours pouring over anything I could find, I only discovered more glowing articles about how she was raised in a perfect loving family. I learned about her father William, a Professor of Accounting at the university; her mother Linda, a stay-at-home mom and an avid reader who was devoted to ensuring Margaritta and her older brother Peter, received the best education possible. What the classroom could not provide, Linda provided at home to both children. They graduated with near perfect marks from high school. Margaritta was the valedictorian for her graduating class and received a full scholarship to Buckley University, majoring in English. Her brother Peter became a physician and married his high school sweetheart, Sandra and they had two boys, Bruce and Freddie, who were adults now. Margaritta's parents, now in their mid-eighties, lived in the same town as Peter and Sandra, about twenty minutes from Buckley Brook.

"Nothing!" I said, slamming my hand too hard on the table. I was accessing archives of local town newspapers on a library computer. There were only three people around me, but the noise from the table jolted them all from what they were doing. I could feel three pairs of eyes staring daggers at me as I looked down at the table, my head in my hands. I looked up at them apologetically and sheepishly whispered, "Sorry." All eyes slowly reverted back to where they were and I was left to stew in the stillness of the library again. Surrounded on two sides by the tall stacks of books, I put my elbows on the table and my head in my hands and sighed. "What am I doing?" I whispered out loud.

"I found this article," said a quiet voice behind me. I lifted up my head and turned in my chair to see the eager young librarian who had been helping me dig into Margaritta's life. I had told her that the purpose of my research was for an editorial about my 'favorite professor' for the local newspaper.

She set a printed page down in front of me. I thanked her and my eyes dropped down to see a picture of a much younger Margaritta standing beside a man with his arm around her. They were both smiling for the camera. I looked back up at the librarian and thanked her for the article.

I turned back to the article. Its caption read, 'Buckley University student wins prestigious National Literary Award.' I stared more closely at the fuzzy picture examining its details. From the date of the article, Margaritta would still have been a young student, but the man was far too old to be a student. What was his connection? Was he the one giving her the award? I sat back and crossed my arms, continuing to ponder this article. They looked pretty cozy together. If this man worked for the university, a relationship with a student would have been strictly prohibited. Who was this man, I wondered and what was his relationship with young Margaritta? This could have caused a world of trouble for both of them. It still could. I chuckled quietly, delighting in my potential discovery, my imagination running away with how I might use this information to bring Margaritta down off her pedestal.

I decided to pause my search for the day to find some food and began to pack up my things. I carefully folded up the article about Margaritta and the mystery man and put it safely in the front pocket of my bag. I took the elevator down to the main floor, my mind wandering. Still lost in thought and relishing my newfound information, I walked out of the elevator in a fog.

"Mona!" I heard an excited voice announce my name. I looked up to see Max's friendly face smiling at me. Beside him, holding Max's hand, was the most beautiful woman I had ever seen. She was taller than me, yet petite, with long arms and legs like a dancer. She had thick black hair reaching almost to her waist. The most remarkable thing was her skin, which was absolutely flawless. She looked like an exquisite porcelain doll.

"This must be the great Tish." My stomach sank and my mood soured even further. Instantly filled with the feeling of total inferiority, I realized I hadn't said a word in return. Instead, I stood stunned in the library foyer with my mouth hanging open. I quickly composed myself. "Oh, hi Max. Sorry, I was in a daze," I said awkwardly.

"This is Tish!" he said, his arms outstretched, proudly presenting her like a gift to the world.

She beamed at me with warmth and radiance that triggered just the faintest glimmer of guilt for my instant dislike of her. She reached out and gently touched my forearm and in a softer, kinder voice than I expected, said, "Mona, it is such a pleasure to meet you. Max speaks so highly of you. It is truly, truly a pleasure."

Taken aback, I stammered like a fool. All I could manage was, "Uh, thank you, Tish. Uh, nice to meet you."

Max jumped in, "I am so glad that the two of you are finally meeting. We are headed upstairs to my favorite spot for a few hours," he said with a big smile. "Easing our way back into university life after three weeks of being spoiled at Tish's parents' house at the lake."

Ready to get out of the conversation and away from Max's goddess girlfriend, I made up a story on the spot, forcing a big smile, "It's nice and quiet in the library this week. I am just finishing some research myself. I . . . uh . . . need to ask the librarian a question. Nice to meet you,Tish. Enjoy your afternoon." Max and Tish said goodbye and I walked to the library desk. I waved as Max walked into the elevator and Tish bounced after him, giving him a big hug as the doors closed. Yuck.

Now, completely miserable, I remembered the fuzzy picture the librarian had given me. Maybe she will know who the mystery man is standing beside Margaritta. As I sat my bag down on the floor and removed the folded article from the pocket, I heard the bubbly voice of the young librarian again. "You're back! Was that article helpful?"

Despite my current mood, as I stood up, I forced a smile in return. "I am not quite sure yet. I am trying to identify the person standing next to Margar . . . er . . . Professor Merchante," I corrected myself. "Do you know who this man is?" I asked, as I passed the printed copy of the article to the librarian to examine.

She frowned and looked intently at the photo. "This article is over forty years old. The copy is not very clear at all. I think I need to do some digging to uncover the answer to your question. Do you mind? If you leave me your phone number I can call you if I can come up with anything." I complied and thanked the eager librarian. I tucked the article back into the pocket of my backpack.

I trudged out of the library and made my way home. The hot summer day looked like it was about to produce a heat storm . . . one of those amazing light shows where there are flashes of lightning all across the sky. Sometimes it doesn't even rain, it just gets really quiet and the sky darkens to an eerie yellowy-orange color, peppered by light streaking across the sky.

Then there are the tremendous summer thunderstorms that rattle your bones, especially when they happen in the middle of a summer night. These are usually accompanied by rain so hard you think it will wipe everything out in its path. It's best to watch these from inside through a window or even better, from a covered porch where you can really experience the power of the storm, but stay sheltered from the rain.

I watched the clouds start to darken as I walked, quickening my pace. I had a feeling that we were in for a doozy of a storm. I glanced at the parched grass on the lawns as I walked by and noticed how needed the rain was, but hoped it would hold off until I could get home. I heard a large crack of thunder above my head and jumped, startled at its proximity and started to jog the rest of the way home, hoping to beat the rain that was sure to follow. The drops started to fall: big cold drops, first a few, then more until the pavement was covered. I could see the house and made my final dash for the covered front porch, across the garden path and up the stairs just as the torrential rain descended on everything.

I stood on the porch–damp, but not totally soaked. The hot, humid air was cooled, but the heat was still swirling around in waves. I paused for a moment to enjoy the sights and sounds of the summer storm from the safety of the porch, relieved that I had narrowly missed getting caught in it. I decided to drop my bag inside, grab a blanket and sit on the swing to watch. The air was heavy and damp, but I was close enough to the window to stay mostly dry. With the soft wool blanket pulled tight around me, I stayed dry and warm. I sat cross-legged in the middle of the swing, mesmerized by the rain and the sound of the thunder breaking through the air as I gently swayed back and forth. It was unusually dark for an early summer evening, but this only accentuated the flashes of light blazing through the sky inter-mittently.

I thought about my trip to the library, my findings, running into Max and Tish. I felt sad, and unsettled. Why was I wasting my time and mental space on any of it? I was in a new town, a fresh start, in a beautiful apartment, overlooking a stunning garden. What was I doing? I stared off into the garden, frustration rolling around in my mind. Maybe I should set this whole thing aside, be the bigger person and just ignore Margaritta. But then I remembered how she treated her student the day we ran into her at the library–her cruelty, her arrogance, and I was back to where I started.

I couldn't shake the urge to find out more. I was confident she was not the picture of perfection that the papers painted her to be and I couldn't help but think it was all connected to that locket. Maybe I was chasing nothing, but I saw how Margaritta had reacted to Randy finding the locket. There was sadness, almost desperation, too. There had to be a story there. But, what did it say about me that I was so intent on discovering dirt on this woman to shake up her life?

For hours, I continued to sway back and forth on the swing, staring at the garden with the blanket wrapped around me. The storm passed and the sun set, leaving me in the quiet summer night air, contemplating my situation. It had a calming effect until the mosquitoes arrived. I gently brushed away the first one, and the second, but then they arrived as a pack and I had to make a run for the door to escape. I slid inside, hoping I hadn't brought any of them in with me. Knowing my luck, one stealth mosquito would hide and hunt me down after I went to sleep.

I walked to the kitchen and grazed on a few things at the counter, calling it dinner. After walking around aimlessly for a few more minutes, I decided to call it a night and go to bed. Always inviting, I jumped into my new bed with my overstuffed duvet and fluffy pillows, feeling like a princess nestling down for a long slumber. My subconscious got the best of me, though. Jumbled thoughts mixed together into vivid dreams about evil queens, flying toilets, and a handsome prince named Max. I tossed and turned most of the night, moving between a dream state and restlessness.

CHAPTER 8

By morning, all I could do was lie in bed and deny the arrival of the sun. It was the most bizarre sleep I had had since I arrived in Buckley Brook. Still trying to escape the thoughts that tormented me, I finally made the decision that this pursuit of Margaritta's past was not a healthy endeavor and it needed to stop. I longed for a distraction. I didn't know quite what that was yet, but I knew I needed to get Margaritta out of my head, move on and put my energy into finding a new focus.

Energized, I jumped out of bed and put on some light summer clothes. I decided to skip my standard mint tea and make some strong coffee to take out onto the porch. The stormy weather had completely cleared out and left clear air and a hot sun to dry everything off. I could only imagine what the heat would be like in a few hours.

I perched in the middle of the swing, carefully crossing my legs as I held my steaming mug of fresh coffee firmly with two hands. I closed my eyes and breathed in the amazing aroma, feeling the warm sun on my face. This was the joy of summer.

"My dear Mona Lisa, I see you are soaking up the morning sun today," said a familiar deep voice.

I opened my eyes and smiled as Nathan walked toward me down the path from the sidewalk. He was grinning, his arms full of groceries.

"Oh, you have been shopping! Were you at Paul's?" I asked.

"Why yes!" he responded proudly, as he stopped at the bottom of the stairs, set his groceries down and rested his left foot on the bottom step, leaning his arm up against the railing. "There was a sale on meat today, so I stocked up. I told you they have sales. You really should go over there. They have the best cuts of meat and when you can get them on sale, it's even better," he added.

I chuckled and assured him I would wander over and take a look later. We chatted about the summer weather and the big storm from the previous night. Then he started talking about Margaritta and my stomach sank.

"It sure is nice not having that old bat hanging around right now," he started. "I can finally live in peace without her going on, criticizing my every move. She really is a piece of work," he continued.

Despite my earlier resolution to get Margaritta out of my head, I couldn't resist adding to Nathan's comments, "Yes, it has been a lot more peaceful without her here. Maybe she won't come back."

Nathan jumped on this idea. "No way! She has tenure, don't forget. She is never leaving. She is going to haunt this place forever," he said, with venom in his voice.

Ethyl's voice came around the building toward us. "Mona, Mona!" she said excitedly. "Oh, good, you are here. I have such wonderful news to share!" She noticed Nathan chuckling at her and added, "Hello Nathan, lovely to see you. Sorry to interrupt you two, but I have big news!" Then she turned back to face me, looking like she was going to burst if she couldn't share her news. "Mona, the most incredible thing has happened. Do you remember when we first met? We talked about your aunt and the amazing lemonade she would make from the lemons on her tree."

"Yes."

"Well, before she left Buckley Brook, your aunt gave me a

cutting from that tree. I nursed that cutting at our farm and got it to grow, but it never produced any fruit. When we moved here, I thought the new protected space in our back garden might spur it on, but still no fruit. Eighteen years, Mona. No fruit. Nothing for eighteen years . . . until today!" she proclaimed, holding three small lemons up in the air toward me. "I walked to the back of the garden to take a look at the tree. Since it hasn't produced any fruit, I often forget about it. I'm not sure what made me go over there today, but I am glad I did. These little lemons were growing on the tree. There are quite a few more coming along, too!" she exclaimed.

I sat there enjoying Ethyl's excitement, trying to make sense of what had happened. "You have been caring for the lemon tree for eighteen years?" I asked, amazed.

Nathan interjected, "She is a dedicated gardener!"

Ethyl smiled and said, "Every year I hope that a lemon will grow. Then, this year you arrived, Mona and they did! I think it is you!"

I blushed at the compliment. "Aunt Audry would be so thrilled," I said softly, remembering my sweet aunt. Then it dawned on me, "I think I have her recipe for her lemonade."

"Really? We have these three little ones. We could make up a small batch to test it out," Ethyl suggested.

"Let's go look. I have a box with loose recipes on the shelf in the kitchen. I am pretty sure I saw a recipe for lemonade."

"Well, I will leave you two to concoct your lemonade," Nathan said, as he bent down to pick up his groceries. "I have to say, I do like a good lemon meringue pie, if you are feeling really adventurous," he added.

"Nathan Laine, if I can get you to cook one of your unbelievable meals for us, I will make you all the lemon meringue pies you want!" Ethyl declared.

"Ethyl, you know I will cook for you and Randy any day," he said confidently. "I better get these groceries put away. Good luck with the lemonade!"

Ethyl bounded up the stairs to the porch as Nathan waved goodbye. "Okay, let's go look through the box. If we are lucky, the recipe will be in there," I said as I got off the swing and headed into the apartment, holding the storm door for Ethyl to come inside.

I walked into the kitchen with Ethyl close behind. Reaching above the sink onto the small shelf above, I pulled out a light blue box, slightly smaller than a shoebox and set it onto the counter behind me. I took the lid off the box and we both peered inside at the jumble of folded newspaper cutouts, recipe cards, and scribbled notes on pieces of loose paper.

"This was my Mother's recipe box. She loved to cook," I said fondly, remembering how excited she used to get about finding new recipes to try. "I didn't inherit her skills in the kitchen," I added, laughing.

Ethyl smiled. "Sometimes the right recipe can guide you to perfection. I do hope we can find the lemonade recipe in here," she said, looking into the box with anticipation.

We both started sorting through the pile. We carefully scanned each one, hoping we would discover the coveted lemonade recipe. After a few minutes of searching, we each had a little pile on either side of the box. Pausing for a moment, Ethyl asked, "Where did your Aunt Audry go after she left Buckley Brook?"

"I was still quite young, so I don't remember a lot of details. She moved closer to us, but to an apartment of some kind. I think there was nursing care there. I went with my mother to visit sometimes. She always had treats for me," I said smiling. "She died only a few years after moving there, unfortunately. I think she was my mother's favorite aunt. It was a really sad time when she died, especially for my mother. Great Aunt Audry was the last of the elder family members to pass away."

We continued searching through the box for a few more minutes. Then Ethyl hooted in delight, "I think this is it, Mona!"

We both took a closer look at the small, weathered recipe card. "This is Audry's writing. She had such perfect cursive writing," Ethyl noted.

She flipped over the card to look at the back and sure enough, it read, "Audry's Famous Lemonade–Sure to make your cheeks pucker and your mouth water every time!"

We both laughed, "That was Audry, always having fun, even with her recipes," Ethyl said, smiling fondly at me. "Well, should we attempt to make this?"

"I don't know, I meant it when I said that I did not inherit the gift of cooking."

"How hard can it be? It's lemonade!"

"Audry's lemonade, remember . . . with the only three lemons you have produced in eighteen years!" I added.

"Okay, I will attempt the recipe on my own then," Ethyl conceded. "You will come to sample it on our patio after it's done, though. Can I borrow the recipe card to make a copy of it?"

"Of course," I said, handing Ethyl the little card. "Good luck!"

We walked outside together and stood chatting at the bottom of the steps for a few minutes about the weather, and her beautiful garden. The sun was in full force now. We were in store for another hot day.

"I should get back to my kitchen to work on the lemonade," Ethyl said with a big smile, waving the recipe card in the air. "With Audry's recipe, it is going to be fantastic. I just know it." Continuing in a more serious, earnest tone, she looked at me. "Mona, I really meant it. You are the magic touch this house needed. After 18 years and two different houses, the tree is producing lemons. It really is truly a wonder."

I smiled back at Ethyl, not knowing how to respond. This was one of the kindest things anyone had said to me in a long time. All I could do was whisper. "Wow, thank you Ethyl. That is very nice of you to say. The pleasure is all mine to be here in this wonderful house overlooking your beautiful garden."

"Give me a few hours to get the lemonade just right, then we will enjoy a glass on the back deck this afternoon and toast your Great Aunt Audry," Ethyl promised.

Ethyl bounced off around the corner of the house, waving the recipe around in the air with her tiny hand. I paused to chuckle for a moment, standing at the bottom of the stairs. "This place really is magical." Out of the corner of my eye, I was sure I saw the garden gnome wink at me again. I shook my head and laughed, not even bothering to look back at him this time, then walked back up to the porch.

I noticed my now-cold coffee on the table. "I need to invest in smaller mugs if I am going to live here; there is too much action to enjoy a full mug of coffee or tea in one sitting," I proclaimed.

I sank down into my very cozy spot this time and stretched my arms. "Maybe I need to find something active to take my mind off my obsession with Margaritta; nothing too crazy like axe-throwing or archery, though. There must be a nice yoga studio in Buckley Brook that I could try out. Yes, yoga would get my body limber and calm my mind at the same time."

I ducked inside to grab my phone. Then I plopped back down to search for yoga studios nearby. I was surprised to find several in Buckley Brook. I started looking at the one closest to the house, 'Zenza Yoga Parlour.' I wasn't so sure about the 'Parlour' reference, but it was close, so I decided to give it a whirl. How bad could it be? Looking on the map, I could see that it was only a short walk past Paul's Grocery. I searched the site for a schedule and noticed that there was a drop-in class that day before lunch. I looked at my watch. I had just over an hour to get ready and make my way to the class. I had taken the occasional yoga class in the city, but the classes were often full of pretentious, skinny girls– more focused on looking good and showing off their gumby-like physiques than focusing on the yoga. I had tried a few different yoga studios, but the experience was the same every time, so I gave up. It had to be different in Buckley Brook.

I jumped up, realizing I needed something to wear. I walked inside and down the hall to my bedroom. I found a pink tank top and some basic black yoga pants to go with it. Since it was so hot outside and the studio was so close, I decided to walk over in my yoga clothes. I grabbed a small bag and put my wallet, keys and a bottle of water into it, pulled the door shut and skipped down the stairs.

As I walked into the garden, I saw Randy walking purposefully toward me from Merl's house next door. "Hi, Randy. How are you doing today?" I said happily. As he got closer toward me, I could see that he was not in any mood for cordial chit-chat.

"Hi, Mona," he said, straining to be polite.

Rather than follow my better judgment, I persisted. "You look a bit upset, Randy. Is everything alright?" As the words left my mouth, I realized what I had done.

"Alright? Not alright at all. I am far from alright. I just opened up the water bill for Merl's property and it was through the roof. Insane–off the charts. It was three times the amount that it should have been. I went over to talk to Merl and hammered on the door, but there was no answer. I have to get in there to check out what is running the water bill up so badly. I can only imagine," he said, rolling his eyes. "I would just go in, but for the life of me, I can't find the key. That Merl never leaves the house. I don't know why he wasn't answering. He probably saw me coming over and decided to run and hide."

I realized that if I kept standing there, I was going to be late for the yoga class. I tactfully said, "I am sorry Merl is causing you so much aggravation. I hope you can find the key to figure out if there is a problem inside."

"Oh, there is a problem alright and if I can't get into that house, Merl is going to have even bigger problems!"

I started inching away along the garden path and Randy finally noticed. "Mona, I am keeping you. I am sorry. You don't need to get into my problems," he said.

Feeling terrible for being rude, I quickly said, "No Randy, it's not that. I like talking to you. It's just . . ." I paused, slightly embarrassed to admit that I was on my way to the 'Yoga Parlour.' I decided to go the healthy route and said, "It is just that I thought I should take better care of my health, so I'm on my way to a yoga class."

I could see Randy holding back a snicker, but he stifled his giggles and responded emphatically, "That is great, Mona! I hope you really enjoy it. Don't let me keep you, now."

I smiled and thanked him as I slid out of the garden onto the sidewalk. Luckily, I only had about seven minutes to walk, according to the directions on my phone. If I walked quickly, I could get there in five or six minutes. As I walked past Merl's house, I noticed the stillness of the house. A big old house with just a man and a large cat living there didn't have a lot of action going on on a hot summer day, I guessed. For some reason I was struck by the quiet as I passed though.

I picked up my pace so that I would arrive before the class. The heat from the sun was intense and I started to sweat as I walked. "Perhaps the pink tank top was not a good idea," I thought, as I looked down to see dark pink splotches emerging all over the shirt. I was going to look like I had already taken a yoga class by the time I arrived.

I finally reached my destination and slowed my pace, stopping in front of another century home that had been renovated, with an addition across the front of it. The whole house was clad in white siding, accented in black around the windows, the metal roof, and all the eavestroughs. It had a very different look from the other brick homes that lined the street. There were two front doors in the middle of the building painted canary yellow. To the right of the doors in the windows were letters in a thin curvy script displaying the name 'Zenza Yoga Parlour.'

I started to walk up the wide set of stairs to the front entrance. Before I got there, the door flew open and I saw Max staring down at me. "Mona! I didn't know you were a yogi!" he said excitedly.

I pondered how to answer this, discarding all the sarcastic answers that flew through my mind. I smirked a bit and settled on, "Well, Max, I would not go that far, yoga and I aren't best friends yet, but I figured I should get out and do some exercise. What brings you here today?"

"My girlfriend Tish is teaching the class this morning," he said with a smile.

I tried not to let my face display the instant horror I felt. Of all the yoga classes in town, I had picked the class taught by Max's goddess girlfriend. Feigning enthusiasm, I responded to Max, "Oh, what a coincidence! This is so great! What are the chances that I would end up here in Tish's class?"

"Don't just stand there, come right in and get settled. The class will start soon." Max answered, as he stepped back and opened the door wide. I entered through the canary-yellow door and turned to my right into the front entrance area. There was a heavy smell of sweet herbs in the air and quiet acoustic guitar music coming from a small speaker in the corner of the room. The walls were lined with hanging crystals and rocks on every flat space I could see.

I stepped up to a glass counter at the far wall and smiled at the petite young girl sitting behind it. "Hello, I am here for the drop-in class. Do I pay for it here?" I asked.

Before she could respond, Max jumped in excitedly, "Lindy, this is Mona! She lives in one of the apartments in the house that I live in. Mona, this is Lindy."

Lindy was wearing a light cotton wrap around her shoulders and had her hair twirled into a fancy knot on her head. Looking at Lindy's hair reminded me that I had forgotten to do anything with my hair. It was not particularly long, but I should have tied it up or something. I would have to manage.

Lindy smiled at me, "It's nice to meet you Mona-from-the-same-house-as-Max," she giggled. "That will be thirty dollars for the class today. I have books of ten classes for two hundred and seventy dollars, if you decide that you would like to come back," she said enthusiastically.

"Thank you, I will remember that," I responded, as I slid thirty dollars out of my wallet and handed it over to my perky new friend. This class better be fantastic for thirty bucks.

Max piped up behind me, "You are going to love Tish's class. It is such an experience."

Experience? What kind of experience were we talking about here? I didn't dare to ask, so I kept my enthusiastic facade going, "I am so excited. What a fun coincidence!"

"Come, let's get you set up with a mat. Follow me," Max said, waving to me to follow him. We walked through a doorway into a dimly-lit area where I took off my shoes. There were benches along the wall and hooks above them for coats. Little wood boxes lined the opposite wall, some with locks on them. "You can tuck your shoes under the bench and put your bag into one of the boxes. Don't worry about a lock. This is a trustworthy group," Max whispered.

Once I was down to just bare feet, yoga pants, and my pink tank top, Max slid open a heavy dark purple velvet curtain hanging across a rod in the doorway and revealed 'The Parlour' and fifteen extremely fit women with mats placed in a semi-circle facing the opposite wall. They were all sitting in a cross-legged position on their mats, in some sort of contemplation pose. It was at this moment that I decided this was a very bad idea. I couldn't flee, though; there was no way Max would allow that to happen. I searched my mind for an excuse to run out of The Parlour but my mind was blank.

We entered the dead quiet room and turned to the left of the door, where there was a stack of mats. Max gestured to me to pick one out. I stood looking at the pile of random colors and thicknesses, not sure which one to take. Too thin and I would be grinding my bones into the wood floor; too thick and I would fall on my face during the balance poses. Max leaned in, grabbed a lime-green, medium-weight mat and smiled at me as he handed it over. Then he took a gray mat for himself.

We found a spot on the floor in the semi-circle, close to the back, thank goodness. I was already planning my escape as we rolled out our mats. Not wanting to be out of place, I assumed the cross-legged position, like the others. My knees were screaming, but I managed to smile at Max, gave him two thumbs up and a big, goofy grin. Then I proceeded to contemplate just how terrible this idea was.

At about the time my knees and thighs were about to exit out of contemplation pose, with or without me, in walked Max's goddess girlfriend in an entrance I wish had been recorded. From behind another heavy purple velvet drape, the goddess stepped into the room. She was dressed in a black one-piece footless leotard held up with tiny spaghetti straps along her shoulders. As she entered, she paused in place to survey the room, taking time to make eye contact with all her adoring students. When she turned to put down her water, I noticed that her black leotard was open at the back, right down to her waist and was held closed by alternating criss-crossing spaghetti straps all the way down her back. I instantly felt unworthy. At least it was finally clear why Max kept coming back for more.

Then the goddess spoke in a low, sultry voice, "Welcome to the parlour, everyone; the parlour, a space where everyone is welcome. Welcome, to be free. Free, to be yourself and to explore your abilities. The ability to shine, and let your radiance glow. We are one today and together we will make magic here, in the parlour," she said, pausing after every other word for dramatic effect and raising her hand in reverence at the end.

I was overcome with a wave of the giggles. Was this chick for real? I bit my tongue hard to control myself as Max looked over, wondering what was going on. I didn't want to offend Max. He was so sweet, even if his girlfriend was a little out there. I bit my tongue harder, which caused me to let out a noise that sounded like a bird squawking, but luckily it was at the same time that Tish's fans started fawning over her and raising their hands up in joyous harmony, including Max, who was right into this thing.

Finally, all the love in the parlour settled down and Tish asked us to stand up on our mats. "Stand with your feet shoulder-width apart, soft knees anchored to the ground like your feet are one with the earth's foundation, fixed and solid in place. Now bend your knees deep and swing your arms around, free like a chimpanzee in the wild," she said, walking around the room as everyone began to swing around their mats like chimps.

That's when I heard, "oo oo oo oo," from across the room. The call of a chimp, I supposed. It was echoed by several other sporadic chimp calls, and then Tish followed, "That's it! Be free, show us your inner animal!" This continued for a few minutes until things settled down. It was everything I could do not to run out of the room until I looked over at Max who was giggling while doing a half-hearted chimp. He looked back at me with a big smile and laughed and I couldn't help but stay.

"Okay," said Tish. "Let's anchor our feet to the floor. Stand tall in your mountain pose and be still. Channel the energy you just found from your inner animal into strength that will propel you forward in your practice today. Now draw in a big breath and take yourself to the top of the mountain. Now breathe out. We are going to add arms, now. Big breath in, sweeping your arms up to the top of the mountain. Look over the edge, now dive over like a bird, fly little birds over the mountain and be free!" she declared.

I looked over at Max, and I mouthed desperately, "Dive?"

He smiled and mouthed back, "Follow me," then tipped over and dove forward into a bend, pausing, then folding in half, touching his legs with his face and dangling his arms around his feet. "Impressive," I thought, pausing to admire his flexibility.

Relieved that this was all that we were doing, I tipped over and followed Max into a dive forward. I couldn't bend the same way as he did, though. My fold was a desperate flail toward my toes with a bit of wishful thinking. I settled on half the distance as Max, touching my shins with my hands instead.

Not tying my hair up came back to haunt me at that point. The room had gotten really hot for some reason and I was sweating profusely. My damp hair was hanging all over my face and slid its way into my mouth. I tried to spit it out, but every time I breathed in, I sucked more hair into my mouth.

Tish continued, "Now enjoy the rest here and breathe; focus on the breath filling your lungs and energizing your every cell."

I tried to relax and go with it, while subtly extracting the hair from my mouth.

"Now, let's climb that mountain again, slowly rolling up this time, lifting your arms up in the air at the top and your head last. Now take a moment to survey the land below and breathe. Here we go. Dive, my lovelies, dive," Tish belted out across the room.

I stifled a groan as I prepared to tip over again. I paused partway, quickly glancing over at Max who was lost in his dive, clearly lapping up all his goddess girlfriend had to give. "Men," I thought. Seriously, how does a man so brilliant in every other area of his life, go so wrong in the love department? As we climbed the mountain again and Tish walked past us touring around the room, I caught the view of the back of her black leotard. "Fine," I thought.

We climbed and dove over the mountain what felt like a hundred times before we finally moved into a series of what I would call more traditional yoga poses. Each time, Tish offered her own unique twist, though. Finally we arrived at savasana, the universal signal that the class was almost done. As I lay on the now very-sweaty mat and contemplated the wild journey I had just been on, I noticed that I felt pretty relaxed, but that might have been relief, or delirium. How hot was the room, anyway?

I looked over and Max was smiling at me. "Wasn't that great?" he asked enthusiastically.

Not wanting to offend him, I answered, "It certainly was like no other yoga class I have taken."

"Yes, Tish does put her own spin on traditional yoga," he said proudly.

I smiled and nodded. "That's one way of describing it!"

"We better clean our mats and put them away. I'll go grab the spray and some towels. You look like you need a towel for yourself, too."

"Oh, great," I thought. I looked so bad that Max was offering me a towel. I decided laughter was the best path and added, "This class should come with a heat warning."

Max laughed in agreement and headed over to the corner to find some towels and the spray to clean the mats.

As we walked toward the purple velvet curtain after cleaning up and putting everything away, we heard a voice from behind us, "Mona! You came to my class!"

We turned around to see Tish's smiling face. She gave Max a hug, then turned to me and beamed, "I didn't know that you were a yogi!"

"I like the occasional yoga class," I replied. Technically, that was true.

"How did you enjoy my class?" Tish asked.

"Uh oh," I thought, as I searched for the right response, "Well, it was a hot one! Your approach to yoga is very creative, Tish. I could see your students really responding to your teaching," I said earnestly, hoping she would buy it.

Tish raised her hand to her chest, "Oh Mona, that's so nice of you to say. Thank you," she replied, visibly touched by my words. I felt a little guilty for selling her such drivel, but buyer beware, right?

Max looked at us excitedly. "I loved the class, Tish." Then he turned to me and said with a big smile, "Tish and I have a big night planned. We are going out on the town."

"Oh, about that, Max . . ." Tish said–a bit too casually.

"Here we go again," I thought, as I watched Max's face fall.

"My energies are just not in alignment today. I think I better go home and rest, Max. You understand, right?" Tish continued, patting his arm for good measure.

Max sighed, "Yes, of course I understand."

Caught in a more than awkward moment, I started to creep toward the purple velvet curtain, "I'll let you two chat. Thanks for the class, Tish."

Neither Max nor Tish responded. They seemed to be caught in a silent stare. I took one last look at them as I slid through the purple curtain and breathed a sigh of relief to have escaped 'The Parlour.' "Poor Max," I whispered, as I sank down onto the bench to rest for a moment and slid on my shoes. He had looked so hurt.

Everyone had left and I was alone in the little change room. I strained to try to hear Max and Tish talking. I could only hear urgent whispers, though. Finally, Max yanked open the curtain aggressively across the rail and stomped into the room. Seeing me, he drew up short and stopped, composing himself. He took a breath and ran his hand through his hair, "Don't even start," he said to me in frustration. "I know what you are thinking. Why do I put up with this?"

I looked at him and responded, "I don't even know what is going on here, Max. I came here for a yoga class that I found on an internet search."

He sighed and dropped down onto the bench beside me. "No, I know. I'm sorry you had to witness that," he said, looking at me.

"From my perspective, you don't have anything to apologize about. Let me guess; you created a big plan for tonight and you were hoping to propose again."

Max nodded his head, and quietly said, "Yes."

"Well, let's not hang around in this dark changeroom all day. It's a beautiful day. We should go enjoy it," I added, hoping to get Max's mind off the situation.

Max smiled, "Okay. Thanks Mona," he said quietly, going along with the plan.

We put on our shoes, gathered our belongings and headed out of the yoga 'parlour' into the beautiful, hot summer afternoon. We were both famished after the wild yoga class. When we saw Paul's Grocery, our stomachs started to rumble for deli sandwiches.

As we were waiting for our sandwiches to be made, I blurted out in excitement, "I forgot about the meat sale today!"

Max laughed, "You sound like Nathan."

"Well, it was actually Nathan who told me about the sale. He stopped to talk this morning on his way back from shopping."

"What are we waiting for? Let's go find some steaks to grill tonight!" Max responded, joining in my excitement.

"Hold on, how do we grill them? I don't have a barbecue; do you?" I asked.

"Don't worry about that. Ethyl and Randy have a big barbecue at the back of the house in their yard. They are always inviting everyone to use it. They won't mind at all," Max said, reassuring me.

"Do they like steak?" I asked as we walked toward the fridge.

Max laughed, "Do they ever!"

"Should we pick up two steaks for them?"

"It can't hurt. Even if they have dinner plans, they can put them in the fridge or freezer for another day."

"Okay, let's do it!" I said enthusiastically.

We picked up ribeye steaks, our sandwiches, and made our way to the checkout to pay. A fridge containing smoked fish caught my eye. "Smoked fish! It has been so long since I have had smoked fish!" I exclaimed excitedly. I scooped up a small piece wrapped in brown paper and put it in the basket.

As we waited to pay, Max glanced out the window and said, "It is such a beautiful day; do you want to eat our sandwiches here on the patio?"

I took a look at my watch, "I would love that, but Ethyl is making very special lemonade and I promised to meet her on her deck for a glass," I explained.

Looking confused, but curious, Max asked, "And what makes this lemonade so special?"

I laughed. "It's a long story. How about I tell you on the walk home? We can take our sandwiches over to Ethyl and Randy's and have some lemonade with them on their deck."

"Sounds like a plan," Max agreed.

After paying for all our delicacies, Max and I walked back to the house. The early afternoon heat was intense. It hit us like a wave as we left the cool air of the store and walked out into the summer sun. For late August, the hot weather was still in full force.

Max and I bantered back and forth as we walked. I shared the lemonade story and he was amazed. There was a lull in the conversation until Max spoke up. "I'm sorry about that stuff back at the yoga parlour earlier," he said sheepishly, looking down at his feet as we walked.

Confused, I responded, "What do you mean?"

"I just wish you hadn't witnessed that whole thing. I was a bit snarky with you when I first came into the changeroom. I am sorry."

I shook my head and finally seized the moment, "Honestly, Max, you don't need to apologize to me. You didn't do anything wrong. I have to ask you, though, if Tish keeps treating you like this, why do you keep giving her more chances?" I held my breath and waited, knowing I had probably crossed the line of our short friendship.

There was a long pause in the conversation as we walked in silence. My stomach churned; I was concerned that I had upset Max. At the same time, I meant every word I had just said. "Why did he keep letting Tish walk all over him?" Then I remembered the black backless leotard, long black hair, and sultry voice.

Finally Max spoke and to my relief, he wasn't angry. "Mona, I don't know why I keep giving Tish more chances. She has cast a spell over me. I just keep forgiving her and going back."

"Forgiveness is important, but not when it's one-sided," I offered, surprising myself. Where had that pearl of wisdom come from?

Max sighed, still looking down at the sidewalk. In barely a whisper he added, "I know you are right."

Looking for a way to escape this awkward topic and not wanting to push any further, I attempted to change the subject. "I am sure Ethyl's lemonade and the sandwiches will help cheer you up!"

Max laughed. "Subtle, Mona. Really subtle. A nice glass of homemade lemonade after this hot walk will be nice, though," he agreed.

Before he could say anything else, we turned the corner onto our street approaching Merl's house and were greeted on the sidewalk by the big black and white cat.

"Oh hello, Mister," I said, happy to see the cat again. I crouched down to pet him and he slinked around my arm, his fluffy fur puffing up around him.

"He really likes you, Mona," Max said, surprised. "Don't let Randy see this," he cautioned.

I laughed. "Never! Randy has declared war with this guy. Last time I saw them together he was chasing this boy around the garden with a pot and a hammer."

The cat started to take a liking to my shopping bag of treats, pushing at it with his nose. He looked up at me with his big green eyes and I decided to give in. "I know what you are interested in . . . the smoked fish!"

"Not your smoked fish, Mona. That fish cost you a small fortune," Max reminded me.

I dug through the bag and found the wrapped fish. "I'll just give him a little piece." I unwrapped the fish inside the bag and carefully separated out a small piece from the bones. As I pulled it out of the bag, the fluffy cat perked up, his eyes following my hand. I held out the fish on the palm of my hand and he gently ate all of it. He even licked my hand clean of the oil after all the flesh was gone. The cat leaned up against my knees, rubbing his head on my hand, and started to purr loudly.

Max looked down at us, smiling. "I think you made a friend, Mona."

"I think my smoked fish made a friend!"

I stood up and we started walking toward the house, the cat prancing beside us. When we arrived at the bottom of my stairs, I looked down at my cat friend. "You are in dangerous territory. If Randy comes around that corner and sees you . . ." my voice trailed off as I imagined Randy's reaction.

"It will be goodbye, kitty," Max jumped in.

The cat slinked around me again, brushing his soft fur along my legs. Even through my yoga pants, his fur tickled my skin. I smiled and watched him walk toward the garden where he curled up on the wood chips around the garden gnome. The cat pawed lightly at the wood chips beside the gnome. Then he got up and started digging with purpose at the feet of the gnome, leaving a growing pile of dirt on the path behind him.

"Uh oh, now this cat is going to get in trouble with Randy and Ethyl the gardener, too. Stop, kitty. Don't dig up Ethyl's garden!" Max cautioned.

I walked closer, "Come on, stop digging. You are going to get yourself in hot water," I said emphatically to the cat.

Despite our urging, the cat's digging became more aggressive. Then he stopped and stepped back, revealing something metallic. I leaned in for a closer look and noticed a single key on a simple metal ring. As the cat and Max watched, I bent down and picked up the key and held it out on my index finger to examine it.

I looked back at Max with a puzzled look, holding the key in the air. "Do you recognize this key? How do you think it got into the garden?" I asked, as I turned to look back at the cat and the garden gnome. The cat stared up at me with innocent eyes. I gave it a suspicious look, leaning in closer, "Did you hide this key in the garden, kitty? If this is the key to next door that Randy is looking for and he thinks you hid it, you are going to be kitty bbq!" I turned around to face Max. "I think we better show this key to Randy. It could be the one he is looking for."

"Let's go back to see Ethyl. Maybe Randy will be there and we can ask him."

"Okay," I agreed. "I'll run the steaks and the smoked fish up to my fridge. We can bring the sandwiches with us."

I ran into the apartment, dropped my bag under the kitchen counter and put the food that needed to be chilled into the fridge. I still had the key the cat dug up in my hand. I lifted it up and took a closer look and decided to rinse it off before showing it to Randy.

After drying it off, I took another look. "How did this key get into Ethyl's garden," I wondered, puzzled at the situation. Remembering that Max was waiting for me in the hot sun, I put the key in my pocket and walked quickly outside, pulling the doors tight behind me. I found Max on the porch sitting on the swing. "Oh good, you found some shade," I said, smiling at him.

"This is a great porch, Mona," he said, scanning the length of it. "You have both sides, too. My basement apartment didn't come with a porch, unfortunately."

"Yes, I have really enjoyed this spot. I will miss it in the winter when it's too cold to come out here. You are welcome to use it any time you like, Max. There is more than enough sitting room," I offered.

"Thanks, Mona. I just might do that," he answered enthusiastically.

"Shall we go visit Ethyl and Randy?"

Max jumped up. "Absolutely, I have been craving a glass of lemonade ever since you told me about those lemons!"

We walked down into the garden and I noticed that the cat was gone. I turned and looked at Max, "What did you do with the cat?"

"We had a heart-to-heart while you were inside and he went home. I think he decided that Randy having a kitty barbecue was a real possibility."

I laughed. "Thanks for convincing him."

"I don't even know that big cat's name," I mentioned as we walked around the house to the back. I'll have to ask Merl if I ever cross paths with him in the yard."

"That guy is a funny one. He rarely leaves the house. I have only seen him a few times the whole time I have lived here," Max said.

"Well, he has a cute cat."

Max laughed as we turned the corner at the back of the building, arriving at Ethyl and Randy's apartment. I stopped for a second to admire their back yard. It was much bigger than I realized. There were flower patches all over and a large vegetable garden in the middle. To the right of the garden were two trees with a hammock strung between them. There was a stone patio to the left of the garden in the middle of a cluster of flowers. It had a black iron table with four chairs around it and a large red umbrella covering the table to offer some shade.

As we were taking in the beautiful surroundings, we heard a voice. "Oh, there you are, Mona. You brought Max, too!" Ethyl called out to us from the large deck stretched along the back of the house. Smiling, Ethyl walked down the stairs extending from the middle of the deck directly opposite the entrance door to greet us. "I think I have figured out Audry's lemonade recipe!" Ethyl said confidently.

"I heard about your lemons, Ethyl. I can't wait to try the lemonade!" Max added.

"Come on up," Ethyl said, gesturing toward the deck.

We followed her up the stairs. I took a moment at the top to admire the large sitting area overlooking the gardens. It was a similar structure to the front porch with a covered section immediately outside the door, but the deck continued past the covered area by the house, opening up as a sunny seating area. "This is quite something, Ethyl," I said, taking it all in.

"Thank you, we love it. This is why we haven't left this house. We loved the front porch so much we tried to duplicate it back here. Then we built this extension so that we could enjoy the sun a bit more." Ethyl paused and then declared, "It's time for lemonade! Give me a moment to bring it out. Have a seat."

Max and I placed the bag of sandwiches on the table and took a seat at the edge of the deck, looking out at the yard in silence. "It's so peaceful back here," Max said quietly. I nodded in agreement.

Ethyl came outside, carrying a glass pitcher. I jumped up to meet her, taking the pitcher from her and placing it on the table. She went back inside and came back with a tray of four tall green glasses, which she set down on the table.

"I brought a glass for Randy. He is somewhere around here. Hopefully he isn't planning on tangling with those bees today." Ethyl poured three glasses of lemonade, setting one in front of each of us. She lifted her glass to us and we followed suit, lifting our glasses in the air. "A toast to Audry and her lemon tree. After so many years, our paths cross again. Here's to the magic of old friends and new," Ethyl said warmly. We all smiled and took a big sip of the lemonade.

It took a moment, but then it hit us. We all screwed up our faces, puckered our lips, and opened our eyes wide with surprise. I was trying to figure out the taste. It was sour, but also salty and sweet. I looked over at Max and I could see horror creeping onto his face as he fought to hide the reaction and be polite, but faces are hard to control sometimes, especially when reacting to eating something sour.

Finally Ethyl spoke. "Whew! That packs a wallop!" she said with a smile. "Take another sip. Trust me; it grows on you."

I giggled. I couldn't help myself and I took another big sip. Max raised his eyebrows and looked at me, silently questioning why I was torturing myself with another mouthful. This time I was ready for it, though. After the initial assault on my taste buds, the flavors levelled out, leaving a smooth lemony after-taste. I looked at Ethyl. "The first sip was a shock, but then it mellows. How does this batch compare to what Audry used to make?" I asked Ethyl.

"I think Audry's was a little smoother. I wonder if she left out a secret ingredient," Ethyl said, laughing. "It would just be like Audry to slide one ingredient off the recipe card into her back pocket. What a character she was." Ethyl smiled, looking off into the garden. "Did you see the lemon tree? It's just to the left of the vegetable garden over there."

We followed Ethyl's gaze into the garden and spotted the tree gleaming in the sunshine. As we admired the lemon tree, we all heard banging coming from the side of the house. Bang, Bang, Bang. "What on earth is that noise?" Ethyl asked, looking at us.

Bang, Bang, Bang, we heard again. This time it was more urgent followed by a muffled, "Ethyl! Help me, I'm locked in."

"Randy!" Ethyl jumped up and ran down the stairs with Max and I close behind. As we turned the corner into the parking area, the banging became louder. "Help! I'm stuck," called Randy from inside the garbage shed.

Ethyl walked up to the door of the garbage shed and politely knocked in reply, and said, "I'm here. Are you okay?"

"No, I'm not okay, I'm locked in the shed!" said Randy, followed by a few muffled words none of us could hear. I suspected this was probably for the best.

"How is the door locked on the inside?" Ethyl asked, puzzled.

"It's one of those locks that doesn't unlock. It stays locked all the time. I was cleaning the shed since all the garbage bins are out on the road today. The old doorknob was loose and I thought I would replace it. I was in the middle of installing it when the door swung closed and locked me in."

"Uh huh," Ethyl replied, shaking her head at us. "Do you have a key?"

"No, I don't have the key. I didn't think I would need the key INSIDE the shed!" Randy said, exasperated.

Ethyl looked down at the doorknob and reached for it, then turned the handle and opened the door. An irritated Randy stood inside the shed staring back at us.

"Well, come on out. This shed has got to be 150 degrees. You'll melt your brain spending any length of time in there."

Randy came out of the shed and fiddled with the doorknob. He looked at us and then at Ethyl and scratched his head with his left hand. Still holding onto the doorknob, he said, "Backwards. I put the darn thing on backwards."

"You still need the key, though, Randy. How will everyone get into the shed?" Ethyl added.

"Maybe I should just go to the store and buy one of those

keypad ones, so we don't need a key," he said, thinking out loud.

"I don't think anyone is itching to steal our garbage, Randy," Ethyl responded, with her hands on her hips. "Do you really need a lock on that door?"

That's when I remembered the key in my pocket that the cat dug up. "Speaking of locks and keys," I said, digging the key out of my pocket. "Do you recognize this key, Randy?"

Randy squinted and blinked a few times, then walked closer, "That's the key to next door that I was looking for!" He took the key from me and looked at it in his hand, then looked at me, puzzled, "I have been looking everywhere for this darn key. Where did you find it?"

I hesitated, not wanting to reveal the antics of my cat friend next door. I glanced quickly at Max and said, "It was the funniest thing. We were walking through the front garden and something metallic caught my eye. I reached down into the wood chips and lifted up the key."

"Huh. Well, isn't that odd," Randy said looking down the driveway. Then his face changed and he looked back at us, "Now I can go find Merl. I'm going to give him a piece of my mind for whatever is going on in that house that is causing the water bill to go through the roof. I have had just about enough of that guy and his irresponsibility."

Randy started marching toward the front of the house when Ethyl called back to him, "Randy, what about this door?"

He called back over his shoulder as he walked, "It's fine like that as long as no one shuts the door while they are inside."

Ethyl looked back at us and shook her head, "I better go make a sign to put on the door." She stepped around us and headed toward the back of the house. Smiling, she said, "Thank you for enjoying the lemonade with me today." Then she winked at Max. "I'll keep working on the recipe to make it a little smoother." We heard her laughing to herself as she disappeared behind the house.

Max looked down at my right hand and laughed. "You grabbed the sandwiches?" We both heard my stomach rumble. "I think you need to eat one of those."

"Let's go eat on my porch."

"Okay, I'm famished."

We walked to the front of the house and settled at the table on the porch. We were enjoying the first few bites when I noticed Randy stagger out of the house next door and walk toward us.

"Something is wrong," I said, concerned as I stood up from the table.

Max and I walked down the stairs and toward Randy. As he got closer, it was clear that something was definitely wrong from the look on Randy's face. He gave us a blank, hollow stare and said in a low voice, "Merl . . . Merl's dead."

"What?" That was probably not the most helpful response.

"I found him in his chair, in front of the TV., I don't know how long he has been like that," Randy said vacantly.

"What do we do now?" Max asked.

"We need to call the funeral home. I have the number. I better go tell Ethyl. I can call from inside the house."

"Are you okay, Randy? Do you want one of us to walk back with you?" I offered.

"Thanks, Mona. I'm okay. Just a little shocked, I think."

As Randy walked around the house toward the back of the building, Max and I were left staring at each other. There was nothing to say.

Then we heard Nathan's voice from the balcony above us, "What's going on? You all look like someone died!" he shouted down jovially.

Max and I just looked at each other, not sure how to respond to that comment. After a minute, I answered. "Your choice of words is convenient, Nathan. It's Merl next door. Randy just found him dead in the house."

"What? Oh, my goodness. Hold on, I'm coming down."

After a few minutes, Nathan arrived at the front of the house. As he got closer, he asked, "So what's happening now? Where is Randy?"

"He went to call the funeral home, and to tell Ethyl the news. I imagine they will be back here soon," I explained.

"How long has the old guy been dead?" Nathan probed.

"We don't know anything. We only talked to Randy for a moment. He was pretty shaken up," Max responded.

Then it dawned on me and I wondered aloud, "How has his big cat been wandering around outside if he was in there, uh . . ."

"Expired?"

"Yes that," I said, shriveling up my face in distaste at Nathan as he continued.

"That cat is pretty independent. He has his own escape hatch on the back door. He comes and goes as he pleases," Nathan said nonchalantly.

"I wonder where the cat is now," I said, concerned. "The poor cat has lost his owner."

As we were considering this point, Randy and Ethyl appeared. I reached out and touched Randy's arm and quietly asked, "How are you doing, Randy?"

"I don't really know. That guy was a pain in my rear, but I didn't want him to die."

"The funeral home said they will be here soon to take care of Merl's body." Ethyl said, as we stood silently looking at each other in the heat of the summer sun.

We noticed a vehicle arrive next door and two men clearly from the funeral home got out and looked around. Ethyl and

Randy walked over to meet them. As Nathan, Max and I watched the events unfolding next door, the heat beat down on us and I suggested that we move to a shadier spot on the porch. I put the sandwiches away in the fridge, as neither Max nor I were hungry anymore. I returned with cold drinks for the three of us and we congregated around the table on the porch.

I was settling into my chair when we heard a car turn into the driveway of our house. We turned to look at it and everyone realized whose car it was. "Well, look what the coast blew in?" Nathan proclaimed. "The wicked witch from upstairs."

My stomach dropped and I began to sweat, even more than when I had been standing in the sun earlier. "This is turning into quite the day. First the bizarre yoga class, then Merl, now Margaritta returns," I mumbled.

Nathan laughed, looked at me and exclaimed, "Don't tell me you went to one of Tish's far-out yoga classes!"

I gave Max an uncomfortable side glance and then responded, "Yes, I thought I should do something healthy."

Nathan was now in a fit of laughter, "I'm sorry, Max, I know she is your girlfriend, but those classes are out of this world and full of nuts."

"You took one?" I asked inquisitively with a wry smile. The image of Nathan in a one-piece, backless, black leotard filled my mind. Ugh. I quickly tried to think of something else.

Nathan looked over and gestured at Max, "This guy thought it would be good for my health and convinced me to tag along one day. I lasted ten minutes before I called it quits and went home. Too 'out there' for my liking. I will stick to my daily walk around town, thank you very much. So where is the lovely Tish now?" Nathan said, directing his gaze squarely at Max.

Max looked down at his hands and shook his head in response. Nathan glanced over at me and I gave him a look, trying to silently tell him that he was heading down a bad road. Unwavering, Nathan continued, "She ditched you again, didn't she, my friend?"

Max shook his head again, but this time, looked up at Nathan in frustration. "Will you quit it? You are always poking at Tish. Enough!" Max stood up quickly, scraping the chair loudly along the deck. He turned away, grabbed the railing and looked off into the distance.

Caught in the middle, I sat uncomfortably between my two newfound friends. Not wanting to make anything worse, I just said nothing, shifting my eyes between Max's back and Nathan's face.

Nathan raised his hands up in front of himself in defence, "Hey, I'm just telling you how it is. I'm sorry." Nathan paused for a moment, then continued with a chuckle, "I love the fire, though, man. Now you gotta direct that fire at the lady who is breaking your heart."

Max let out a long sigh and continued to stare off toward the house next door.

"You are a good guy, Max. You deserve to be treated how you treat everyone else in the world," Nathan told Max.

Max turned around and looked at Nathan. "Thank you. I'm sorry I lost my cool."

"Nathan let out a big laugh, "I'm not! It's about time. How did it feel?"

Max laughed and rejoined us at the table. He thought about Nathan's question for a minute and then responded with a wry smile, "Pretty good, actually."

Nathan banged the table with his hand, causing me to jump and we all laughed at my skittish reaction. Then Nathan said, "Exactly! It feels good to stand up for yourself. Now, you need to practice this more often. Both of you do, actually." I looked at

Nathan, surprised to be sucked into this.

"What do you mean?" I asked.

"Oh, don't start with me, lovely Mona Lisa. I have seen how you shrivel up when that wicked witch upstairs gets near you. You should have seen your face when she drove in a few minutes ago. I thought you were going to pass out."

There was no use protesting. Nathan was right. Now it was my turn to look away toward the house next door. "This would be a really good time for Ethyl and Randy to come back," I thought to myself.

"I'm not trying to be the bad guy here, you two," Nathan protested, drawing our eyes back to him. He softened his tone and continued, "I like you both and it drives me crazy to see people treat you badly. You deserve better. That's all I am saying."

He stood up and pointed at the house next door. "Looks like they are taking Merl away." We watched the funeral home staff finish up their work and close the doors on the van. Ethyl and Randy stood in the driveway and watched them drive away. They stood for a moment before turning to walk back toward us.

"I wonder what they are thinking right now?" Max whispered.

"Could be a lot of things. Death is a funny thing. You can never predict how someone is going to react or the crazy things that go through your mind when it happens," Nathan shared. I glanced over at him, wondering what was underneath that comment—what loss he had experienced.

Ethyl and Randy made their way across the garden path and we walked down the stairs to meet them. "Hi, Nathan," Ethyl said, "I guess you heard the news."

"Yes, I'm sorry to hear about old Merl. Do you know what got him?"

"We don't. He wasn't in the best of health, unfortunately.

Could have been a lot of things," Ethyl shared.

"I'm sorry this happened and I am really sorry, Randy, that you had to discover him," Max added.

Randy shook his head, "It's a good thing I got in there today! If it hadn't been for that darn water bill, I might not have gone in there for weeks. Can you imagine the mess there would have been then?" I shivered at the thought.

"Well, I'm beat. I'm going to go back and lie in my hammock to rest for a bit. Unless something changed, I'm Merl's executor. Tomorrow could be an interesting day, dealing with his estate," Ethyl said, as she started to walk toward the back of the house.

"Oh, I'm sure that old coot left us a mess to clean up. He better not have left us a bunch of bills we have to pay. It would be just like him to do that," Randy added, as he followed behind Ethyl.

"Randy, enough. His body just left the property. You could give it 24 hours before you speak ill of the dead!" Ethyl snapped.

Nathan laughed and said quietly to Max and I, "Nice to see Randy has bounced back quickly." We shook our heads and agreed with Nathan.

Suddenly, I had an idea. I walked toward Ethyl and Randy and called out, "Ethyl, why don't I help you sort out Merl's estate? I have time right now and depending on the state of his finances, I can put my bookkeeping skills to good use to help sort this out with you."

"Mona, you don't have to do that," Ethyl responded, her voice weary from the day's events.

I walked closer to Ethyl and in a softer voice added, "I want to help you, Ethyl. You have been so kind to me, welcoming me into your home. Let me help you this time."

Ethyl smiled and agreed with a nod. "Can you come by our apartment tomorrow at 10 a.m. to talk about where to start?

Maybe I can figure out how to smooth out the lemonade and we can have a glass of it while we work."

"It's a plan. Get some rest and I will see you tomorrow."

I watched Ethyl and Randy disappear around the house and then I rejoined Max and Nathan in the garden.

"Well, I have a steak calling my name!"

My stomach rumbled loudly, hearing the word 'steak' and we all laughed as my face turned red with embarrassment. "I think you are speaking my stomach's language," I said.

"I guess our barbecue plans are out, Mona. I would feel kind of weird heading back to Randy and Ethyl's to use their barbecue under the current circumstances," Max said.

I winced in realization and nodded, "We can save it for another night. There are still deli sandwiches in the fridge."

"Nonsense! I'll cook for you. It's pretty tiny upstairs, though. Can we eat down here? What did you get to grill?" Nathan inquired eagerly. He was practically drooling with anticipation.

"We picked up ribeye steaks from Paul's," Max proclaimed.

"Ohhh, very good choice, my friend!" Nathan responded, high-fiving Max.

"What is it about men and steak? I just don't get it."

"We should have some vegetables and sides with them," I suggested.

Both Max and Nathan looked at me like I had two heads. They finally conceded that we should have something else in addition to grilled meat. I took on the vegetables and Max offered to cook his special baked potatoes. I ran into my apartment and retrieved three ribeyes to give to Nathan to prepare. Then we agreed to meet back on the porch in about 45 minutes, to give Max enough time to doctor up some potatoes and bake them.

I walked into my kitchen and poked around the fridge. Finally, I decided that a simple tossed salad with a citrus-based dressing inspired by Great Aunt Audry's lemons would do the trick. As I whisked the ingredients together, I paused to stare out the window at the garden, thinking about the lemon tree and Ethyl's attempt at lemonade. I recalled Max's puckered expression and chuckled to myself.

I finished up the salad and put it aside on the counter. I carried plates and cutlery outside to set the table. The steaks cooking on the barbecue upstairs smelled amazing. The aroma caused my stomach to really rumble.

Nathan called down to me from the balcony, "I hope you like your steak rare."

I bellowed back up, "Nathan, I am sure I will love anything cooked by you!"

He laughed, "These will be done any time now."

"I can't wait!" I said, as Max came up the stairs to the porch with three extremely large foil-wrapped potatoes in a basket. "Those are the largest potatoes I have ever seen! There is no way I can eat a whole one of those, plus steak, plus salad!" I exclaimed, laughing.

"You see, Mona, this is exactly why Nathan and I tried to dissuade you from adding vegetables to this meal," Max responded with mock outrage.

I smiled and shook my head, adding, "I am sure I can save half the potato for tomorrow."

Before Max could respond with something witty, Nathan came around the corner carrying a platter of steaks, with a presentation like that of a five-star restaurant.

"Steak is served," Nathan declared, as he walked up to the porch and set the platter down on the table.

"That looks amazing. I cannot wait," Max said.

"Let me go grab the salad. Start serving yourselves while I bring it out," I said as I walked to the door.

When I returned outside with the salad, there, sitting at the top of the steps, was the big cat from next door. I stopped and looked at Nathan and Max,who were sitting at the table smiling at me.

"Someone else appreciates good cooking and decided to show up for dinner," Nathan announced.

"I forgot about him. He's probably hungry. There is no one to feed him," I said sympathetically, while I set the salad onto the table.

I turned back to look at my cat friend and Max added, "Well, he did get a little smoked fish from someone here, whom I won't name."

"You didn't! Now you have done it. He's going to show up at every meal," Nathan said, teasing me.

"In all seriousness, who is going to take care of him, now that Merl is gone?" I asked.

"Not Randy, that's for sure," Nathan said.

We all laughed, but I was left wondering about this. "For tonight, you can dine with us. I'll go get you some more smoked fish. Maybe Nathan can spare a little steak," I said, looking at Nathan with a smile.

"We will see about that!" he answered.

Once I got the cat some fish to munch on, I joined Max and Nathan at the table. The food was unbelievable. Starved from interrupted meals all day, I barely said a word. I just sat and enjoyed every bite in silence. After cleaning my plate, I sat back and declared, "That was the best meal I have had in I don't know how long. Thank you both."

"I agree, it was fantastic and Mona, as much as we gave you a hard time about vegetables, that salad was perfect with the steak and baked potatoes," Nathan admitted.

Max agreed. "The steak was unbelievable, Nathan. Where

did you learn to cook like that?"

Nathan smiled, but there was a sadness in his eyes and then he said quietly. "My wife Sam. She was something else."

Picking up on the past tense that Nathan used, I hesitated to respond. Instead, Max and I smiled silently back at Nathan.

"Sam was in a car accident eight years ago. The other driver was a man who had a heart attack while driving. His car went out of control and into oncoming traffic. Sam was hit head on. They said she died instantly."

"I am so sorry," I offered, in a whisper.

"Thanks. It seems like a lifetime ago now. I kinda shut down after Sam passed. All I wanted to do was escape. Everything reminded me of her. I sold everything, our house in the city with everything in it, our boat, the cottage at the lake, and left town. I don't know how I ended up in Buckley Brook. I was in a fog. I got in my car, went out for a drive and ended up here."

"I started driving around the streets admiring the old houses. When I stopped for gas and some food, there was a local newspaper on the table in the restaurant. I flipped through it absentmindedly to pass the time while I was waiting for my food and stumbled upon a 'for rent' ad. Without even really thinking about it, I called the number in the ad. Ethyl answered and we made arrangements for me to see the apartment. One thing led to another and my lost soul found this home. There is something about this place," he finished, lost in thought.

"Yes, there is definitely something about this place," I echoed quietly, in agreement.

We sat in silence for a few moments before Nathan changed the subject, "Well, that's enough about me. Tell me, Mona Lisa, what prompted you to go to Tish's yoga class today?"

"I didn't actually know it was Tish's class. I just did an internet search and picked the one closest to me. They happened to have a class this morning and I thought there was no time like the present, so I went. It really was a spur of the moment decision."

"Why yoga, though?" Nathan persisted.

"I don't know. I just thought I should do something to fill my time and it might as well be something healthy."

Nathan looked at me with a hard stare and then asked, "Why did you leave the city?"

I laughed, caught off guard by the change of subject. I looked into the garden and thought for a few moments before I answered. "I don't know, I just needed some space. Everyone is crammed together, moving too fast to have real relationships. It was all about money and power. I just needed to get out and find more substance. That probably sounds crazy," I said cautiously, glancing at Nathan and Max. "I had such fond memories of Buckley Brook from when I was child that I was just drawn here. There didn't seem to be any other option."

"So, here you are . . . what now? There is more here than yoga, you know," Nathan said, chuckling.

We all laughed. Memories of the morning yoga class as we dove over the cliff, flashed back in my mind. "I had great ambitions of going back to school at the university. I have always wanted to study there," I added quietly, as I stared off into the garden.

Nathan got excited at this idea, "Oh well, there you go! You should do it."

"I don't know. Classes are almost starting. I'm sure I have missed the admission window for this year."

"Nonsense, my dear Mona Lisa. I have a friend over at the university. I'm sure he can help you figure that part out. All you have to do is start. Pick one class."

"Maybe," I smiled, entertaining Nathan and regretting bringing it up. Then an idea came to mind. "Hey, why don't you register with me?"

Nathan let out a big chuckle, "This old bird? No way."

Max jumped in. "Do it, Nathan. You guys can be study buddies."

We laughed and Nathan rolled his eyes and groaned. "I don't know."

"If you will commit, I will."

Nathan shook his head. "Alright, I'll phone my friend tomorrow morning and investigate."

We started to clear up the dinner dishes from the table. As I stood up to walk into the apartment, I remembered the big cat who was sitting on the deck staring up at me, eagerly awaiting more fish. "What are we going to do about the cat?" I said.

"He has the cat door at the back of the house. He'll be fine for one night. We can figure out new accommodations tomorrow," Nathan assured me.

"Really? Are you sure he will be okay by himself in there?"

"I'm sure. Cats are very self-sufficient, especially that one," Nathan said, gesturing down at the big guy.

The cat meowed loudly, participating in the conversation. Then he turned and pranced across the deck to the far end of the porch, jumped into my cozy spot and curled up. I laughed as he put his head on his paws, looking back at me with not so innocent eyes.

"Alright cat, you can stay for a while, but you are sleeping at home. My allergies will be a mess by morning if you sleep in my apartment.

"Meow."

"Oh, you are going to end up with a cat if you don't watch out. Randy will not like that one bit," Nathan warned.

"It's just for tonight."

"That's how it starts, my dear. That's how it starts."

We finished cleaning up with the big cat looking on from my chair. Nathan and I made plans to discuss the course the next day, after my meeting with Ethyl about Merl's estate. Then Max and Nathan said farewell and walked back to their apartments. I stood at the railing of the porch and watched them disappear, then stared out at the beautiful garden. The sun had ducked behind the trees across the street, turning the scorching heat of the day into a comfortable evening temperature. Even in the fading light, the colors of the flowers seemed to sparkle throughout the garden. My mind ran through the events of the day and I smiled, thinking about my new friends.

I looked over at the big cat, staring at me from his new spot. "I have created a monster, haven't I?" I said teasingly, walking toward the big cat. I leaned over and stretched my arm out toward him, being careful not to get too close with my face. I scratched his head. He closed his eyes and began to purr loudly. "I'm definitely going to regret this," I whispered out loud, smiling at the big guy in my chair.

CHAPTER 9

The next morning after enjoying breakfast out on the porch and an entire cup of tea in my cozy spot, I tidied up and made my way to Ethyl and Randy's apartment. As I was walking through the garden up to the parking area, I stopped dead in my tracks as Margaritta exited the side entrance. For a fleeting moment, I wondered if I could turn and run around the corner before she saw me, but I was too late, her eagle eyes landed on their prey.

"Mona Lisa Brown, how lovely to see you, my darling." I cringed at the sound of her voice. "I am back from writing my latest book at the beach. Did you manage to find something to occupy your time this fall?" she asked oh-so-sweetly as she slid down the stairs toward her car. I stood frozen in place like a fool, my mind absolutely blank. "Mona? Cat got your tongue, today?" Margaritta laughed.

"I have plenty to occupy my time, thank you very much," I finally said coolly.

Margarita's eyes popped open as she drew her right hand up to her chest in mock shock, "My, my, no need to be rude, Mona Lisa Brown," she continued, taking time to roll the 'r' on Brown, crawling even further under my skin. She opened her car door to get in and called back to me in the same patronizing tone of voice. "Maybe you will have more to say when I get back. Will you still be here, thinking about it, when I return?" She slammed the big door of the old Mercedes and sped off down the driveway, leaving me standing there steaming with anger.

My feet finally released from the walkway. I wanted to scream or cry, or both. I stomped toward the back of the house, fuming from my encounter with Margaritta. Before I turned the corner to Ethyl and Randy's, I stopped, closed my eyes, and took a deep breath to calm my nerves before seeing Ethyl.

As I walked around the corner to the back of the house, I noticed that Ethyl and Randy had a storage building at the end of the path. I hadn't noticed that last time. It had a roll-up door, twice the size of a regular door with a handle on it. It looked like a mini-garage at the back of the house.

I walked closer and reached the bottom of the stairs leading up to the deck. Suddenly, with great dramatic flare, the roll-up door flew open and I heard the roar of a chainsaw. Out stepped Randy, in full chainsaw gear from head to toe. He had on big steel-toe boots, heavy black pants, a flannel shirt with the sleeves rolled up, and some sort of orange suit that wrapped around the front of his legs and chest. His hands were covered with thick, large black work gloves and he had a yellow hard hat on his head, but the best part was the pair of reflective aviator glasses on his face.

As Randy revved the chainsaw a few more times, clearly enjoying its power, he finally noticed me, standing gobsmacked at the stairs. He turned off the chainsaw and set it down outside the mini-garage. "Mona, I didn't see you there. Are you here to see Ethyl?" he said, pushing his sunglasses onto the top of his head and leaning up against the edge of the deck.

I smiled and responded, "Yes, I am helping her sort out Merl's estate."

"You really don't have to do that."

"I know. I want to help. You both have been so welcoming to me. It's the least I can do. I have the time right now and you might as well put my bookkeeping skills to good use." I continued hesitantly, "Uh, Randy, what's with the chainsaw get-up? I know it's still early in the day, but aren't you roasting in that suit?"

Randy laughed. "I have to go take care of some fallen branches in the back. It might be hot, but this suit keeps me protected." He lowered his voice and leaned toward me, "To be honest, Ethyl bought this for me so I would be safe." He stood up straight again and continued, shaking his head, "A guy has one accident . . ." I tried to hide the concern I was feeling as I imagined the details of the 'accident.'

Randy continued, whispering, "I'll let you in on a secret." He pointed across the lawn to the forest behind the house, "I have this tree just inside the forest where I stash half this stuff while I am in there cutting. I can't move with all this on."

My mouth dropped open and I started to laugh while shaking my head. I wasn't sure how to respond to the little secret Randy had just shared with me. I was saved by Ethyl. We turned and looked up the stairs at Ethyl as she came out onto the deck.

"Mona, is Randy holding you up?"

"Not at all, Ethyl. He was just instructing me on all the latest chainsaw safety techniques he uses."

Randy gave us both a big smile and added, "The latest techniques!"

Ethyl put her hands on her hips, narrowed her eyes, and gave us both a suspicious stare. Then she focused on Mr. Chainsaw. "Randy Martin Findler, are you making fun of me? I will have you know it was not me who nearly cut his hand off with that very chainsaw," she said, pointing to the chainsaw on the ground.

"That was a fluke accident! I couldn't do that again if I tried! I didn't know there was a squirrel's nest in the tree. They are nasty little creatures, Mona. Don't tangle with a mother squirrel and her babies.They are almost as bad as that cat next door!"

My face must have given away my horrified reaction as Ethyl quickly added, "The squirrels were fine. It was Randy who was nearly maimed."

Changing the subject, Ethyl looked at me and said, "Well, you didn't come over to hear near-death chainsaw stories. Come on up. Can I get you something to drink?"

As I walked up the stairs to meet Ethyl, I heard her say to Randy, "And you . . . please, please will you be careful this time?"

Randy reached up and flipped his aviator sunglasses down on his face and picked up the chainsaw. "Careful is my middle name, my sweet," he said in a serious voice. Before Ethyl could protest, he swung the chainsaw in the air, pulled the cord, and revved it a few times. Randy turned and gave her a big smile as he strode across the back of the property toward the forest, challenging anything to get in his way.

Ethyl turned around and shook her head. "That man is going to make me a widow one day."

I turned and watched Randy as he disappeared into the forest, knowing he would soon be removing layers of protective clothing and stashing them in a tree somewhere.

Ethyl's voice pulled me back. "I managed to find Merl's will. At least, I think it's his will. Marise had asked the lawyer to update Merl's will after she passed. She knew he would not take care of it. Even in death she was taking care of other people. The lawyer sent it over and I filed it away. Luckily, I remembered where and found it this morning. I suppose we better start with reading this. Why don't we sit out here?" she said, gesturing to the table and chairs on the deck. "Can I get you something to drink? I modified the lemonade recipe last night if you would like to try it again."

"Thank you! I would love some," I said enthusiastically,

walking toward the table and chairs.

Ethyl handed me the long envelope containing the will and walked back inside. As I sat down, I turned my attention to the thick package in my hand. I opened the flap at the top and slid the folded papers out. I flattened them out on the table and started flipping through the pages. My eyes slid over the usual legal text. I scanned the pages, not really paying too much attention. Then on page seven, I spotted a picture of my big cat friend next door. "That's unusual," I thought. "I haven't read very many wills, but I have never seen a picture as reference inside a will before." I looked more closely at the page and read the text beside the picture. "As guardian of 'Mr. Prince', a rare Maine Coon cat, I appoint Mr. Randy Martin Findler."

"Oh no, this isn't going to go over well," I said out loud, as Ethyl came outside with the lemonade.

"What, Mona?" she asked, looking concerned as she sat two glasses of lemonade down on the table.

I turned and looked at Ethyl with a tentative look on my face. "I think Merl just got the last laugh on Randy."

"Why? What do you mean?" Ethyl responded, confused.

I hesitated, looking back at the text to make sure I was not dreaming it up. "He . . . he appointed Randy the guardian of Mr. Prince."

"Who is that? Don't tell me Merl had some love child out there we did not know about!"

"No, no, it's his big cat!"

Ethyl's eyes popped open. The shock and realization of the situation covered her face, "Oh! Oh dear. The cat. This can't be right," she said, leaning over to take a look at the text on the page. She picked up the papers, sat down and stared at the text. She thought quietly for a moment, then whispered while slowly shaking her head, "Oh Merl, what have you done?"

"How are we going to tell Randy? He is going to lose it."

"Well, we are certainly not going to tell him with that chain-saw in his hands," Ethyl responded.

We both sipped the lemonade, letting the matter sink in.

"This is delicious, Ethyl. What did you change?" I asked.

Ethyl smiled conspiratorially. "And that, my dear, will re-main my little secret."

I laughed. "The Chef's Secret."

"Mona, I was at the kitchen window when you walked over. It overlooks the side of the house," Ethyl said quietly, pointing to the corner of the house. "I think I caught the end of some-thing between you and Margaritta. You looked quite upset as you walked over. Do you want to talk about it?"

My heart stopped for a moment and my stomach sank. All I could think to say was, "She's not very nice."

Ethyl smiled, "She has some rough edges that could use smoothing."

"To say the least! She is a monster," I said, frustrated that Ethyl didn't see how terrible this woman was.

"Monster might be a bit strong. You just need to learn how to interact with her," Ethyl said patiently.

"Me! Why me? I am the one minding my own business, be-ing accosted by this woman every time she sees me. Why do I have to change?"

"Because you can, and she sees no reason to. You are the one getting hurt. Something has to change and so it's in your hands. That's why."

We sat in silence drinking our lemonade for what felt like an eternity. Finally, I broke the stillness with barely a whisper, "What do I have to do?" I asked. Ethyl looked at me, puzzled, not saying a word. I repeated my question, but far more force-fully than I meant to, "What do I have to do?"

Ethyl stared at me. "Wow, she has really gotten under your skin," she responded in a calm, soothing tone.

I sighed heavily, staring down at my hands in my lap. "Yes, she has," I acknowledged softly.

"Look who's back," Ethyl announced, pointing across the yard at Randy as he walked confidently toward us in full chainsaw gear. Spotting us looking at him, he revved it up a few times while waving it in the air, showcasing its power.

He reached the path below and looked up at us. "So, have you sorted out old Merl's affairs yet?" he asked cheerfully.

We both smiled at him. "Something like that, yes. You must be sweltering. Why don't you put that chainsaw away and peel that suit off before you pass out. I have a new batch of lemonade for you to try," Ethyl offered sweetly.

"Well, I can't argue about the heat. It certainly is a hot one today, but you can keep your witches' brew. That first batch nearly killed me yesterday," he said, walking toward the mini-garage. Ethyl and I gave each other a look, knowing she had just bought us some time before having to share the news with Randy.

I noticed Randy patting himself down. He sat the chainsaw down on the ground and started turning out all of his pockets. We both let this go on for a few minutes until Ethyl could no longer resist, "Are you okay there, Randy?" she called out.

"Do I look okay over here? I can't find the blasted key."

"Where is your spare? I will go get it for you from the house," Ethyl offered.

Looking really irritated now, Randy turned to face Ethyl with his teeth clenched and responded in an irritated voice, "I don't have a spare. It's a special key."

"So what are you going to do? How do you get into the building?"

"I'm gonna find the key!" Randy said, exasperated. "I must

have dropped it or something," he added, looking at the ground around him.

Ethyl stood up and shook her head. "I will come help you. Two pairs of eyes are better than one."

I stood up and followed Ethyl down the stairs to help. "Make it three."

We searched in front of the building for a while, but found nothing. Finally Randy suggested another idea. "Well, I better retrace my steps," he said, pointing to the forest at the edge of the lawn.

"Do you think it might have fallen out of your pocket when you were working out there?" I asked Randy. Without being able to suggest it out loud while Ethyl was standing with us, I tried to give him a look that suggested that it could have come out of his pocket while he was removing all of his safety layers and stashing them in the tree.

"Oh, heavens!" Ethyl spouted, now beyond frustrated with the situation. "If you lost it out there . . ." she said, waving her arms at the thick forest. ". . . Then it's gone. You are not spending all day retracing your steps to find that key. Just call the locksmith and have him come over here to open this door so we can get on with our day."

"Leave it with me," Randy grumbled. "I will retrace my steps once and if I can't find it, I will call the locksmith."

"Alright, but first, go take off that get-up you have on before you overheat, then come have a drink on the porch to cool down."

"Fine, but none of your witches' brew," Randy said, looking suspiciously at Ethyl.

As Randy walked into the house, Ethyl turned to me and asked, "Are you sure you want to be here when I tell him he is the new caretaker of the big cat next door?"

"I don't mind. Maybe he will temper his reaction if I am here."

"It's always a possibility," Ethyl acknowledged. "I better go find something refreshing for Randy to sip on when he gets out here. Maybe that will cool him down a little before breaking the news.

As Ethyl disappeared into the house, I looked down at the ground around me, searching again for the key to the mini-garage. I stared across the lawn toward the forest. The heat from the sun was blazing. I tried not to think about the fact that we only had a few weeks before the weather would change again. I decided to stroll toward the forest, following the route Randy had taken with the hope that maybe I would stumble upon the key. The likelihood was low, but it was worth a try. The warm sun overhead was heating up my shoulders. I hadn't bothered with sunscreen that morning and I had a feeling that I was going to pay the price for walking around outside without it.

I lingered for a moment at the iron patio set. The big red umbrella was tied up from overnight and there were still a few drops of dew resting on the tops of everything. I kept walking through the thick damp green grass toward the forest. As I got closer to the entrance, I was surprised to see the big cat from next door walking out toward me. "What are you doing here?" I said, surprised to see him. "This is really not a good time for you to be here," I cautioned, bending down to greet the cat while sneaking a look over my shoulder at the house.

Ignoring my warning, the big cat snuggled up to me, rubbing his head into my outstretched hand. "Really? It is obvious what you want, cat," I said, snickering while complying with his demand to rub the top of his head. "I understand your name is Mr. Prince. What a good name for you." The big guy purred loudly in response as I rubbed behind his ears.

The cat turned to face the entrance to the forest. It was dense with the green summer foliage in full growth. The cat leaned into my hand, urging me toward the entrance. I came back to reality and said again, "This is not a good time for a stroll, cat. You should make yourself scarce right now." The cat ignored me, though, and sauntered into the forest. He stopped right at the entrance and looked back at me, then disappeared, moving along the path. I couldn't resist. I had to find out where he was going. I hurried forward to follow the cat.

Just inside the dense brush, I found the cat at the bottom of a huge oak tree. At about the height of my shoulders, the tree split into two large trunks, each measuring at least a foot in diameter. They formed the two halves of the rest of the huge old tree. Where they met there was a nice flat v-shape. The cat looked up at me and pawed at the tree. I stepped back to get a better view. "What are you trying to tell me, big guy?" I scanned around the other side of the tree and spotted it; a small branch broken off, about the height of my waist. It was like a peg on the tree and hanging off of it was a leather lace. Looped through it was a key that I suspected matched up to the mini-garage door.

I stepped forward and slowly lifted the lace off of the tree. I held it in my hand, examining it for a moment. Then I stepped back and looked up at the tree. "This must be where Randy stashes his 'safety gear' when Ethyl is not watching." I looked down at the big cat in total amazement as he slinked around my legs purring. "How did you . . ." I started to ask, then stopped, realizing I was talking to a cat. I shook my head in disbelief. "Well, you might have helped your case with Randy today, cat. I still recommend you skedaddle, though."

He answered with a loud, "Meow," as he looked up at me with innocent eyes.

"I'm serious. Save yourself, go," I urged forcefully.

He turned and boldly pranced back up the path toward the edge of the forest. I stood in place at the base of the tree watching the curious creature walk confidently up the trail, disappearing out of view until I was jolted back into reality by a giant wail from the house.

"You have got to be kidding me!"

Ethyl must have shared the news with Randy. I ran down the path hoping to prevent him from seeing the big cat. As I reached the edge of the forest, I realized I was too late. Mr. Prince was sitting in the middle of the lawn, baiting Randy.

"This ends now, cat!" Randy called out in his deep booming voice.

The chainsaw fired up again. From across the yard, Randy brandished his weapon of choice, revving it over and over as he walked across the lawn with long, purposeful strides directly toward the big cat. I was frozen in place, watching the horror unfold. The cat didn't move. He sat with his eyes locked on Randy until he was about ten feet away. Then he took off in a sprint around the garden.

Randy took the bait and began to chase him, waving the chainsaw awkwardly in front of him. Round and round they went until Randy started to slow down. The cat ran toward the iron patio set, leapt onto a chair and then onto the top of the table, appearing to taunt Randy. With a burst of energy and more speed than I thought he was capable of, he charged toward Mr. Prince. Just as Randy got close enough to lunge toward him, the cat leapt off the table and sprinted toward me at top speed.

I stepped out of the path, anticipating the cat would try to run into the forest, but instead, the cat leapt onto the trunk of a large maple tree and scrambled up the tree with ease. Higher and higher he climbed until he reached a large limb that stuck out over the edge of the lawn. The cat scurried out onto the limb and stopped.

Randy arrived at the bottom of the tree. He was steaming mad as he stared up at the cat, swiping wildly at it with the chainsaw over his head. I dove to the side for cover, hoping not to be a casualty of Randy's wild efforts to get the cat above him. It was as if the big cat realized he was safely out of Randy's reach because he sat down on the branch and smuggly swished his big fluffy tail back and forth.

Randy let out a yell that was part exasperation and part fury. With rage in his eyes, he swung the chainsaw in the air and fired it up again. Like a madman, he charged toward the base of the tree and started to swipe at the bark. As he did this, the sound of an air horn cut through the noise of the chainsaw. Randy stopped in his tracks, stood up and turned around. We both looked across the grass to see Ethyl steaming mad, charging toward Randy, sounding the horn.

"Really, Randy! Were you really just about to cut down that beautiful tree to win your war with the cat? Have you completely lost your mind?" Ethyl spoke with disdain overtop of the low rumble of the chainsaw.

Exhausted from the chase, Randy silenced the saw completely and sat it on the ground. Realizing his victory, the big cat stood up and looked down at Randy below. Then he walked to the end of the branch with swagger, leapt onto the adjacent tree and tiptoed down to the ground on a limb that had partially fallen. Slowly, confidently, he moved toward the house next door. "Is it odd for me to envy the confidence of this animal?" I wondered.

We stood in silence for a moment, then Ethyl spoke. "Come on, let's put that thing away," she said, gesturing to Randy's weapon on the ground.

"I would love to," Randy responded sarcastically. "But, I lost the key to the shed!"

Realizing I had the key, I jumped into the conversation, "Is this it, by chance?" I asked, lifting the leather lacing in the air.

Randy's eyes grew large in surprise. I could see him trying to put together in his mind how I had the key he was missing, again.

He responded in a stunned voice. "Yes, that's it! How . . .?" is all he managed to get out.

"It's a long story, but the credit actually goes to your big furry friend whom you just tried to do away with."

Randy squinted at me, confused. Behind him, I could see the big cat in the distance; he had stopped to look back at us. Out of the corner of my eye, I am sure he gave me a wink. I quickly shook my head. "Get it together, Mona."

"Mona? Are you alright?" Ethyl asked quietly.

"Yes, I think it's just the heat out here and maybe the excitement of the day."

"It's been quite a day, alright–and it's not even noon yet!" Ethyl agreed.

I handed Randy the key. "Thank you, Mona," he said, still staring down at the key in his hand. Looking up at me, he added with a smile, "Another time you will have to tell me how you found this."

"Indeed I will," I responded, smiling back at him.

Randy picked up the chainsaw with his right hand and the three of us walked back to the house. Stopping at the walkway below the back porch, I turned to Ethyl, "Did you read any more of the will?"

"I didn't get a chance. I ran across the lawn trying to stop the chainsaw catastrophe I saw unfolding," she said, giving Randy a perturbed look. "I'll give it a thorough read this afternoon."

"Okay, just let me know how I can help. I hope you don't find any more surprises," I offered. From behind me I heard Randy grunt in acknowledgement as he finally unlocked the door to the mini-garage, rolled it open, and disappeared inside.

"I will be sure to let you know what the rest of the will says, Mona. Thank you for coming over to help me today. I am sorry for all the drama," Ethyl said earnestly.

"Not at all. This morning was entertaining to say the least. I am glad no one got hurt."

"One of these days, Randy might not be so lucky," Ethyl added.

CHAPTER 10

We said goodbye and I walked back to my apartment, eager to sit in my cozy spot with a quiet book for a few minutes. As I rounded the corner of the house to the front garden, I saw someone waiting for me on the front porch. Sitting on the top step was Mr. Prince. I laughed, shaking my head at him. "That was quite a show back there," I said, as I climbed the stairs and sat down beside him.

He responded with a loud, 'Meow,' in agreement as I rubbed his head. "Boy, this cat has me trained."

"You know, given the circumstances, you might need to work on endearing yourself a bit more to old Randy." The only response I got this time, though, was purring, as he lay down and stretched out beside me.

We sat on the stairs while I rubbed the big cat's head and looked out at the rainbow of colors in the garden. The cat purred loudly beside me. I could have stayed in that spot forever, soaking up the warm sun and the sweet scents from the flowers, but my nose started to tickle and I was overcome by a large sneeze.

"That's your cue, cat," I said, looking down at him as my eyes begin to water. "You are adorable, but my allergies are demanding that we separate for a while."

He looked up at me and acknowledged with a loud, "Meow," but didn't move.

"Really, it's not you, cat, it's me. There is just something about your fur that makes me sneeze."

"Meow." He licked his lips and got up.

"Are you trying to tell me that you are hungry?" I walked into the house and began digging through the fridge. As I put fish on a plate for the big guy outside, I called out to him from the kitchen. "Don't tell Max I am giving you more fish. He knows what I paid for this." Then I muttered to myself, "I am talking to a cat and feeding it gourmet smoked fish. Mona, you need to get out and meet more people."

From the door, I heard Nathan's familiar voice, "Well, my dear Mona, then I have just the plan for you!"

I looked up and was greeted by his wide smile. I looked at him suspiciously, "Nathan! That big grin you are wearing looks like trouble. What plan have you cooked up?"

"I talked to my friend at the university and he found us a class. It is a financial literacy class and a prerequisite to any of the finance programs. It's perfect."

I gave Nathan a skeptical look, "So the old dog has changed his mind? Going to broaden his horizons?"

Nathan laughed enthusiastically, "It's never too late to expand one's mind."

Now it was my turn to laugh. I stopped what I was doing in the kitchen as I laughed at Nathan's pursuit of my academics. "What has gotten into you? Last night, you didn't want anything to do with this idea." Then it dawned on me, "Hey, is there an attractive woman involved in this plan?" I said, giving him the all-knowing eye.

Nathan laughed again. "Nothing could be farther from the truth, Mona, unless you are referring to yourself."

I tried to hide the blush that crept across my face as he continued.

"I thought about the conversation at dinner. It's time that I step out of the comfort of my surroundings. What better way than to take a class at the university with you?"

I narrowed my gaze. "Are you sure there isn't more to it?"

"Scout's honor," he said, raising his three fingers in salute.

"Okay, so tell me more about this class. Why this one?"

"It is 'Financial Literacy for our Times.' It is a generalist course that they use as a prerequisite to all the financial programs; a good one to ease our way back into the world of academics. It takes place Monday and Wednesday mornings and starts next week. Being so close to the start of the school year, many courses are already full. My friend will fast-track us through the admission steps, so we can register for this one."

"I don't know, Nathan. I appreciate all the work you did to organize this for us. But I just don't know. It sounded like a good idea in conversation yesterday, but now that it's real, I don't know if I am up to this."

Just then, I heard a loud, "Meow," from the door.

"Oh, the cat." I called out to him in a louder voice, "Just a second, Mr. Prince." I returned to the plate of fish I was fixing, picked it up and walked outside.

"Mr. Prince? Did you give him that name?" Nathan asked, amused.

"No, it's actually his name. He is referenced in Merl's will."

"Well, that is certainly a fitting name. He has you wrapped around his paw. Is that more smoked fish?" Nathan asked in a surprised voice.

We heard another demanding, "Meow."

I gave Nathan a look of acknowledgement as he folded his arms and looked down his nose at me.

"Fine, I may be under his spell," I said, as I ran outside with the plate of fish.

"So what happened with Merl's will? Did you and Ethyl find anything interesting besides this big guy's regal name?" He followed me outside.

I stood up from setting the plate of fish down on the deck, as Mr Prince gobbled up the expensive treat. I looked up at Nathan. "The will, now that was an episode," I smiled knowingly.

"Come on, out with it!"

"Turns out, Merl declared Randy as the guardian of Mr. Prince."

"No way!" Nathan exclaimed.

"That was pretty much Randy's reaction. Well, that times ten," I laughed, remembering Randy chasing the cat around the garden.

"I wish I had seen that. It sounds like my morning was way too tame compared to yours."

"Yes, it was entertaining, to say the least. This guy decided to show up in the middle of it, just to rub it in Randy's face a little."

Nathan's eyes bugged out as he looked down at the cat. "Seriously, you are a gutsy creature."

The cat responded with a loud, slow, "Meow."

We both burst out laughing. Then Nathan stopped, and a serious look came over his face. "So, what is it going to be, Mona Lisa? Are you registering for this class with me or not?"

"I just don't know, Nathan."

"What is holding you back?"

"Well, isn't that a loaded question on so many levels?" I responded, trying to lighten the mood without revealing how accurate Nathan's comment really was. I turned and walked over to my cozy spot and flopped myself into it. Mr. Prince galloped over and leapt onto me. He tiptoed around in a few circles, then lay down and curled up on top of me. I laughed and shook my head, adjusting my positioning to accommodate the big cat while I smoothed his fluffy fur with my hand.

"You have found a friend, my dear," Nathan said, as he sat

down on the swing beside my chair.

I continued to stroke the cat's luxurious fur coat and I nodded in agreement, "So I have. The only issue is that I am terribly allergic to my new friend."

"Meow." The cat answered as he lay his head down, closed his eyes and purred loudly.

"If it wasn't for my allergies, I would adopt this big guy in a second," I said, as my nose began to tickle and my eyes started to itch.

"Well, this is a predicament, then."

"Yes, it is."

"Back to the course. You can't change the subject that easily."

I groaned in response.

"This is the last thing I am going to say and then I will leave you to think."

"Alright," I agreed, wrinkling my nose as I fought back a sneeze.

"Sometimes in life, opportunities arise. It is important to spot them. I don't know your concern with taking this class, but I do know that one of your goals when you moved here was to study at the university. This is your chance to start. It's just one course and we will do it together."

I smiled at how eager he was to sell me on taking the class with him.

"Why are you smiling?" Nathan asked.

"I am just amused that this went from Max and I trying to get you to take a class with me, to you trying to get me to take a class with you. I find it funny. Give me the day to think and take a look at the course outline. It's been a crazy morning. Can you email me the link so I can read it?"

"Deal! I will be back tomorrow morning to get your answer,"

Nathan said, as he stood to leave.

As he walked down the stairs, I called out to him, "Nathan, thank you. I do appreciate that you are looking out for me."

He smiled at me and gave me a wink. "Of course, until tomorrow, Mona Lisa."

After Nathan disappeared behind the house, I sat quietly for a while, staring into the distance, absentmindedly petting Mr. Prince and fighting the urge to sneeze." So, cat," I finally said.

He answered with a loud, "Meow."

"I don't know about this name of yours. It might be too regal."

"Meow."

"What if we shorten it to just 'Prince'?"

"Meow."

"Okay, it's settled then. We will call you Prince." I shifted under the weight of the big guy on top of me and he took this as a cue to move along. He stood up and jumped down onto the deck, then stopped and sat, facing me. I stretched my arms and legs out in front of me and then curled back up in the cozy chair. The sun was beginning to come across the house and move into its hot afternoon position, shining straight onto the deck. For now, the temperature was just perfect. I laid my head down on the edge of the chair and smiled at my furry friend.

"What are we going to do with you? You can't keep going back to that empty house over there and you can't go anywhere near Randy, regardless of what was in Merl's will. I would invite you into my place, but my allergies will run wild." The cat tilted his head to the side and stared at me with large innocent eyes. "Oh, don't start that. I might not look tough, but neither of us are going to be happy when my allergies kick in."

"Meow."

Realizing that I was talking to a cat again, I got up and walked past him to the top of the stairs. I bent down to pick up his well-cleaned plate and heard giggling coming from the sidewalk past the garden. I stood up, holding the plate and looked out to see who was so jovial. Walking toward the house were Max and Tish, hand in hand, enjoying an inside joke. I watched them for a few moments before they noticed me staring at them as they walked along the garden path toward me.

"Mona! How lovely to see you today!" Tish called out with her syrupy sweet voice.

I forced a smile and waved, then focused my gaze on Max. I guess they were back on again. Either Max had caved into Tish's antics or he had taken my advice and 'had the talk.' But if he had actually told Tish how he felt, I am not sure that she would be this happy.

I forced another smile and made some small talk. "Another beautiful day in Buckley Brook," I said, matching Tish's tone. Did I actually just say that? I groaned and scolded myself.

"Why, yes it is! It is a splendid day. I'm going to need a nap later, though. Max and I were up half the night last night," she said, giggling as she slapped his arm flirtatiously.

"Ick, I didn't need that piece of information," I thought. Max continued to stand in the same spot, staring at me with a stupid big grin on his face.

"Really? Exciting night?" I finally said cooly, not quite knowing how to correctly respond, but instantly regretting my words.

Tish grew very serious–well, as serious as Tish could get, "Oh yes, we were up talking for most of the night. It was a very deep conversation, Mona."

It was all I could do not to roll my eyes. Instead, I feigned interest and matched Tish's seriousness. "Oh, sounds important."

"Oh, it was. Max really opened up to me last night." She

smiled warmly, looking at Max with adoring eyes.

I raised my eyebrows, looking at Max as he started to shrink at Tish's honesty.

"Wow, sounds like it was quite a conversation," I continued.

"Oh, it was. Max talked all about the parts of his personality he is working on, like how he gets so upset when I need time to rest and have to cancel our plans. He is really working to understand my needs and improve himself."

It was all I could do to prevent my eyes from popping out of my head. I had to bite my tongue hard not to lash out. How did she not comprehend that what she had just said was the most self-absorbed, ignorant statement to come out of anyone's mouth? Stunned, I stared at Max, who was looking intently at something on his sandal. Finally, he spoke up quietly, "We should go, Tish."

"But I haven't thanked Mona yet. I understand this whole talk was your idea. Thank you, Mona, for encouraging Max to be so honest with me. You get all the credit."

My shock turned to a flash of anger. "Credit! Really, me?" I laughed out loud. "I get the credit for Max not having the guts to tell her what a flaky bimbo she is," I thought. I was doing everything I could to contain myself.

Reading my face, Max jumped in. "Really, Tish, we should go now."

Continuing to stare firmly at him, I thought, "Yes, you really should go, Max."

"But Max, I want to properly thank Mona," Tish continued, completely unaware of what she had stirred up.

I decided to end this awkward moment and responded in a slow, earnest tone, "Tish, no need to thank me at all. I am just glad that the two of you could have such a good talk. It is wonderful to see you both today. Enjoy the rest of this fantastic weather." I forced a huge smile onto my face as I waved and walked confidently into the house, still holding the empty plate.

As I opened the door to go in, Prince darted across the deck and slipped in ahead of me. Needing to escape the porch as quickly as possible, I let it slide. Without even looking back, I shut both doors behind me and walked, steaming, into the kitchen. Groaning with frustration, I absentmindedly put the plate into the dishwasher and started preparing food for myself, all the while muttering away. "Seriously, how do I get credit for Max practically taking responsibility for Tish's bad behavior? How?"

After a few minutes of this, I stopped and asked myself, "Why is this bothering me so much? It is Max's problem to solve. If he doesn't have the guts to address things with Tish, then it is his issue to live with, not mine. I can't get past this frustration, though. Max is such a great person. He deserves better."

After a few half-hearted bites of my sandwich, I stopped and looked across the room. The big cat had taken up residence in the corner of the sofa close to the window. He was curled up with his head on his paws looking straight at me. I smiled and shook my head, calling out to him, "You really made the most of that situation out there, sneaking inside with me at just the right moment. You can stay for now. I guess the room is large enough to prevent my allergies from being triggered."

My comment was met with an appreciative, "Meow."

"I am talking to a cat again," I grumbled as I walked toward the front room with the rest of my sandwich and sat at the other end of the sofa. I sighed heavily as my nose prickled, then I let out a huge sneeze.

CHAPTER 11

The next morning I staggered out of my bedroom, still in my summer pajamas. As I walked down the hall toward the washroom, I heard someone in the bathroom. I froze and jumped into action mode. "An intruder has broken into my apartment," I thought. "Who breaks into an apartment to use the washroom?" I shook off this notion as I switched into action mode and ran down the hall back to my room on my tiptoes, trying not to make any noise to indicate my location. I darted straight to my sock drawer and slid it open as quietly as possible and started digging through it. My hair was flying around my face obstructing my vision, so I grabbed a long knee sock and tied it around my forehead, anchoring it with a knot at the back of my head.

Finally, I found what I was looking for in the drawer–my trusty sock full of batteries. My father always worried about me in the city, so when I moved there, he stuffed one of his old socks with a handful of old batteries, tied it up and gave it to me as a house-warming present. I pulled out the bright orange sock knotted in the middle and felt its weight for a moment. I held it with two hands and assumed a fighting stance, swinging it around the room a few times. I had never needed this before, but maybe today was the day.

I tiptoed slowly back down the hall, adrenalin pumping. There was still noise coming from the bathroom. As I got closer, I heard the toilet flush. I stood right outside the door, poised for battle, sock held high above my head with two hands. I swung it round and round, building momentum as I got ready to strike when out of the washroom walked Prince. My mouth dropped open and I lowered my weapon. The big cat walked into the middle of the hall and stopped to look at me. I could only imagine what I looked like to him in full commando pajama mode.

He let out a loud, "Meow," then turned and walked back to the front room.

I stood there wondering what just happened. I peered into the washroom. Everything seemed fine. "Did that cat just use the toilet, and flush?" I walked back into my bedroom to return the sock to its proper hiding place. While taking off the sock tied around my forehead and looking for some clothes to change into, I processed what just happened. "The cat is toilet-trained and I almost clobbered it with a sock full of batteries." I sighed heavily at what could have happened. As I left my bedroom, I mused, "At least my new house guest doesn't need a litter box."

I walked into the front room and stared at Prince curled up on the sofa in the same place I had left him the night before. I was greeted by another, "Meow," like nothing had happened. I guess to the big guy, that's business as usual, except for the part about me mistaking him for a burglar and nearly smacking him over the head.

I decided that coffee was required after that start to the morning and moved to the kitchen to prepare a pot of it. All night I had tossed and turned, thinking about Tish and Max, which was ridiculous. "It is his relationship and if he wants to keep subjecting himself to her shabby treatment, then so be it." As I searched for something to eat for breakfast, there was a knock on the door. I looked down at myself. At least I was dressed. I walked toward the door and on my way, stopped for a second to try to make my hair somewhat acceptable.

I opened the door and was greeted by Nathan's smiling face.

"Nathan, you are up and about early this morning," I said warmly, as I opened the storm door to let him in.

"Sorry to come by so early. I was hoping you would be up."

"I just made some coffee. It looks like another beautiful day. Would you like to join me for coffee outside on the porch?"

"Sounds like a lovely idea, my dear."

I walked back into the kitchen and heard from behind me, "Oh, look who made his way inside!"

I turned and looked at Nathan approaching the big cat on the sofa. "I was hoodwinked. I won't get into how it happened, but yes, he has infiltrated the palace."

Nathan laughed as Prince lifted himself up, jumped off the sofa and ran into the kitchen. I looked down as he gave us a loud, "Meow."

"What are you feeding the big guy? I think he wants more."

"Are you hungry?" I asked my new house guest.

"Meow."

I looked up at Nathan and explained, "All I have is the smoked fish."

"Woowee, no wonder he followed you inside. Do you have a can of salmon or tuna? That might be a little cheaper until you get to the store to buy some cat food," Nathan suggested.

We heard a low disapproving, "Meeooow," in response to this idea.

I looked down at the cat. "Look, this is my apartment and you are cleaning me out of my expensive smoked fish. I didn't even get to try it yet." I walked over and rooted through the cupboard, pulling out a large can of salmon. "Look, delicious!" I said showing the cat the can.

My comment was met with another low disapproving, "Meeooow."

"Just try it," I said sternly, opening the can and dumping the contents onto a plate. "I'll get you some proper food at the store later today."

Nathan and I took our coffee outside to the porch. I held the door open for Prince to come out and then I set the plate down beside us. He stood there and looked at it with disdain for a moment, but eventually hunger overtook his stubbornness and he dove in.

We settled in on the deck with our coffee. I curled up in my cozy spot and Nathan took the chair opposite to me. We sipped our coffee in silence for a few moments, enjoying the quiet of the morning and the warm late-summer air.

"Today is the day, Mona, my dear. You need to decide if you are signing up for this course with me."

I sighed heavily. "Oh, that. I thought you might forget about that idea," I said with an awkward chuckle.

"What is the issue here, Mona? This was your idea originally. It is one class, what is the big deal?" Nathan was showing his frustration, "I don't get it. You said that you want to continue your studies, so I jumped into action, called in a favor and found us just the right class. Now you are telling me that you are backing out? I hope you understand how irritating this is from my position, Mona. I am trying to help you here."

"Stop, Nathan, just stop," I said, trying to stop him before he got whipped up into a frenzy.

"Then tell me what is the real problem here because I don't get it."

I cut him off before he could continue, and blurted out, "I'm afraid!" I could feel the heat of embarrassment rise in my face and I started to sweat. I took a sip of coffee, trying to hide my anxiety and whispered, "I'm afraid I won't be able to keep up, that I will be out of my league and lost." I looked down at my coffee intently, having revealed my worst fear.

When I looked up, I could see that I had completely disarmed Nathan. He looked at me, stunned. I could tell he was searching for the right words. I looked out across the garden and summoned the courage to speak.

"I have always wanted to go to Buckley University, ever since I was a little girl. We would drive by it when we would come to visit Great Aunt Audry. I used to peer out of the window from the back seat of the car and stare up at the old stone buildings and imagine myself there as a student," I shared softly, processing the memory as I was speaking.

Nathan listened intently, not uttering a sound.

"Years went by and it came time to apply for colleges. My mother was quite ill at that time and I really was torn. How could I leave her and my father to go to school? I finally conceded to my mother's urging to go and pursue my dreams and applied to schools, one of which was Buckley University. I got so excited during the process, thinking again what it would be like to go to classes in those old stone buildings."

"So, what happened?" Nathan asked, on the edge of his seat.

"I didn't get in."

"To Buckley?"

"To any of them, Nathan. I was denied entry to all of them! Every single university I applied to respectfully declined my application," I said firmly, choking back tears at the end of the statement.

"I don't understand. What happened?"

I sighed. "I don't know. My grades, I assume. I definitely could have done better in my last year at high school, but I was distracted with everything going on at home."

"What did you tell your mother?" Nathan asked softly.

"I didn't, really. I just said that I found a fantastic bookkeeping program at the college in our town that would allow me to live at home, save money, and learn more to expand the book-keeping business I had started. I thought she would be happy to have me close. We never really talked about it beyond this."

"I don't understand why you don't want to take this chance now, Mona. You can finally go to Buckley University. I will be with you every step of the way as your friend."

Nathan's comment flooded me with warmth. I gave him a big smile and sighed again. "It defies logic, I know. Nathan, I am terrified. My confidence is broken, even after all these years."

"How about you trust me on this one? We will register to-gether and I will be there every step of the way. I know it's scary, but it is time to face your fears. Just imagine how excited you will be when you show yourself that you can master your first class? I wouldn't be surprised if you get an A," he said confi-dently.

His statement was echoed by a loud, "Meow," causing us both to burst into laughter at his timing.

"See! Even the big guy agrees," Nathan added, as he turned and looked over his shoulder, winking at the fluffy cat. Prince was standing at attention beside the empty plate, looking expec-tantly up at Nathan who continued, "Hey, I like your style, man, but Mona is your meal ticket."

Nathan turned back to me and silently stared as he finished off what was left in his coffee mug.

I finally broke the silence, "I know. You want an answer."

"I do, but I am also not going to force you into anything. I just think it would be a shame to waste this opportunity."

"Fine! I'll do it," I blurted out.

"Really? You aren't just saying this to get me off your back, are you?" He gave me a skeptical look.

I smiled and shook my head. "As terrified as I am, you have convinced me. This is my decision, though. You have my word."

"Scout's honor?" He asked, raising three fingers in the air.

"Scout's honor," I said, sitting up tall and mirroring his salute.

Nathan jumped up and grabbed me in a big hug, "I will get everything arranged today. You will not regret this, Mona, I promise."

"What's all the excitement?" Nathan stepped back and we saw Ethyl standing at the bottom of the stairs, smiling up at us.

"Come on up, Ethyl. We are having coffee. Would you like one?" I asked. "Nathan, can I refresh your mug?"

"Absolutely," he said, holding up his mug.

"You two are up early today. What are you up to?" Ethyl inquired again as she came upstairs to join us.

"We are making big plans, Ethyl," Nathan responded conspiratorially, in his deep voice.

Ethyl laughed. "Oh, really? Secret plans? Do tell!" she said, joining in the fun.

"That's up to Mona," he said, as he turned in his chair and looked at me.

I smiled. "No secrets from Ethyl." I hesitated for a moment, knowing as soon as I shared the news, it would be real. I took a breath and slowly breathed out, preparing myself. "Nathan and I . . ." I stopped, pausing to reconsider for a split second. "Nathan and I are going to take a finance course together at the university."

"That is wonderful, Mona! How lovely!" Ethyl said, beaming at us.

I smiled back at her, feeling relieved, then ducked inside to get coffee for us all. When I came back, carrying a tray with three coffees, cream, sugar and spoons, I found Ethyl and Nathan laughing away at something. "What did I miss?" I asked, as I set everything down on the table in front of us. I looked up at

Ethyl, who had settled in comfortably on the swing with the big cat sitting next to her. Prince looked up at me with a smirk on his face revelling in his spot next to Ethyl.

Ethyl gave me a look and gestured to the big guy. I innocently looked back at her. "What?" I asked.

"I hear someone has moved in," she said, grinning. I looked over at Nathan and gave him a look of disapproval for sharing my secret.

"Hey, I just tell it as I see it and from what I can see, the big boy has moved in," he responded, putting the palms of his hands up in front of him to shield himself.

"Nice. I will remember to be careful around you, Nathan Laine," I added, in mock disdain.

"Seriously though, are you going to let this big guy move in? What about your allergies? It might be fine in the summer, but what about the winter months? You are going to be miserable."

As if her words were summoning the universe to action, my nose began to tickle. I closed my eyes, gave in and let out a huge sneeze.

"See? This is not a practical solution at all," Ethyl declared.

I sighed. "I know, but for now, Prince needs a place to live. Heaven forbid that he wander back behind the house into Randy territory."

"Oh, you let me deal with Randy. He is not going to harm this cat," Ethyl reassured me.

I looked at her skeptically, "Really . . . what do you call the near-death incident with the chainsaw yesterday?"

"I will give you that. It was a close call, but I have spoken to Randy and he assured me he will stay away from the cat."

"Well," Nathan said, as he stood up from his chair, "I had better go call the university and confirm we are registering for the class. I will pick up our books this week, too."

"Thank you; let me know about payment," I said, smiling up at Nathan.

We said our goodbyes and Nathan set off to finish organizing the class registration. I was filled with dread as I contemplated what I had gotten myself into, but I quickly pushed those thoughts out of my mind. "Did you finish reading Merl's will?" I asked, as I turned to face Ethyl, who was softly petting Prince's fluffy coat. He was curled up beside her on the swing and I couldn't help but smile at the two of them. "What a shame he couldn't move in with Randy and Ethyl," I thought to myself.

"I did finish it and luckily there are no more surprises. There is only one bank account to close. No real complicated accounting at all. Everything seems to be quite simple, beyond the issue of this guy, of course," she explained, looking down at Prince as she continued to stroke the soft fur around his ears. We both sat quietly staring at him as he purred loudly in contentment.

"I need to get him some food and supplies," I said absently, but more as a reminder to myself. "He has been dining on my smoked fish from Paul's. He is an expensive beast. I forced him to eat fish from a can this morning and he was none too pleased. The sooner I break him out of the gourmet meals, the better."

"I have to go to the store today. Let me pick up the supplies for you. After all, Randy is technically his guardian. He should open his wallet and help out." We both had a good laugh at this. "What do you need? Food, a litter box, what else?"

I interrupted Ethyl at her mention of the litter box, "I think we can skip the litter. Apparently this sophisticated cat is toilet-trained."

Ethyl's eyes grew large and she gave me a disbelieving stare. "You are kidding me," she said, amazed.

"Not kidding, I discovered this little secret this morning on my way to the bathroom." I was flooded with a pang of guilt, the events replaying in my mind, including nearly smacking the large feline over the head. I shook off the thought, relieved that it had turned out the way it did.

Ethyl moved in her seat to face the cat curled up next to her. "You are full of surprises, mister," she said to him as she continued to ruffle his fur while he purred away joyfully.

"That he is," I added, smiling at him.

As we both sat quietly, enjoying the moment together on the deck, we heard a voice from the garden, "Hello, my dears, lovely to see you both on this sunny day."

My gut filled with dread when I recognized the voice. I was filled with an overwhelming feeling of longing for the railing around the deck to be solid, so I could hide in my cozy spot. Instead, I looked through to the garden and locked eyes with Margaritta. "Just when I thought this was going to be a great day," I grumbled in my mind.

Thankfully, Ethyl spoke first, "Good morning, Margaritta," she said, pleasantly. "What have you got on the go today?"

"Well, I am off to the university to get things in order before classes begin next week. I am teaching a new class this term and I have the best curriculum planned for my students," she said, stressing the word, 'best.' It took all my willpower to prevent myself from groaning and rolling my eyes.

"I am sure your students will just love it," Ethyl chimed in after Margaritta finished gushing over herself.

"How does Ethyl do that?" I wondered. "She truly seems to see the best in everyone. I wonder if there is anyone at all that she dislikes?"

I was pulled out of my lovely moment of contemplation by Margaritta's sharp voice. "Earth to Mona Lisa Brown, come in, Mona Lisa Brown," she said, laughing, dragging me right back into reality.

I gave her a weak smile through the railing. "Pardon, can you repeat the question, Margaritta?" I asked, with full awareness that I was about to hear some holier-than-thou reply from her. Heaven forbid she not command full attention from all those in her presence. As I braced myself for her witty barb, she spared me and moved on. Shocked, I proceeded to give her my full attention now, wondering what could possibly be more important to Margaritta than being able to insult me.

"Ethyl," she began, dragging her name out and then pausing as if the next thing she was about to say would be earth-shattering. She shifted her weight back and forth. Was it possible that the great Margaritta was uncomfortable? Maybe this day was going to turn out well after all. Ethyl and I both leaned in, totally focused on Margaritta, wondering what could possibly be coming next.

"What is it, Margaritta?" Ethyl asked charitably. "Is everything alright?"

"I was sitting in my apartment last night and I had made a lovely cup of tea from a medley of Egyptian spices that I picked up last summer at a market."

"Oh, here we go," I thought to myself.

"I had just sat down in my favorite chair by the window to read the latest works by Louise Foistingham. Shis is such an inspiring writer. Mona dear, you really should look for her work. It's not too dense. I think you could handle it."

"Here we go, just when I thought I had escaped the witty barbs." I wanted to scream at her. I breathed in slowly as Margaritta looked at me through the railing.

Sensing my discomfort, Ethyl jumped in, "Sounds like a lovely way to spend an evening. I am sensing it did not go as planned."

Looking awkward again, which eased my fury slightly, Margaritta hesitated. "Yes, you are correct, Ethyl. As I read and sipped a heavenly cup of tea, I heard scratching and scurrying above me. At first I thought there were squirrels on the roof running around gathering nuts, but this sound was too close. I think they have nested, Ethyl." She paused for dramatic effect, then continued. "They have nested in the attic right above my apartment!"

The look of dismay on Margaritta's face was fantastic. I thought to myself, "I am not sure squirrels in the attic require such drama and apprehension."

"Well, that is just terrible. Don't you worry, Randy will convince those squirrels to find a new home. I will get him on this right away. He'll have his way with them," Ethyl said confidently. Then she turned ever so slightly toward me and gave me a quick wink.

While I chuckled quietly to myself, imagining Randy convincing the squirrels to leave, I could see that Margaritta was visibly relieved. She thanked Ethyl and wished us both a good day, then walked with purpose to the street. As we watched her disappear down the street, I turned to Ethyl, "She seemed really concerned about squirrels in the attic," I said sarcastically.

"She does indeed. I'm glad she said something because those little critters can wreak havoc with a building if they get inside. They can chew wiring to bits. It can be quite dangerous. When we lived on the farm, our neighbor's barn burned down because something got in and chewed the wiring. It was a terrible thing. Luckily, the barn was empty at the time and no one was hurt."

Feeling a little pang of guilt for my snarky comment and a little nervous that there actually could be squirrels in the house running wild in the attic, I sat quietly and stared across the porch out at Merl's old house. "What are you going to do with that big house next door?" I asked, relieved to have thought of a good way to change the subject from destructive squirrels, burning barns, and Margaritta.

"Oh, no, you don't. I can see what you are trying to do, missy."

I gave Ethyl a confused look.

"You are changing the subject. I saw what went on there between you and Margaritta just now. She does get under your skin, doesn't she?"

I sighed and returned to staring across the deck again. "She is mean, Ethyl!"

"Yes, she can be. She can also be charming, and vulnerable. You are missing this."

"Why are you taking her side?" I sputtered in frustration, pouring out all my anger for Margaritta in the statement.

Ethyl smiled at me calmly, not even bothered by the toxicity of my comments. In a warm, soothing tone she said, "She is only mean if you let her have power over you. Take back your power, Mona."

I said nothing in return. I just looked at Ethyl, trying to absorb the full gravity of what she had said.

She gave me a big grin, "I better go break the news of the squirrels to Randy. I also have some supplies to buy for this big guy," she said, ruffling the big cat's fur.

As if Prince understood Ethyl's words, he stood up and stretched before jumping down onto the porch deck. Then he tiptoed around behind me and walked to my door.

"I think someone needs to use your toilet. How sophisticated," Ethyl said, snickering.

"He continues to amaze me."

As Ethyl walked down the stairs and I rose to let the Prince use the royal loo, she continued, "To answer your earlier question, we don't know yet what to do with the house next door. I guess we will let it sit for now. We are right over here. It's not a bother to take care of it for a while. It does seem a shame to leave it empty, though."

"Did Randy ever figure out why the water bill was so high?"

"Oh, yes!" Ethyl responded with excitement looking up at me from the garden path. "It was a running toilet in the basement. Would you believe it? Merl probably never even used that washroom down there," she finished, shaking her head.

"I'll remember that. If the toilet starts running, call Randy right away."

"That's right! Well, call me, but if you see Randy, I'm sure he won't mind if you flag him down. Just hide the cat first."

I smiled. "Thanks for the advice," I responded, hesitating for a moment. "All of it."

We said our farewells and Ethyl went on her way. As I cleaned up the coffee mugs, I considered what Ethyl had said. "Take back my power. How on earth do I do that?" I asked out loud.

I heard a loud, "Meeeoooowww," from the door.

"Okay, Okay, I'm moving," I said, opening the doors for the cat who darted inside and went into the washroom. "I know who has the power in this relationship."

I took all the dishes into the kitchen and started cleaning up when I heard my phone ring. I walked over to the counter to answer it.

"Hello, is this Mona?"

"Yes, this is Mona."

"Oh, good. This is Mary-ela from the Library. I was helping you research Professor Merchante when you were at the library. You asked me to look into a photo for you. Unfortunately I misplaced your phone number. I just found it today though. I am sorry for the delay in getting back to you."

"That's okay. I appreciate the phone call. Did you find anything?"

"I did! Do you have the article handy? I want you to look at something."

"Just a moment. I will go get it." I put the call on hold, excitement stirring in me. I walked down the hall to my office to find my backpack. As I passed the bathroom, I heard the toilet flush. I looked back over my shoulder and out strutted the big cat back toward the sofa. "You are quite something, cat," I called back to him.

I heard, "Meow," in response as I walked into my office.

Locating my backpack and the folded article in the front pocket where I left it, I put the call on speaker, setting the phone on the desk, "I'm back. I have the article here," I said, as I sat down in my office chair, unfolding the article and smoothing it out across my desk.

"Okay, first you asked about the gentleman in the picture standing next to her."

My heart raced, anticipating the dirt I had been digging for. "This is it," I thought, barely able to wait.

"The image is really fuzzy, but if you look closely, you will see the family resemblance."

"What?" I screamed in my head as my excitement deflated as fast as a balloon touching a hot lightbulb. I forced myself to keep listening as I examined the image in front of me more closely.

"Yes, this is Margaritta's father William, another Professor Merchante," the perky librarian continued, clearly thinking she was sharing something wonderful with me.

Not able to match her enthusiasm, I tried to respond in a kind tone, "Thank you. This was helpful, Mary-ela."

"There is more, though."

"More?" I asked, hopeful again.

"Yes, the woman in the background caught my eye. Do you see her? It's her expression. She is happy like everyone else, but she also looks a bit, I don't know . . ." She paused, then continued, "She looks kind of sad, don't you think?"

I looked more closely at the woman in the background and tried to make out her expression. The image was so unclear. I could barely see her expression. "I am having a hard time with this printed copy."

"Why don't I email the article to you instead so you can see it on screen? You will be able to see the details much better."

"Okay, that sounds like a good idea, but before you go, did you find anything out about this woman?"

"Oh yes, I almost forgot that part! I found references to Professor Merchante having a sister.

"Which Professor Merchante, the father or daughter?"

"Sorry. Yes, this is confusing. Professor William Merchante. His sister's name is Beth. The woman in the photo looks older than Margaritta. Perhaps she is her Aunt Beth."

"Hmm, I wonder what the story is there?"

"Yes, I will keep digging, so you can get the full story for your article."

I thanked the eager librarian and gave her my email address. Ending the call, I stood and noticed Prince sitting at the door to my office, giving me a look of dismay or as close to what a look of dismay could be from a large cat.

"What?" I said to him, laughing smugly. "Ethyl told me to take back my power."

"Meow," the big cat uttered, in a low disapproving tone. Then he turned and pranced down the hall.

I shook my head as he pranced slowly down the middle of the hall with me trailing behind him. He gave me a look over his shoulder as he entered the front sitting room. "Are you seriously judging me, big guy? I'm just doing a bit of research."

"Meow."

"Don't take that tone with me."

"Meow."

He walked across the room, jumped up on the sofa, and curled up, giving me a long look from across the room. Then he rolled onto his back and passed out.

"I guess we are done, then. Good talk, cat."

I was left standing there, staring at him, my thoughts drifting to the connection between Margaritta and Beth Merchante. Maybe she was simply Margaritta's aunt. I couldn't help but wonder if there was more though–a bigger story to uncover.

CHAPTER 12

Bang, bang, bang, bang. My eyes flew open as I tried to orient myself. I slowly sat up and looked at the table, noticing my now-cold cup of tea. Disoriented, it started to come back. I remembered going outside to read and enjoy a cup of tea in my cozy spot on the porch. Bang, bang, bang, bang. I heard the noise again. "What is that?" I muttered to myself, wondering how long I had been asleep. Bang, bang, bang, the noise continued. This time it was followed by cursing.

"For crying out loud. You'll never get back in here, you worthless excuse for a four-legged creature!" I shook my head, starting to realize what was going on and walked down the stairs, through the garden, toward the street. I turned and looked back at the house and saw Randy suspended halfway down the steep roof by what looked like an old rope. He was crouched awkwardly over the skylight above Margaritta's apartment hammering away. Bang, bang, bang.

"What's going on up there? Is everything okay?" I called up to Randy with concern.

He stopped and looked down at me from the roof. "Oh, hi down there. Sorry for the noise. How are you doing today, Mona?" Randy said casually, as if hanging out on a steep roof was an everyday affair.

"I'm doing well, thank you. I heard there are some critters causing problems," I responded, trying to be careful not to upset Randy.

"That there are! Do you know what they have done up here?" Randy asked emphatically, pointing down at the roof.

"Uh, no . . . What?"

"I'll tell you! They have chewed a hole in between the roof and this skylight, peeled it right off. These things never seal well from the elements as it is, but now I have to contend with this damage! They better not have gotten into my wiring in the attic or there will be hell to pay, I tell you. Hell To Pay!" he said punctuating the last statement.

I hesitated slightly, but I had to ask, "Uh, Randy, is that a rope around your waist?"

He looked down at it, then responded, "One of my finest! I'm still pretty nimble, but Ethyl would kill me for being up here without being fastened to something. I banged the other end in with a spike, at the top of the roof up there," he said pointing to the peak of the roof.

"Well, it's good that you are being safe," I responded tentatively, not at all convinced of his safety measures. "Did you see what caused the damage up there?"

"Not yet, but I will find them. This has to be the work of squirrels." He paused and then called out confidently, "Do you hear that, squirrels? I will find you!" He bellowed like a soldier going into battle. I said a secret prayer for the squirrels, hoping they would move somewhere else instead of tangling with Handy Randy and his arsenal of who-knows-what in the shed out back. The fight hardly seemed fair.

"Well, good luck with the roof repairs. I hope you can persuade the squirrels to relocate," I said, forcing a bubbly tone.

Randy laughed. "This might be their last location, if I have my way." I swallowed the lump in my throat, whispered another prayer for the squirrels, and gave Randy a smile and a wave as I started walking back to the house. Still focused on Randy and the roof, as I was making my way around the garden path, I heard a voice from behind me.

"Hi, Mona. What's going on?" I stopped and looked behind me to see Max. My first reaction was irritation, as the events of our last encounter with Tish flooded through my mind. Before I could say anything, Randy started up again. Bang, bang, bang, bang. I waved hello and indicated we should move inside to quieter surroundings. Max followed me up the front steps, through the doorway and into my apartment. He shut the storm door behind him, which cut some of the noise down. "Is there a leak?" he asked.

"Not yet, but it sounds like it was heading in that direction due to the handiwork of some squirrels." Max nodded in response as I continued, "Are you coming from the university?" I asked.

"Yes, I was over there getting ready for next week. I am teaching a new class this fall and need to prepare."

"Where is Tish today?" I asked, making conversation, not really interested in the answer.

"She is teaching today," Max answered. I nodded, still annoyed. We stood awkwardly in the sitting room looking at each other when Max noticed Prince curled up on the sofa across the room. "You have the cat from next door in your apartment!"

"Yes, he slid in here without me noticing. Sneaky guy."

"Do Ethyl and Randy know?" Max asked, concerned.

"Ethyl yes, Randy no."

"Huh. What about your allergies?"

"I'm surviving so far. I'm not sure this is a long-term solution, though."

I finally gathered the courage to speak my mind.

"Max . . ," I paused, trying not to chicken out. I took a deep breath as he stared at me, waiting for the rest of my sentence.

"I have to ask, what was all that with Tish the other day on my front porch?" I said, surprised at my boldness. I could feel heat coming to my face as I waited to hear his response.

Max shifted his weight from foot to foot nervously in the silence that followed. "Yeah, that."

I looked at him expectantly, raising my eyebrows. "Yeah, that!" I responded, frustration creeping into my voice.

"I'm sorry, Mona. I started to talk to Tish and then everything got twisted around."

I was hit with a pang of sympathy as I saw Max's discomfort. "Can you tell me what happened? How did my name get into the conversation?"

He sighed and raked his fingers through his thick brown hair. "I don't know. It was such a jumbled mess. I brought up some examples to explain how she makes me feel. At first she did not understand, but I gave her more details and then she started to get angry, saying this was not like me at all, grilling me on who put me up to this."

"And you said it was me!?"

"Not exactly. Well sort of."

"Max!"

"What? Wait. I knew what I had done as soon as your name came out of my mouth, so I tried to rescue the situation and I guess I ended up twisting the message completely."

"Uh huh," I responded, crossing my arms across my chest, totally unimpressed.

"I'm sorry, Mona. At least Tish doesn't think badly of you."

"Max, I don't care what Tish thinks of me. In fact, I would rather be viewed as the bad person who put you up to telling her the truth than what you are describing. I don't know why I am getting credit for anything here. It was Nathan who put you up to this!"

"It was stupid, Mona. I'm sorry. I messed up."

Disarmed by Max's apology, I paused, searching for the right words, aware that he was visibly anguished over the situation.

We were interrupted by more noise from the roof. It was different this time–a scuffling sound like something was being dragged, followed by yelling.

"Help! Help!"

Max and I ran outside and down to the garden, knowing whose voice we were hearing.

"Help me!"

We looked up to see Randy hanging off the roof, clinging to the metal eaves along the edge of the building, a few feet from Margaritta's balcony. The rope was still tied around his waist, but not attached to the roof. Instead, it was hooked on the edge of the balcony railing, the end dangling in the air below.

"Help me!" Randy called out desperately.

"We are here, Randy!"

"I don't know how long I can hold on. I'm going to break my legs if I drop," Randy said, panic in his voice.

"Can you reach Margaritta's balcony?" Max suggested.

"I think I'm too far. If I try to swing over there and miss, I will fall on my head for sure."

"What is going on?" said Nathan from his balcony.

We pointed frantically at Randy hanging off the roof and I called up to Nathan, "We have a situation here!"

"Oh dear, we do. What have you done, old man?" Nathan yelled to Randy.

"I was fixing the roof. We can get into that later. Right now, I need to get down without breaking a limb or worse!"

"We walked closer to Nathan, then looked back up at Randy from a different angle. "If we can get onto Margaritta's balcony, maybe we can use the rope to pull Randy closer. Margaritta is out, though. I saw her leave earlier."

"There is a ladder on the other side of the house. The one I used to get up here."

"Quick, you two go get the ladder. I'm coming down," Nathan barked as he exited his balcony.

Max and I ran around to the parking area and spotted the huge ladder leaning against the building. We stood at the bottom, looking up at it, unsure how we were going to move it. Then we heard Nathan's voice from the side entrance. "Just lift it off the building, it's lighter than you think."

Max and I exchanged doubtful looks. Nathan jumped in and the three of us managed to move the huge ladder off the building and around to the front of the house, setting it against Margaritta's balcony. Randy appeared to have given up on us and was reaching his long left leg out towards the railing. I could barely watch for fear that his hands were going to let go.

"I'm coming up! Hold tight," Nathan called out.

"I better hold tight. The alternative is not looking good from up here. Hurry, though, I am not as strong as I used to be."

"Maybe you should have thought of that before falling off the roof, old man!" Nathan bellowed up to him. "Mona, Max, hold the ladder still, I'm going up."

We both steadied the ladder from either side as Nathan scampered up, looking spry and youthful, like he did roof rescues everyday. Reaching the top, he immediately grabbed the dangling rope and secured it tightly to the heavy metal railing, demonstrating some impressive knot-making skills. He hopped over the railing onto the balcony and called out to Randy, "I have tied the rope to the balcony just in case you fall, but let's not tempt fate. How about we get you over here? Can you reach the railing with your foot?"

"If I could get onto the balcony, I would have done it five

minutes ago!" Randy snapped back impatiently at Nathan as he jabbed his left leg over and over toward the balcony railing to illustrate the problem.

Nathan grabbed Randy's leg and held it. "You just need a helping hand. Lean on me and inch your hands this way."

"I don't know if I can hold on much longer."

"You're tied in now. Just try it. I got you."

Like a mountain climber with impressive strength, Randy lifted his left hand and moved it swiftly along the edge of the roof in one big desperate movement toward Nathan. At the same time, his right hand gave out and he dropped like a stone from the roof, his left leg sliding out of Nathan's grasp as if it was covered in butter. My heart skipped a beat as we watched him fall. Luckily the rope caught him just below the deck of the balcony.

We all froze in silence and watched Randy swing in the air from the balcony like a rag doll.

"WoooooooooWheeeeee!" he wailed. "I'm good! I survived!" he cheered, looking up at Nathan who was gazing down at him, stunned by what had just taken place and likely saying a prayer for his knot-making skills.

This was the exact time that Ethyl walked around the corner of the house carrying her big basket of gardening tools while whistling a show tune of some sort. She first looked at Max and I, who looked back at her wide-eyed, frozen in place, holding the ladder. Then she noticed Randy hanging from the roof. Ethyl shrieked and dropped her basket. She ran toward Randy, yelling, "Get down from there right this instant!"

"What do you think I am trying to do? There is no other place I would rather be right now than on terra firma."

Ethyl stopped talking, placed her hands on her hips and called up to Nathan with desperation in her voice. "What are we going to do?"

Before anyone could answer, there was a cracking noise as the rope ripped apart just above Randy's head. Nathan grabbed desperately at the rope, but it was too late, Randy dropped down onto the sloped roof of the porch below. As he dropped, he twisted himself around and managed to land on his side with a thud.

We all cringed at the sound of the impact, fearing the worst, but Randy sprang into action and flattened himself out on the steep roof to keep from sliding off. He spread his arms and legs out wide across the shingles, gripping whatever he could to hold himself in place.

After a few moments, Nathan called down, "Are you alive down there, you crazy old geezer?"

A muffled voice followed. "I'm a survivor. Who are you calling long in the tooth, anyway? I'm younger than you."

"Oh, you might have survived that fall, but you will be wishing you hadn't when I am through with you! Now get down here this instant," Ethyl yelled up to him.

"I don't know. This rooftop is pretty comfortable. It's certainly warm. Maybe I'll stay up here for a bit and get a suntan."

Nathan crawled over the balcony railing and onto the ladder. "I'm coming down to get you. Don't move."

"Don't worry. I won't."

Nathan climbed over the balcony railing back onto the ladder and lowered himself down to the ground. We helped him shorten the ladder and reposition it against the roof of the porch. Holding it steady from the ground, he called up to Randy, "Can you get onto the ladder from where you are?"

Randy slowly lifted his head and surveyed the situation. He crawled across the roof and slowly slid his body onto the ladder. Gripping the ladder with his hands, he paused for a moment to steady himself, then began to move down the ladder toward the ground.

Ethyl walked over to the ladder and stood at the bottom with her arms crossed in front of her. Hanging back from the action, Max and I gave each other a concerned look, fearing what was coming next. Looking grateful to return his feet to the earth, Randy stepped off the last rung of the ladder onto the ground and faced Ethyl. They gazed at each other with Nathan, Max and I staring apprehensively at them. We were waiting for Ethyl to blow her stack, but she didn't say a word. Instead, she pulled Randy into a big hug. Shocked, he bent down toward her and embraced her. No one said a word, all of us aware of how close a call that was for Randy.

After a few minutes, Ethyl stepped back and smacked Randy across the chest with the back of her hand.

"Ow! What was that for? Be gentle with me, I just had a near-death experience!" Randy said.

"Oh, YOU did? I nearly had a heart attack watching you!" Ethyl shouted back.

"And you didn't even see the part before," Nathan said under his breath. Randy gave Nathan a look, trying to tell him to pipe down.

"Exactly! This is the last straw. We are going to get someone to help around here." Randy sighed, saying nothing. After today's events it was hard to argue with Ethyl. "What would have happened if your rescue crew hadn't been around. You surely would have fallen to your death!"

"Stop being so dramatic. I'm like a cat. I bounce," Randy smiled and pawed the air like a cat.

"Your hands! Oh my goodness, let me see them."

Randy extended both his hands out in front of him palms up, examining them both for the first time. Both of Randy's wrists and hands had deep scrapes across them and were bleeding.

"Huh, look at that," he said casually.

"Nice work. Those are some serious scrapes," Nathan commented.

Ethyl threw her hands up in the air and shook her head as she walked back to her basket. As she collected everything that had fallen out, she turned and called back to us, "Nathan, we really owe you one. Thank you. You too, Mona and Max. Thank you all. Let us thank you with a big barbecue at our place."

"You don't have to do that. I couldn't leave my old friend hanging off the roof, could I? Anyone would have done what I did. I can't possibly refuse a barbecue, though," Nathan said with a big smile.

Ethyl turned to Max and me. "Will you join us, too?"

Max and I both enthusiastically agreed. We set the date for a few days later to give Ethyl time to prepare and Randy time to recover. He might have bounced off the roof, but he surely would be mighty sore over the next few days.

"Alright, let's get you patched up, mister," Ethyl said, turning to Randy as she picked up her big basket of gardening supplies. They bid us farewell and Randy dutifully fell in step behind Ethyl. Before they disappeared around the corner, Randy turned and gave us a mischievous grin and a wink. Then he waved farewell with a goofy salute and dropped out of sight behind the house.

I looked at Max and Nathan in amazement. "What just happened? I think it gets more bizarre here every day."

"Yes, possibly true. This was one for the record books, for sure. Unfortunately for Randy, I think Ethyl is correct, they are going to have to get some help around here," Nathan added.

"Maybe there is someone who can help him, but let Randy direct," Max suggested, ever the placater.

"Like an assistant?" I offered.

"Yes, exactly. There must be someone in Buckley Brook who

could be Randy's assistant," Max continued optimistically.

Nathan and I gave each other a skeptical look. "I don't know, Max. I've only known Randy a few months, but something tells me it might be hard to find Randy an assistant who will stick around."

Nathan nodded in agreement. "Regardless, today was a close one. I hope there are no more roof rescues in our future," Nathan said.

We turned our gaze to the ladder which was still leaning up against the porch roof. "What do we do with this ladder?" I asked.

"I'm sure Randy will remember it and come back for it. We better leave it, so he can put it back the way he wants it stored," Nathan stated.

A thought ran through my head, "I wonder if Randy finished the roof before he fell off of it."

Nathan and Max looked at me, unsure of what to do next.

"I'm just wondering because he said there was a big hole around the skylight. I would hate for it to rain and cause damage in the attic. I can see all his tools still up there too."

"Ah, Mona. Now why did you have to go and do that? I can't in good conscience walk away knowing this," Nathan said, looking annoyed at the realization.

"And you know, if we tell Randy, he is going to go charging back up there, no matter what any of us say," I added.

"We could hide his ladder," Max suggested.

"Max!" I exclaimed. "And what exactly is that going to achieve other than to make Randy really angry?"

"Well, at least he will be angry on the ground," Max responded.

I gave him a disapproving look as Nathan jumped into the conversation, "I think you are right. If we leave this ladder here,

Randy is going to go back up to retrieve his tools and do Lord knows what else up there while he is at it."

A car pulled into the driveway and we turned to see who it was. Max waved enthusiastically at Tish and went to meet her in the parking area. "Wonderful. That's all we need . . . the great Tish gracing us with her presence," I muttered under my breath.

Nathan snickered at my comment. "She is a winner, alright. I don't know why he stays with her."

"You do have eyes, right?" I responded sarcastically.

"Oh I do, but I've been around the block a few times. I can spot that type from a mile away. She is nothing but trouble. Leave-your-heart-torn-up-on-the-floor kinda trouble. I've tried to tell him that, but he's still young."

I sighed heavily in response. "Okay, are we taking care of this situation or what?" I responded, intentionally changing the subject.

"Yes, ma'am. Are you going up the ladder this time?" Nathan asked, laughing.

"I just might," I said in a tone of mock offense. "You don't think I can go up a ladder, too?" I was mustering way more confidence than I was feeling.

"Right, it's fine. I'll do it," Nathan said as he lifted the ladder back up to the main rooftop and rested it to the right of Margaritta's balcony.

"What? The girl can't go up the ladder?" I continued to protest.

Nathan gave me a look over his nose conveying that I was being ridiculous. "This is not a girl thing, Mona. It's also not something to be trivialized. You saw the trouble Randy got himself into up there. This is an extremely tall building. Look at the ladder. It barely reaches." I glanced up at it and acknowledged in my head that he was right. "Unless you are experienced with ladders and roofs, I suggest you stick with holding the ladder. Can you do that for me?" Nathan asked, softening his tone.

I sighed, knowing he was right, wondering why I even put up a fight as I realized how high the ladder really stretched to get up to the top of the roof. "Do you think it is safe for any of us to go up there?"

Nathan smiled. "It's okay. As long as you are holding the ladder at the bottom to keep it steady, I will be fine."

"How are we going to get Randy's tools down?"

Nathan pointed to the frayed rope on the ground that Randy had tried to use to secure himself to the roof. "That rope still has plenty of strength to it. I can lower what is still up there down to you. You could even come up the ladder partway to get them if you like," he said, giving me a wink.

"Oh goody." I rolled my eyes, but couldn't help smiling back at him.

Nathan secured the ladder in place and stepped onto the first rung of the ladder, as Tish and Max came around the corner of the house into the garden.

"Hi, guys! So good to see you! What's going on?" asked a perky voice.

Nathan and I both cringed as he stepped back onto the ground, trying not to look annoyed.

"Tish, lovely to see you my dear," Nathan said in an overly sweet tone. "Actually, I am glad you are both here," he continued enthusiastically. I gave him a puzzled sideways glance, curious as to what idea he was cooking up.

"Really? It is so nice to see you, too, Nathan!" Tish responded, oblivious to Nathan's ulterior motives.

"Oh yes, Mona and I are trying to help poor Randy who just narrowly escaped death by falling off the roof."

"Oh dear! Poor Randy. My goodness. I hope he is okay. How

can I help?" Tish offered, showing great concern.

Unable to bear it, I turned away and rolled my eyes.

"Randy's tools are still up on the roof. I am going to go get them and lower them down. It would be a lot faster if Mona could come partway up the ladder to receive them. Could the two of you hold the ladder steady at the bottom for us?"

"For sure. We can do that, right, Tish?" Max responded enthusiastically.

"Okay," Tish said, hesitant now that she was aware of the task.

"Thank you, Tish! Mona, shall we?" Nathan asked. "I'll go up to the roof first. You come up partway after me and wait for me to drop the first load down with the rope, okay?"

"Absolutely," I responded, excited to have a larger role in Nathan's plan.

Wasting no time, Nathan expertly scaled the ladder while Max and I held it steady at the bottom. As Nathan hopped onto the roof, he looked over the edge and gave us a thumbs up before he disappeared to survey the state of things left by Randy.

"Okay, Tish, we are counting on you. Take my spot, so I can go up and help Nathan," I said, deciding to pour it on as thick as Nathan.

"I can do it," Tish said confidently, with a big smile.

I grabbed the ladder with both hands, took a deep breath, stepped onto the first rung and began my climb. By the fourth rung, I felt a flutter in my stomach as I looked down and realized that I was already pretty high off the ground. I fought to keep my gaze fixed above me.

When I arrived at the level of Margaritta's apartment, I decided to pause and wait for instructions from Nathan. Being careful not to look down, I took the opportunity to peer through Margaritta's window. From what I could see, it had a similar layout to my apartment, except for being a one-bedroom. Everything was stylish, organized and perfectly placed. The place looked like it could be featured in an expensive home decor magazine. A wave of jealousy washed over me, which dissipated as I heard Nathan call my name from above. I looked up to see Nathan crouched at the edge of the roof staring down at me.

"How do things look, Nathan?" I called up to him.

"Randy definitely finished the repair job. I can't see any work left to do, but it's a disaster up here, tools everywhere. I don't know how he gets any work done. He must be constantly trying to find the right tool in a mess like this."

Memories of Randy trying to find his keys flooded back to me and I stifled a laugh as Nathan continued. "I am going to lower Randy's toolbag down. I only put a few items into it, so it won't be too heavy. When you get it, can you carry it down to the ground, empty it and bring it back up? I only have the two tool bags up here. Let's be safe and take a few trips instead of loading them up too full, okay?"

"Okay, Nathan."

"Get ready, the first load is coming down now." As Nathan slowly lowered the tool bag down to me, we heard the unmistakable voice of Margaritta below us.

"Well, well, well, what are you two doing now? Trying to get a break on your rent this month? Do watch out for the clematis on the balcony railing. It is about to bloom. It would be a tragedy to disturb it. Mona Lisa Brown, dear, are you sure you are strong enough to handle that work? I hadn't taken you for one who enjoys heights or ladders."

My stomach churned, and my face flashed red as fire. Before Margaritta could continue, though, Nathan jumped in from above me. "Enough, you pompous old twit. While you have been gallivanting all over town, Randy nearly killed himself falling off the roof. We are trying to recover his tools so he does not go back on the roof and really finish himself off."

Margaritta was silenced with this remark. I couldn't bear to look down at her from that height, so I smiled up at Nathan as he returned to the job at hand. Margaritta said nothing more and stomped off behind the house.

"Well, that took the wind out of the old gas bag!" Nathan said, after Margaritta was out of earshot.

"You are a master, Nathan Laine. A little lower and I can grab that tool bag."

I caught the bag and set it onto the rung above to untie the rope. It was lighter than I thought it would be. As I released the rope and Nathan pulled it up, I slung the bag onto my shoulder and began my descent.

By the third round, I was getting the hang of things and was feeling quite confident about my handywoman abilities. I arrived at the top of the ladder to wait for my next load, trying to not make eye contact with Margaritta inside her apartment who was busy in the kitchen. Hopefully, she would stay out of our hair until we got this job done.

Unfortunately, we weren't that lucky. Margaritta shrieked. I looked into her window, trying to figure out if she was injured or just insane. I could see her darting frantically around the apartment like something was biting her. She kept wailing at the top of her lungs and pointing up at the skylight.

Nathan called from the roof. "Mona, looks like we have a new problem. I don't think it's a squirrel issue."

Confused, I looked in the window as Margaritta came charging toward me screeching something over and over. When she opened the balcony door, I finally understood what she was saying. "Rats, rats, rats are in my apartment!"

Margaritta slammed the balcony door shut, like she was narrowly escaping a lion chasing her and continued to scream at the top of her lungs.

I looked up and saw Nathan as he reached the edge of the roof and peered down at us. "Stop your screaming, you crazy lunatic!" he yelled down at Margaritta.

Finally, tired and breathless, Margaritta grabbed the railing of the balcony, holding onto it for support. Looking up at me, she whispered, "There are rats in my apartment. I saw one. It looked at me with its beady little eyes. There we were, eyeball to eyeball in my kitchen!" She shuddered at the thought and continued to use the railing to support herself. I stared at her in disbelief. I'm not crazy about rodents myself, but this drama was a bit much. The rat was probably way more scared of Margaritta.

"Oh, snap out of it, will you? It's just a couple of rats. They chewed their way in where the roof meets the skylight. Randy must have sealed them into the attic when he repaired the roof. Really, it's not a big deal. The exterminator will have them out of here in no time."

I gave Nathan a skeptical look as Margaritta continued to gaze down over the balcony. I knew how hard it was to get rid of the rats in the city. It could be a long process.

From below, we heard Ethyl and Randy run to the front of the house. "What the dickens are you all doing up there? We heard the screaming from the backyard. Mona, what are you doing on the ladder? Nathan! Are you on the roof?" Randy sputtered, as he took in the whole scene.

Margaritta was the first to speak, of course, "Rats! Randy, there are rats in my apartment! I barely escaped from them to the balcony! Ethyl, I can't possibly stay in my apartment with rats in there!"

"Oh, my dear, that must have been a horrible experience, Margaritta. I can only imagine how terrifying it was for you,"

Ethyl replied earnestly.

I thought to myself, "Ethyl really is smooth," hiding a smile. "Or is she really that kind?" I wondered.

"It was so frightening, Ethyl. I cannot possibly bear to go back in there."

"Unless you want to climb over the railing and down that ladder, you are going to go back into that apartment," Randy said gruffly, visibly impatient with Margarita's antics.

Before Margaritta could reply, Ethyl softly proposed a solution, "Margaritta dear, how about I come up? I will make sure the coast is clear in your apartment, then we can walk out together. We can figure out the next step after we get you safely out of the house. Okay?"

"That will be fine; thank you Ethyl."

While Ethyl walked back to the side entrance, Randy zeroed in on the rest of us. "Now, what are you all doing?" he said, looking first at Tish and Max who were speechless, still gripping the ladder like it was about to topple over. Then Randy focused his gaze on Nathan and me.

"Well . . ." Nathan started. "We were talking about your ladder still being up on the house and then we noticed that your tools were still up here and we did not want you to have to go back on the roof after what happened earlier. One thing led to another and here we are," Nathan said matter-of-factly, with a big smile. "It really should have been a fast job, but Mona and I did not count on the rats showing up. Things kind of unravelled after that."

"That they did," Randy said, looking annoyed. "What, you didn't think I could take care of getting my own stuff off the roof?"

Before we could answer, Margaritta's balcony door opened and out walked Ethyl, who draped her arm around the still-distraught Margaritta. "The coast is clear. Are you ready to go back in?"

"I think so, yes," Margaritta replied breathlessly, milking the moment for all it was worth.

After the door closed, Randy started up again, "You didn't answer my question. Did you think I couldn't get my own tools off the roof?"

Trying to help, I decided to jump into the conversation, "Not at all Randy, we were only trying to help." I made the mistake of looking down from the top of the ladder at Randy as I finished my sentence. My stomach dropped and the earth started to spin. I was filled with panic at the realization of how far off the ground I really was. I quickly focused on the ladder rung in front of me and breathed in and out slowly, trying to steady myself. I knew someone was talking to me, but all I could hear was a loud whooshing sound in my ears.

"Mona, Mona," I finally heard. "Are you okay?"

"Mona, look at me," Nathan barked assertively. I lifted my head and met his gaze. A trickle of sweat rolled down the side of my face. "I want you to keep looking at me and slowly lower yourself down the ladder, just like you did before. Can you do that?" I nodded and began descending, rung by rung, being careful to keep looking up at Nathan.

Taking long, slow deep breaths, I lowered myself down the ladder, thankful when I finally reached the ground. I watched Nathan climb down, carrying the last load of tools. He stepped off the ladder, put down the tool bag, and came over to me.

Feeling extremely embarrassed by my reaction to the height, I sheepishly looked at him. Nathan grabbed my shoulders with a big smile on his face, then gave me a huge hug. "You did great, Mona! Thanks for helping me carry the tools down. It saved a lot of time," he said. I smiled thinly, appreciative that he was choosing to gloss over the situation at the end. "I'm serious, Mona. You really jumped into that. Even though heights aren't your comfort zone, you weren't afraid to try. Thank you. I mean it."

Randy and Ethyl walked over to join us as Tish chimed in enthusiastically, "You were amazing, Mona!"

"How can Tish be so cheery all the time?" I wondered.

I tried to look pleased, but really, all this attention was making me uncomfortable. Luckily, Margaritta chose that moment to tear out of the driveway at lightning speed, spinning the tires as she turned onto the quiet street. Everyone turned to look at her. "Sheesh, she is something else," Randy said.

"I will never understand that crazy . . ." Nathan started to add, but was cut off just in time by Ethyl, who gave him a disapproving look.

"Knock it off, you two. She has had a traumatic day."

"What?" Randy exploded. "She had a traumatic day? She did not fall off a roof! Good grief! Where is she going so fast, anyway? That nut of a woman is going to take someone out with that old tank."

"Margaritta is going to stay at a friend's B&B in town while we take care of the rats," Ethyl said. Then she gave Nathan and I a stern look, "Really, what were you two thinking of, going back up on the roof!?"

"Exactly! I asked the same thing myself!" Randy jumped in, but was silenced by Ethyl's scolding gaze.

Quietly and calmly, Max interjected, "Nathan and Mona were only trying to help. They noticed that your tools were still on the roof, Randy, and were concerned about leaving them up there. It really was as simple as that."

Disarmed by Max's words, Randy paused, looking down at his feet. "Thank you both. It really was nice not having to go back up on the roof today. So, uh . . ." he paused, "How about some help moving these tools around back, Nathan?" Randy said with a bashful smile.

"Not a problem at all. Let's go do that now," Nathan said, looking pleased by Randy's request for more help.

Ethyl shook her head at them and declared that she was going to go call the exterminator to deal with the rats. As they all walked away, I was left standing with Tish and Max.

"Thanks for speaking up, Max. That seemed to diffuse Randy's outrage. Who knew helping someone could cause such difficulty?"

"You did a good job, Mona," Max responded warmly.

"Well, I don't know about you, but just watching that whole thing made me famished. I could really go for a croissant and a cappuccino. How about you, Mona?" Tish asked.

I smiled back at Tish, thinking that there was not even a minute chance I was voluntarily spending more time with her. "You guys go and enjoy. I'm going to get a glass of water and sit quietly for a little bit."

We said our farewells and parted ways. At the top of the stairs, I looked back and watched Tish and Max walk arm in arm down the sidewalk. They looked so happy together. I should have been happy for them. My eyes drifted down into the garden, landing on the gnome. "What's wrong with me? I could have gone for a walk on a beautiful day to enjoy pastry and coffee at a cafe with friends. Instead, here I am, alone, stewing about someone else's girlfriend over whom I have absolutely no control. Seriously, what is wrong with me?"

"Ah, my dear Mona, seriously, there is absolutely nothing wrong with you." Startled by the voice, I turned to see Nathan's smiling face walking toward me. "What has gotten you so stirred up?"

"I just don't get Max and Tish. How . . . how are they even together? Their relationship seems so artificial. How can two people build something on a foundation of lies?"

"What did Tish do now?"

"Nothing, she was perfectly lovely, actually. She invited me to go for a walk with her and Max to find pastry and coffee, in fact."

"Why didn't you go? Just curious."

"Because she makes me crazy. Every word she utters gets under my skin. I couldn't possibly spend another second with her. What is wrong with me, Nathan?"

Nathan smiled, then sighed. "You have seen how she treats Max and the impact this has on him. I can see why you wouldn't want to spend time with her. On the flip side, you don't seem so happy right now by yourself."

"I don't get it. Why does Max put up with her?"

"Here is the thing, Mona, we may never know and you have to figure out how to be okay with it or you can't be friends with Max. Worse, it will eat you up inside. Trust an old man, Mona, let it go. You will be better off."

"You aren't an old man, Nathan. I watched you single-handedly rescue Randy this afternoon. You hopped on and off that ladder like few young men could do. Don't call yourself old."

Nathan gave me a wide grin. "I guess this old body still has a few springs in it," he said, strutting around the garden. "But in all seriousness, I have been around for many more years than you. I've made mistakes. I have harbored grudges. I have been stubborn."

"You? Stubborn? I can't imagine," I teased him quietly.

"Really, it's true, you have your whole life ahead of you. Don't miss out on life, like I did."

I was dying to ask for more details, but I thought better of it and stood silently staring at the gnome in the garden as I digested these words. My heart knew he was right, but my own stubborn disposition just wanted to scream. I could feel Nathan staring at me. As I finally pulled my eyes away from the gnome and looked back at Nathan, I saw the gnome give me a wink.

"Did you see that?" I blurted out, pointing at the gnome.

"See what? Nathan said, confused. But there was nothing to see, of course.

"Never mind, it was probably just a squirrel in the garden."

"Or maybe the rats jumped ship to more hospitable surroundings."

A shiver ran down my back, "Ugh, I hope not. Somehow, I prefer to think about them being locked inside Margaritta's apartment."

"After all the excitement today, I need to go sit and rest," Nathan declared. "It's been a pleasure, Mona. Thank you for getting up to no good with me today," he said with a wink. "Despite the roughing up Randy and Ethyl gave us, I know they appreciated our help."

Nathan gave me a wave as he left. I turned to see Prince sitting on the arm of the sofa, staring out the window at me. "How long have you been up there, Mister? You had a front-row seat to witness all the action around here today."

I went inside to finally get a glass of water and sit quietly. Stretching out on the sofa opposite the big cat, I closed my eyes, the events of the day replaying over in my mind. The images of Randy hanging from the roof, Nathan scaling the ladder, and my near stumble at the top of the ladder rolled through my mind. Then I remembered Margaritta's encounter with the rats, her screeching tires as she fled the property and I couldn't help but smile. I lay there in stillness, but only for a moment before I heard the familiar ding of my phone indicating that I had a new message.

Curious, I got up and found my phone at the end of the kitchen counter. I opened it and saw a new message with, 'More information,' in the subject line. It was from Mary-ela at the library. I felt a pang of guilt, knowing I had not been totally honest with her about my motives, but then Margaritta's face flashed into my mind and the feeling quickly passed. I opened the email and downloaded the article attached, but it was still too small to see the details on my phone.

I walked down the hall to my office to open the email on my laptop, attached to the large monitor sitting on my desk. I skipped the text in Mary-ela's email and moved straight to opening the image of the article. She was right; the details of the picture were much clearer in this version. I focused on Margaritta and the man. I could see the family resemblance now. Frustration came flooding back. "There must be more here," I yelled as I smacked the desk with my hand.

I kept scanning the picture and focused on the woman standing in the background. She was smiling as she watched Margaritta and William pose for the photo. Then something caught my eye. I stopped and squinted, then enlarged the photo on the screen, trying to see the detail. It couldn't be. I looked closer, examining the woman. Hanging from her neck was the locket. I am sure of it. It was the locket that caused all the toilet troubles. The locket that triggered Margaritta to burst into tears.

I sat back in my chair and looked out the window into the garden and smiled to myself. There was a story here, I knew it! Who was this woman and how was she connected to Margaritta?

"Meow," I heard from behind me. I jumped in surprise, whacking my elbow on the edge of the desk. Rubbing my elbow, I spun around in my chair to see Prince sitting in the doorway. With an assertive "Meow," he thumped his tail forcefully twice on the floor, turned and walked back down the hall.

"Come on, buddy? What did I do now? Can I have a hint?"

"Meow," I heard from down the hall.

My phone rang loudly, vibrating across the desk and I jumped again. "Good grief, I need to get it together, here. I am a nervous wreck," I muttered to myself. As I picked up the phone and answered it, I noticed Ethyl's name on the screen. "Hi, Ethyl, how are you doing? How is Randy feeling?"

"Hi Mona, Randy is doing well so far, touch wood, but I know he is going to be sore tomorrow! The day after always does a number on you, especially at our age. I am calling to tell you that I managed to get out to the store to pick up some items for our Mr. Prince. He must be famished by now!"

"Food!" I thought. "How could I have forgotten? I wonder if that is what has him in such a huff."

"Oh, thank you, Ethyl! That is very kind of you."

"It is the least I could do, or technically 'Randy' could do as his new guardian. Is this a good time to come over and drop everything off?"

"Now would be great! I think the big guy is hungry. He has been a little grumpy with me since I came in from the shenanigans on the roof."

"Okay, I will be right over. Thanks Mona."

Ethyl hung up and I walked back to the front sitting room to meet her. As I opened the front doors, Ethyl came around the corner, carrying a big bag of food. I hurried out to take it from her.

"There was a special on the large bag. I hope he likes it," Ethyl said as she turned and walked down the stairs. "I will be right back with the rest."

As I stumbled into the apartment and over to the kitchen with the giant bag of food, I called out to Prince, "Food has arrived;

this should cheer you up." At this declaration, he jumped down from the sofa and ran into the kitchen to inspect what I had brought in.

Ethyl walked in, carrying a few more bags. "Here are a few more things I picked up. Some fancy food for when you feel like giving him a little treat and some toys in case he is feeling frisky. Are you sure we don't need a litter box?"

"Amazing as it sounds, it looks okay so far. No accidents. He even flushes the toilet."

Ethyl started to chuckle at this, letting out a big belly laugh. "That is the best thing I have heard all day." She became serious and looked down at the large feline, speaking directly to him, "You are certainly a miracle creature. Don't worry, Randy will warm up to you eventually. We will see to that."

"And how are we going to manage that great feat?" I questioned, with skepticism.

"I have my ways, Mona. I have my ways," she responded, giving me a coy smirk. "I almost forgot to tell you that tomorrow the pest control people are coming to deal with the rats. They will lay down bait stations all over the house. This should take care of the little pests."

I gave Ethyl a look of concern. "I'm not going to find rat bodies all over the apartment, am I?" An involuntary shiver ran through me.

"Oh heavens, no, Mona. Far from it. This treatment will drive them out of the house. Besides, with this guy in here, they won't bother investigating your apartment." Ethyl looked down at the big bag of cat food. "We should try to make the house as inhospitable to them as possible though. They love pet food. Perhaps put that food in a big sealed container or they may come visit your apartment for a snack. I looked over at Prince as he licked his lips, imagining this snack. A vision crossed my mind of him setting up an elaborate rat trap in my apartment, followed by a rat on a plate with Prince wearing a fancy bib hovering over his meal, a big kitty grin on his face. I shook off the image and agreed to seal up anything that might be appealing to rodents.

We heard a demanding, "Meow," from the kitchen. Prince was standing next to the big bag of food looking impatient.

"Someone is hungry. I better let you go before he breaks into that bag on his own," Ethyl teased. "Before I go, I want to make sure you can still come to the barbecue this weekend. It can be an end-of-summer party for everyone in the house. I'll let you know more details soon."

All I could think of was Margaritta gallivanting through the garden. Maybe she would decline the invitation after the critter invasion in her apartment. I tried to push the negative thoughts out of my mind. "Thank you, Ethyl. That is very kind of you. Please let me know what I can bring to contribute to the meal."

"Okay," Ethyl replied with a warm smile. She gave my arm a squeeze. "Go feed that big guy and we will talk later."

"Thank you again for all the cat food and toys."

"It's the least I could do, dear," Ethyl said over her shoulder as she walked out, closing the storm door behind her.

I walked over to the kitchen. "Okay Mister, I get the message. You are hungry." I found some scissors to open up the big bag of dry food. "This isn't smoked fish, but I am sure Ethyl bought you only the best in dry food," I said, as I tried to find a dish and figure out the right portion of food to serve the big guy.

While Prince nosed the new food in the bowl, my phone rang again. "I wonder if Ethyl forgot something," I said, as I located my phone.

"Hello, this is Mona."

"Hi, Mona, this is Mary-ela calling from the library. I hope you don't mind me calling again. I just wanted to check to make sure that you received my email."

"Hi Mary-ela. That's so nice of you to call. Yes, I opened your email earlier. Thank you. I could see the photo in the article much more clearly on my monitor. The family resemblance between Professor Merchante and her father is clear."

"Did you see my note? I did more research to figure out who the woman looking at them in the background of the photo is. I found a few more earlier family photos of the elder Professor Merchante. Oh dear, that sounds terribly formal. Can we just drop these titles and call them by their first names?"

I laughed. "Of course."

"I am convinced the woman in the photo we have been looking at is William's sister Beth."

"That makes her Margaritta's aunt, then."

"That is what I thought, but I came across Professor . . .err . . . . Margaritta's birth certificate."

My heart jumped in my chest. Why was she telling me this? What did she find?

"It lists her mother as Alyssa-Beth."

"What? No, that isn't right. I am sure Margaritta's mother is Linda."

"Yes, this is puzzling to me too. There are many articles about Professor Merchante. I spent hours digging through them again after I found the birth certificate. All of them refer to her parents as William and Linda."

"Is it possible the birth certificate you found is a fake?"

"Anything is possible," the librarian said, skeptically. "I don't know. The image looks very real to me. It sure looks like someone scanned an original copy."

"If the information on this birth certificate is true, then the woman standing in the background isn't Margaritta's aunt at all. She is her mother."

"Exactly. And William, the elder Professor Merchante is actually her uncle."

Totally confused, I walked back to my office, continuing to listen to Mary-ela recount her research. I sat down at the desk and touched the mouse, bringing the large monitor on my desk back to life again. I stared at the picture in the article. Trying to make sense of this new information, I had so many questions flying through my mind. Did Margaritta know who her real mother was? If she did, then why would she pretend her uncle and aunt were her parents? Why would her birth mother go along with the plan? If Margaritta did not know who her birth mother was, then who had the birth certificate and how did it end up on the internet?

"Alyssa-Beth would be the best person to explain the story, but she died a few years ago." I heard Mary-ela say, jolting me back into the phone conversation.

"Oh," I responded, with disappointment. My eyes drifted to the locket hanging around the woman's neck in the image on the screen. "I don't understand how Margaritta's birth certificate would find its way online like this. It's so strange."

"Yes, given what we have found, I think it is safe to assume it wasn't Professor Merchante."

"Do you know who scanned the birth certificate? How did you find it?" I asked, grasping at any detail that could connect the dots.

"It was a search engine result. I kept digging through the results, page by page. Not many people do that, you know, go to the third and fourth page results. They stop at the first page and give up."

"It's just a single document?"

"It is an image on a website. I didn't investigate the site. It is public though, so the search engines are picking it up. I may be able to figure out who is connected to it by analyzing the url."

Thrilled, my stomach fluttered. I didn't know what the tenacious librarian had stumbled upon, but this could be quite a juicy story. I sat in silence for a few moments contemplating. I should have been thrilled, but my instincts were telling me to stop; leave it alone.

"Mona, are you still there?"

"Sorry, I just need a moment to think." I paused. It couldn't hurt to dig a little bit deeper into this. At least we could find out who posted the image of the birth certificate. What harm could there be in that?

"It won't be any trouble to keep working on this, Mona. This is a fun research project, actually," Mary-ela said, reassuringly. I continued to refrain from sharing why I was hesitating.

"Okay, but only if you don't mind," I responded smoothly. A sharp sting hit my stomach as I realized how insincere I was being. I couldn't shake the urge to know the truth, though. No harm had come from the information we had gathered so far. We didn't even know the whole story yet.

"Thanks, Mona. I will contact you as soon as I learn more. Have a nice day!"

I ended the call and set my phone down on the desk. "Something doesn't add up with you, Margaritta. Let's see if we can find the truth with a little more digging."

CHAPTER 13

I was furiously preparing a salad for Ethyl and Randy's big barbecue. I had offered to bring a summer salad, thinking that I would do my usual citrus vinaigrette, but something crazy took hold of me when I was picking up ingredients at Paul's Grocery. I was inspired and I couldn't shake it. I saw the fresh goat cheese and the unbelievably ripe summer berries and I was possessed by an overly ambitious desire to create. I was a mad woman, scooping ingredients into my cart: spinach, arugula, pecans . . . . I even bought dried coconut to sprinkle on top. Ten minutes before Ethyl had asked us to arrive, it was a war zone in my kitchen. I couldn't settle for just plain pecans . . . I had to candy them in the oven, while whipping up a strawberry-pomegranate vinaigrette dressing.

As the pecans toasted, I finally assembled all the other in-gredients into the blender for the dressing. I took a breath and started to puree. I stared out the window at Ethyl's perfectly planned garden. There was always something new in bloom, all season. "I am so spoiled to be able to enjoy it, day after day like this." I looked down and admired the blended dressing. "A work of art. Maybe I am getting the hang of this cooking thing." Lost in thought, I smelled something. "What is that? Burning!"

The smoke alarm screeched through the building. I ran to the oven and threw the door open. Too late to rescue the pecans, I focused on clearing the smoke out of the apartment. While the alarm screamed overhead, I grabbed the hot tray of pecans and ran out of the apartment onto the porch. I set the smoking tray down at the bottom of the steps to cool. "Seriously, I could have bought a salad. What am I doing?" I muttered to myself as I gazed down at the charred pecans scattered all over the baking pan. "Pathetic. Why do I even bother trying to cook?"

"Don't be so hard on yourself, Mona. I am sure the rest of it can't be nearly as bad as those poor nuts," said Nathan reassuringly as he came around the corner of the house.

I smiled. "I don't know. It might be an omen. Stop cooking, Mona," I responded with a smile.

"I'm sure it's not that bad. How about we go take a look?"

"Okay."

"But first, let's clear out the smoke and silence that dreadful alarm. I can hardly hear myself think."

"Is it ringing in your apartment, too?"

"Oh, yes . . . it's ringing throughout the whole house."

"Great, everyone knows now what a terrible cook I am."

"Many great masterpieces have a trail of ashes behind them. At least that's the way it is in my kitchen," Nathan responded as he walked up the stairs into my apartment. I followed, happy to have an ally to face the kitchen again. "Where is your broom? We need to knock that button up there on the smoke alarm to get it to stop screaming at us." I hurried over to the closet and pulled out my broom. Nathan lifted up the handle and surgically silenced the alarm.

"Ah, that is better. I can hear myself think now," he said, handing me the broom. "Where is the big guy?" he asked, looking around the room. "I hope the alarm didn't freak him out. Animals really don't like high-pitched sounds."

"He is outside somewhere. I got brave and let him out. Even though I like knowing where he is, that's not what he's used to. He used to come and go every day next door using the cat door in the back. I'm sure he is nearby somewhere."

"He will be back. He has it pretty good with you. Now, let's see what you are cooking."

I showed Nathan my partially completed salad. "I was almost done. I just needed to finish the pecans," I grumbled, as Nathan sneaked a taste of the dressing from the blender.

"Mona, this dressing is exceptional," he responded, surveying the rest of the ingredients. "I agree, the pecans would send this over the top. Do you have any left?" I lifted the clear plastic bag to show Nathan the remaining nuts. Nathan looked at his watch and thought for a second. "I am sure Ethyl won't mind if we arrive a few minutes late. I'll show you my method. I use the stovetop. It is a much more controlled process. Less chance of burning, but still fantastic. Can I show you?"

"Yes, please!" I responded emphatically, pleased to learn a new technique. "I'm really quite hopeless in the kitchen."

"Ah, see? There is your first mistake, my dear. Confidence! You need to come into the kitchen with confidence. Go back outside and walk in here like you are the master chef you are about to become."

"Nathan, seriously?"

"Look at my face. I am dead serious. Do it."

Shaking my head, I walked back outside to the front porch. "This is ridiculous," I yelled over my shoulder.

"Not at all, Mona Lisa. Confidence."

Feeling absolutely ridiculous, but knowing there was no way I was going to get out of this, I took a deep breath, turned around and threw open the storm door. I paused for dramatic effect and gave Nathan a long, lingering stare, then I did my best exaggerated supermodel walk toward the kitchen. I stopped partway across the room to flip my hair, then walked into the kitchen.

"Whoot Whoot!" Nathan hooted in appreciation as he shook

his head. "That was fantastic. I knew you had that in you. How do you feel?"

Laughing, I gave him a big smile. "Actually, pretty good. That was fun."

"Every time you cook, I want you to channel that brashness into what you are making. You own this kitchen, Mona Lisa. Shall we show it who's boss?"

"Yes, we shall!"

We made quick work of the pecans with Nathan's alternative technique. As they cooled, we assembled the rest of the salad ingredients into a beautiful glass bowl. I poured the dressing into a travel container, found some salad spoons for serving and we were ready to go.

"Thank you, Nathan. You rescued the salad–and me, for that matter."

"Mona, you did it all. I just reminded you that you could. For that, you are welcome, my dear. Now, we better get over to Ethyl and Randy's with this gorgeous creation."

As we walked down the stairs outside, I realized Nathan was empty-handed. "Where did you put your culinary creation, Nathan? Do you need to go back up to your apartment to get it?"

"I dropped steaks off earlier today. They are in Ethyl and Randy's refrigerator. I made the most fantastic red wine marinade. Mona, these are going to be the best steaks you have ever tasted."

"I can't wait!" My mouth watered thinking about it.

As we walked into the back yard, we were met with a warm welcome. "You made it!" Ethyl said enthusiastically as she walked over and scooped up the glass salad bowl.

"Err . . . I had a little mishap in the kitchen," I admitted sheepishly.

"Well, it looks like things turned out just fine to me. This salad is beautiful," Ethyl reassured me as we walked up the stairs to the deck.

"I will put the salad in the fridge until we are ready to eat. You can set the other items down over there."

"I have the salad dressing, Ethyl. I'll follow you in to put this in the fridge too," Nathan added as he reached the top of the stairs.

"Mona! You need a beverage." I heard Randy's voice from behind me. I turned and was greeted by his friendly face staring down at me. "Ethyl has another batch of lemonade going. She managed to convince me to taste-test it." Randy leaned in. "Don't tell Ethyl I said this, but it's delicious," he said in a hushed tone.

I couldn't help but laugh in response. "Okay, you have sold me on the lemonade. I'll take a glass," I said, still laughing.

"One special lemonade, coming right up!" Randy announced as he walked to the opposite end of the deck where he had a bar area set up.

"Mona! Hi! Over here," called a familiar voice from the garden sitting area. I looked over. Jumping up and down enthusiastically, waving at me was Tish. I groaned inwardly, but then scolded myself for being a jerk. Max smiled and gave me a wave, too. He was sitting by the table looking peaceful. Things must be good with him and Tish today.

My train of thought was interrupted by Randy returning with a glass of ice cold lemonade as Ethyl and Nathan emerged from the kitchen and joined us on the deck.

"Randy, you look great," I blurted.

Randy gave me a big smile, "Well, thank you, Mona."

I blushed, realizing how my comment must have sounded. "I thought you would . . . er . . . be . . ."

Nathan finished my sentence, " . . . moving a bit slower, my old foolish friend. You just fell off a roof a few days ago!"

"I told you, I'm like a cat," he said smoothly.

"Uh huh," said Ethyl skeptically. "He's just putting on a show for you all. He's been limping and moaning around the house since his great tumble off the roof. If you are a cat, you are on your last life, mister."

"Oh, but I am sure it's going to be a good one, right, Randy?" Nathan said, stirring the pot as he winked at Randy.

"I'm going to go out with a bang," Randy responded, punching the air for effect.

"If you aren't careful, you are going to take the rest of us with you," Nathan added.

"Hey, whose side are you on here anyway?" Randy responded, giving Nathan an injured look.

"No sides for me; I am merely a neutral spectator."

"And an occasional rescuer," Ethyl added with a wink.

Randy laughed, "You both are just jealous of this old guy's vim and vigor," Randy said, taunting Nathan and Ethyl.

Ethyl rolled her eyes. "Does everyone have a drink? Let's go into the garden with Max and Tish. I think it is time for a toast," she suggested, changing the subject.

Randy handed Nathan a beer and we all walked down the stairs toward the garden sitting area. As I stepped onto the stone pathway, I was struck by the beauty of everything in front of me. All the pieces of Ethyl's garden came together in a captivating view. I paused to take in the artistry of Ethyl's design. "Ethyl, your backyard should be in a magazine."

"Yes, it really should. Fine work," Nathan added.

"Thank you. It's a passion."

"More like an obsession," Randy added.

"Possibly, but it keeps me out of trouble," Ethyl said, giving Randy a look.

Just as I was enjoying the warmth and charm of the moment, I turned to my right and noticed Margaritta walking toward me. I cringed. My mouth was suddenly dry and I was frozen in place. "Hellooo, I'm here. Sorry I am late. There was a mixup at the bakery." She was carrying a large white box.

"So glad you could come. Let me take that off your hands and put it in the fridge. I can't wait. I am sure whatever is in here is exquisite," Ethyl said with excitement. She turned to me, "Margaritta has found the most fantastic bakery in town. You really have to check it out sometime, but I warn you, don't go there hungry."

"I'm surprised to see you back, your highness. After your mad dash out of here the other day, I figured you would be long gone. You decided it was safe to come back around?" Nathan said goading her.

Margaritta's eyes narrowed. "I wouldn't expect you to understand, Nathan Laine," she said tersely.

"No? Explain it to me, then? While the rest of us were here trying to help Randy out, you couldn't get out of here fast enough. Explain that to me."

An uncomfortable silence fell over the group as our eyes darted back and forth between Nathan and Margaritta, not sure where this exchange was going. It was Tish's voice that rescued the moment . . . or so I thought as she began to talk.

"Mona! Max tells me tomorrow is a big day for you!" Tish proclaimed with her bubbly voice.

With my hopes of moving past the uncomfortable moment dashed, I gave Max a sharp look. "How could he?" He gave me a guilty smile and shrugged his shoulders, feigning helplessness.

"Really, Mona Lisa Brown, do tell," Margaritta said with her sugary tone, like a vulture circling its prey.

"It's nothing. Let's go into the garden for that toast, everyone."

"You can't just leave us wondering. The suspense is unbearable, Mona Lisa," Margaritta persisted.

"Come on, Mona! Tell everyone that you are starting your first class at the university tomorrow!" Realizing she just revealed the secret, Tish covered her mouth. "Oops! I think I just shared your big news for you."

Margaritta burst into laughter. I felt my face flush instantly. I knew I was turning beet-red. "Why is she laughing?" She wouldn't stop. I looked at her in horror. I wanted to run away and hide as tears started to prickle my eyes. "Don't cry, don't cry. Don't let this miserable woman see that she has made you cry."

Everyone was looking at Margaritta in shock as she finally composed herself. "What?" she asked, looking at us all as we stared at her in stunned silence. "I thought Tish was making a joke."

Finally able to get words out of my mouth, I gathered all the nerve I could summon and asked, "Why would me taking classes at the university be a joke, Margaritta?"

Realizing the statement was far from a joke, Margaritta drew herself up into her usual perfect posture, looked at me and said, "I hadn't thought of you as Buckley University material. It is a school for the elite, you know. The cream of the cream."

I inhaled quickly as I felt a stab in my stomach. Every doubt I had about attending the university flooded back. She was right; this was a terrible idea. I didn't belong at this university. They were right when they denied me entrance the first time I applied. My mind couldn't stop the self-doubt flooding in. And then I heard another quiet voice in my head. It was Ethyl saying, "Take back your power, Mona."

I breathed out slowly. "Margaritta, I am attending the university to further my education. In fact, I think they will be quite happy to have me there."

"You're darn right they will!" Nathan added emphatically.

"I think you will be the star of the class, Mona," I heard Randy say with his big booming voice.

"Ethyl, is it time for that toast?" I said, smiling at her.

"I think so. Come everyone, into the garden." Ethyl raised her glass and confidently marched across the lawn, leading the way. She looked small, but mighty, as we all fell in line behind her. Margaritta was left standing on the path and I saw Nathan say something to her. Oh, to have been a fly on his shoulder to hear that exchange. Or maybe a mosquito on Margaritta's neck. As we all gathered in the garden, Ethyl spoke up again, "Does everyone have a drink?"

"Oh, I didn't get a drink," Margaritta noted loudly.

"Of course, held up by her highness again," I heard Nathan mumble under his breath beside me as he rolled his eyes.

"Oh dear, that's not good. Randy, can you get Margaritta a glass of lemonade, please?"

"Coming right up! I need to start the barbecue anyway," Randy said, as he turned and lumbered back toward the house.

As we stood in the garden waiting for Randy to return, Nathan leaned in and said, "Don't let Margaritta get to you. You are the perfect student for Buckley University. You are going to be fine."

"I hope so," I whispered back. My mind couldn't help but question whether she was right, though. Thankfully, Randy's big voice interrupted the thought.

"All set. Barbecue is heating up. Margaritta, here you go. A glass of Ethyl's finest lemonade, if I do say so myself." Margaritta accepted the glass with a smile.

"Oh, you finally tasted it, did you?!" Ethyl asked Randy.

"Err, I mean . . . hear that it is good. That's what I am told."

"Uh huh," Ethyl said skeptically. She smiled, knowing Randy had finally tried her lemonade. "Okay, I think we are all set now," Ethyl said in response. "Everyone, raise your glass."

We all complied.

"Randy and I are so pleased that you could come today. Each of our lives has taken its own path, yet somehow, those paths have led us all to intersect here at our house. Randy and I are honored to know each and every one of you. We have a community here with you, for which we are so grateful. Thank you for adding your uniqueness to our lives and for all that you do to help keep this house running. Even the little things you do, make a big difference. Let's toast the last days of summer, as this week many of you move into a new school year at the university as teachers and students. Here's to enjoying delicious food and savoring the beautiful weather together!" Ethyl smiled warmly and we drank to her toast. I looked over and saw a tear roll down Tish's face.

"Good grief," I thought.

"Oh Ethyl, that was beautiful!" she declared, as she ran over and gave Ethyl a big hug.

Overwhelmed by Tish's display of affection, Ethyl chuckled and awkwardly hugged Tish back. I shook my head and smiled too, trying to appreciate the moment.

I felt something soft tickling my ankles. I looked down and saw Prince had joined the party and was weaving around my legs. Panic flooded me. If he sees this cat, Randy is going to lose it. I carefully nudged Nathan with my elbow.

"Carefully look down at my feet," I whispered.

Nathan sneaked a quick glance down and then looked up at me with wide eyes. "What is he doing here? This cat has a death wish," he whispered urgently.

"Shhhhh, don't use the 'c' word so loud."

"What are we supposed to do now?"

"I don't know. How do we get him out of here and back to my apartment without Randy noticing? If Tish sees him here, she most certainly will blab it back to Randy."

"Meow."

"Quiet, that's enough out of you," I responded to the cat, without looking down to draw more attention to him. I happened to be facing Margaritta standing across from me, deep in conversation with Tish and Max as I made the comment.

"I beg your pardon? I happen to be telling the lovely Tish here about my adventures at the beach this summer. There is no need to be rude."

"How dare she talk to me that way?" I whispered to Nathan. "No need to be rude? After how she treated me earlier? After how she always treats me." Nathan put his hand on my left forearm. I turned to look at him and he gave me a look that reminded me that we had bigger fish to fry or 'cats' . . . than respond to Margaritta's toxic tongue. I hoped there would be no frying of cats. If we could get Prince out of there, it would be just steaks frying. With the thought of steaks, I sniffed the air and looked at Nathan.

"Do you smell burning?"

Nathan sniffed the air, too, looking confused. "Randy, my friend, how's your barbecue doing?" As he said this, we all looked over and saw a huge cloud of smoke billowing out from Randy's barbecue.

Still looking the other way, Randy dismissed the comment, "It's just burning off the leftovers from the last barbecue."

"Oh my! Look, there are flames!" Tish yelled.

"Good Lord, it's on fire!" Randy exclaimed, as he ran toward the house.

"I'm going to help Randy. You take care of that big guy," Nathan directed. As he said this, we looked down and realized Prince was no longer around my legs.

"Where did he go?" I asked desperately.

"Look! He is running after Randy. I don't know if that cat is going to survive this adventure if Randy spots him. Okay, I'll look after Randy, you go get that stupid cat out of here." We both broke into a run, me after the cat, and Nathan after Randy, who was well occupied by his fiery barbecue.

As I ran after Nathan, I watched Prince run up the stairs and leap onto the railing of the deck only a few feet from Randy and the barbecue. Randy had put big mitts on and was venturing to open the barbecue as Nathan arrived by his side. I reached the deck and tried to shoo the cat down from the railing.

He looked down at me and uttered a loud, "Meow."

"Come on, this is not a good place for you."

"Meow."

"Don't make me walk up those steps to get you."

"Meow."

"Seriously, are we really doing this?"

"Meow."

Frustrated, I ran up the short set of stairs toward the obstinate feline. As I reached the top of the stairs to my right, I encountered Randy holding a flaming pan, which I presumed was the source of the fire. Nathan took a step back, his eyes wide.

"What are you going to do with that?" Nathan asked.

"Get it the hell away from my new barbecue," Randy announced. This was when he spotted the cat staring at him from the railing. Eye to eye, they exchanged looks. "What the hell are you doing here, you big fur ball. I am going to get you this time." Randy lunged toward Prince with the flaming pan.

Realizing his time in the yard had expired, the cat ran along the railing toward the barbecue, in the opposite direction to Randy. I hopped back toward the house to get out of the way of Randy and the flaming pan as he ran down the stairs to the pathway below.

At the same time, the cat descended down the railing to the path only a few short strides away from Randy, but he was trapped by the storage building and the tree in front of the garden. His only way out was toward Randy.

"Randy, leave him. Let him go," I shouted in desperation, afraid Randy was going to do something terrible to the cat. As he wound up to throw the flaming tray at the poor cat in front of him, Ethyl came running from the other side of the path, wielding the largest fire extinguisher I have ever seen.

"Not so fast, mister!" she yelled, as she opened up on Randy and his flaming projectile.

"What do you think you are doing?" Randy screamed, covered in yellow foam from head to toe.

"Putting you out, fire man," Ethyl scolded. "Did you not check inside the barbecue before you lit it? And were you really about to throw a flaming tray of grease at that lovely creature?"

"I . . ." Randy started, but stopped. We all stared at Prince.

"Meow." Prince looked at Randy. Then he ran off into the garden.

Shocked, I watched him strut across the lawn, look back, and wink at me. I shook my head, and tried to pull myself together as he disappeared out of sight.

"You didn't have to soak me in that nasty stuff," Randy lamented to Ethyl.

"No? I thought you needed some cooling off. Seems to have

done the trick," Ethyl said, setting the fire extinguisher down at the side of the stairs. Ethyl looked back up at Randy and laughed, "Boy, I really did nail you. Come on, let's go into the house. I'll help you get cleaned up."

Ethyl and Randy walked up the stairs. Randy was quite a sight. The foam was starting to liquify and drip off of him. Ethyl shepherded him carefully into the house, then leaned out the door and said, "Nathan, you are on steaks. I think the barbecue is warmed up and ready for you."

"Alright everybody, show's over. Time for chow. Mona, you are on salad duty. Everyone else, get your side dishes ready, we have some gourmet eating to do. If we time this out right, it will all be ready for when Ethyl and Randy emerge from the great clean-up."

We all sprang into action preparing food. Even Margaritta pitched in to help. By the time Ethyl and Randy emerged from the kitchen, the table along the kitchen wall was laid out with the most lovely food I had ever seen.

"Oh my, look what you have all done!" Ethyl exclaimed as she saw the food on the table. "Wow, you even found plates and cutlery. I can get napkins."

"We have them right here," Max added from behind her, as he set them on the table.

"All you need to do is grab yourself a drink and enjoy this lovely food with us," I said, with a big smile.

"Wow, thank you. Randy, look what they have done!"

"Remarkable! Nathan. How's the barbecue going over there?"

"The steaks are ready. Bring your plates, everyone. You better like it rare. If not, salad is over in that direction," he said, pointing to the side table. Everyone laughed and knew better than to argue with the chef.

We filled our plates and sat down at the table on the deck. A hush fell over the group as we enjoyed the delicious food. Finally, after I couldn't eat another bite, I sat back in my chair to enjoy the warmth of the evening. The sun was on the other side of the house now, but the heat of the day lingered in the air. I smiled as I listened to my friends chatter around the table. The only word I could think of to describe how I felt was content. I had never dreamed of this when I considered moving to Buckley Brook. I'm not sure I believe in destiny, but perhaps fate was working its magic on my life.

Max and Tish departed first. Margaritta, who was remarkably well-behaved after her arrival, left shortly after them. Nathan and I stuck around to help Randy and Ethyl clean up. Then we all walked into the garden and sat on the patio to enjoy the flowers up close.

"That was quite a meal tonight. You outdid yourself with those steaks," Randy declared, looking at Nathan.

"I'm glad you enjoyed them! If only I had written down what I put into that marinade," he said, shaking his head. "Have you recovered from your tangle with the fire extinguisher?"

"Yes," Randy grumbled as he shot a look of disdain at Ethyl. Then he looked back and forth between Ethyl and me, narrowing his eyes. "Now tell me, you two, where are you harboring that cat? I know he is not living in that big house next door anymore and he certainly isn't living in our apartment here. Where do you have him stashed? Fess up."

There was no way I was revealing the location of the cat's safe house, especially since it was my apartment. I looked innocently at Randy, unsure of what to say. I have never had a good poker face, so I knew he could see right through me. All I could do was stare back at him and hope he moved on.

After a painfully long silence, Ethyl finally spoke up, "Oh

Randy, leave the poor girl alone! We will never reveal our secret. The big cat is safe and sound in a secret location living on your dime, Mr. Guardian."

Randy grumbled again in response, "I'm watching you two. I will figure it out. I'm a master detective, you know. I see everything."

A shiver ran down my back with the hope that Randy didn't look too closely for Prince. It's not that easy to stash a very independent Maine Coon cat in the same house.

"Well, fine people, I think I am going to call it a night. Thank you for the food and entertainment." Nathan stood up and patted Randy on the shoulder, "Thank you, Randy. Never a dull moment with you, my friend."

Randy gave Nathan a big smile, "Blame it on that cat. He started it. He always starts it."

"Uh huh," Nathan said, in a mocking tone.

I shivered again.

"Mona, we can light a fire here and I can brew some hot tea if you are getting chilly," Ethyl offered.

"That sounds lovely, Ethyl, thank you," I responded.

"Are you sure you don't want to stick around for a bit longer, Nathan?" Ethyl asked.

"It indeed does sound enticing, but this old guy is tuckered out. Too much excitement for one day, for me. I don't have the same energy as this guy," Nathan added, tipping his head to the side toward Randy. "I'm off. Thank you again, for a really lovely evening. Mona, I will see you bright and early tomorrow. Class starts at nine. I will pick you up at your door at quarter after eight and we can walk over to the university together." With that, Nathan gave us a big wave and turned to walk back to the house.

"Okay, I'll go put the kettle on inside. Randy, can you light the fire pit?"

As Randy walked toward the house, I presumed to get matches or a lighter to start the fire, Ethyl leaned in and whispered to me, "After the earlier events this evening, Mona, you better stay to supervise the fire-making. Keep watch for that cat. He has a tendency to show up at just the wrong time."

Ethyl gestured towards a box at the edge of the garden. "Over in that big storage bin behind the table are our fire blankets. Wrap one of those around you to warm up. I will be back in a minute with tea. Do you like Earl Grey?"

"I do, thank you," I responded enthusiastically.

Ethyl disappeared into the house to make the tea and I walked over to take a peek inside the box, happy to borrow a blanket to cut the chill that had crept into the air. I was excited to sit by the fire. As I dug through the box, I felt my phone vibrate in my pocket. I pulled it out and noticed two missed calls from earlier, both from the same number. I checked to see who had called me and noticed the university's phone number on the screen. It had to be from Mary-ela. I felt a flicker of excitement. I wondered what she had dug up this time? I had to hand it to the persistent young librarian, she was quite the researcher. I put my phone back in my pocket, deciding it could wait until later.

"Okay, let's get this fire pit going," Randy announced as he joined me back at the garden patio. "This is nice. We really haven't used this thing for most of the summer." He stopped to think for a second. "Just kind of fell out of the habit, I guess." He flicked the barbecue lighter in his hand a few times to get a flame, then turned a lever on the fire pit and poof–the pit was a blaze. "There we go. I love this thing. So easy."

We dragged the patio set closer to the fire and arranged the chairs around it, so everyone got a warm spot. I pulled out a heavy woven blanket from the box, wrapped it around me and sat down in one of the chairs next to the table. Randy lowered himself into a chair across from me on the other side of the fire. We both sat in silence for a long while gazing into the fire.

"There is something about a fire," Randy said vacantly.

There certainly is," I echoed, knowing exactly what he meant. "This is really nice, Randy. Not just the fire, but the garden, the house, my wonderful apartment, newfound friends. It is more than I ever imagined I could find when I moved here."

"And Margaritta?"

"Ha." I laughed at Randy's directness. "There is no beating around the bush with you, Randy."

"Life is too short to beat around the bush, Mona."

"You are right there," I responded, thinking about my parents, wishing they could be here right now to enjoy this lovely garden and meet my new friends. They would have loved it here.

"And Margaritta? She does seem to be gunning for you at every turn. What's with that old crow?"

"Old crow! I hope you aren't talking about me." We heard Ethyl's voice from the lawn.

"Not at all, sweet knees. If we were to equate you to a bird, it wouldn't be a crow, more like a hawk," Randy swooped his arms out wide and looked all around. "Or maybe an eagle!"

"Really? I guess there could be worse animals to be compared to," she chuckled, setting a tray down on the table next to me. "So, who is the old crow, then?"

"Our favorite upstairs tenant."

"Ah, Margaritta, I see. What has she done now?"

I sighed. "Nothing more than what you saw this evening."

Ethyl nodded and looked over at the tea. "Do you want anything in your tea?"

"Just a little milk. Thank you." I took the warm mug of tea into my hands and positioned myself in front of the fire. "This is perfect. What a great night." I looked up at the darkening sky, noticing how much darker it was getting each night at this time. "I usually feel sad at this time of year that summer is winding down. I know it isn't over. There are still plenty of warm days ahead, but it's more apparent when the days start to get noticeably shorter and the evenings are cool enough to need a blanket and a fire to sit outside comfortably.

"There is something liberating about the start of summer. Those first hot days after a long winter when you realize you can shed your winter layer of protection. It is almost like finding new freedom. There is no cold barrier between outside and inside, just space, warm space everywhere." I realized my inside thoughts were out loud and I stopped abruptly. "I'm rambling, sorry."

"Not at all," Ethyl responded. "And this year?"

I look at her, confused.

"You said that you usually feel sad at this time of year. What is different about this year?"

I took a long sip of tea. "Mmmm . . . This is yummy. Where did you buy this tea?" I asked, realizing my careless rambling was going to force me toward introspection with Ethyl and Randy. I wasn't about to ruin the night with that.

"Nice try, I asked you a question first." She smiled.

I laughed at how quick Ethyl was to hold me to account.

"Out with it; what is different about this year?" Randy asked. "The hawk over there isn't going to let you off the hook."

"It really isn't a big deal. I just don't feel sad this year. There are so many good things going on. I feel content," I added, borrowing from my earlier thoughts. "Well, perhaps not when Margaritta comes around, but that is a whole other matter."

"Yes it is," Ethyl confirmed.

"Let's not go there tonight. This is such a lovely evening,

why spoil it?"

"You have to go there sometime," Ethyl stated.

I nodded slowly in agreement. My mind turned to the missed phone call from Mary-ela. I was itching to know about the new details she had discovered. I pushed this thought away as soon as it floated through my mind, to focus on the moment and responded to Ethyl with a simple, "I will."

The three of us sat and talked around the fire for hours, unaware of the passage of time. Ethyl and Randy told stories from their past days on the farm and as landlords. I had no idea how many different people had lived at the house–each with their own story connecting to Ethyl and Randy. They had me rolling in laughter until I looked up and was struck by the night sky.

"Wow, look at all of those stars!" I said in amazement. My eyes darted around the sky, trying to take them all in. "I have been here for months. How am I only noticing these stars now?"

Randy chuckled, "You needed to come back here at night. Even that little bit of light from the street in the front changes what you see in the sky."

"Amazing." I stared up at the sky in awe of what I saw. There were no words to properly describe a night sky like this. It's just something you have to experience. What a way to end a great day. "Well, as much as I don't want to leave, I think it's time to head home. Thank you both so much for inviting me."

"You are welcome anytime," Randy replied as he stood up.

"It is quite chilly now. Why don't you wear that blanket back to your apartment? I'll wash up your salad bowl and bring it around tomorrow," Ethyl offered.

"Really? Thank you, Ethyl."

We said our farewells and I trudged across the thick dark lawn toward the path around the house. The dew had started to settle on the grass and I could feel the dampness as I walked.

I felt the cool air on my face and was thankful for the blanket around my shoulders. I thought of Prince. I hoped he was okay. I had left some water and dry food out on the porch when I let him outside earlier today. Hoping he found it, I quickened my pace, worried about my cat friend. As I arrived at the bottom of the steps to the porch, I saw Prince sitting at the door.

"Meow."

"I am so sorry. I hope you are okay. I lost track of time," I said, as I looked to see if he had eaten.

"Meow."

"I hope you aren't starving."

"Meow."

I walked up the stairs and noticed the food I had put out was gone and I relaxed a bit. "I hope you were the one who ate that food."

"Meow."

I put my hands on my hips and stared down at the big guy. "That was quite a stunt that you pulled at the party tonight."

"Meow."

"One day it is not going to work out in your favor." I looked for my hidden key under the front leg of the swing. The hollow inside was perfect for hiding a key, unless of course you were watching me fuss around looking for it from the street. Oh . . . that was a creepy thought. Why did I have to think about that? I stood up quickly and looked out at the street. There wasn't a soul around. Everything was still and quiet. A shiver came over me. Was that the cool air getting to me or the thought of someone watching me triggering that? "Okay, Prince, time to get inside," I announced hastily.

"Meow."

"I'm glad you agree."

I opened the door and let the cat in ahead of me. He darted

across the room and into the washroom.

"Well, at least Randy won't be finding any of your treats in the garden," I called out.

"Meow," I heard from the bathroom.

I walked across the room and reached for my phone, remembering the message from Mary-ela. Excitement came over me again as I called my voicemail to listen to the message.

"Mona, it's Mary-ela, from the library," she said frantically, sounding a bit winded like she had just run up a flight of stairs. "I figured it out. I figured out who posted the scanned birth certificate! The website is owned by Sandra, Margaritta's sister in-law, or cousin in-law, or I don't know who anyone is anymore. She is married to Peter, the son of Professor Merchante . . . er . . . . the senior Professor Merchante, the one who taught accounting. I think I might have overstepped, though."

My ears perked up at this point and I listened more closely. "When I could not reach you after my first call, I went ahead and called Sandra. I was so excited to find someone who might know the truth, that I started asking questions. I was blathering on and on. I didn't stop to think how my questions might come across to Sandra. She got really angry, saying I was invading her privacy. I should have waited for you, Mona, I'm sorry.

"Maybe she will open up if you call her, Mona. This is for your article, so she might respond differently. I am sending you an email with Sandra's contact information. I think you should call her and talk to her. At least she can tell you who everyone is. Maybe there is a logical explanation to all this confusion. Okay, let me know when you get this. Bye."

I deleted the voicemail and ended the call feeling mildly annoyed at the tenacious librarian, but also pleased that she had found a lead. I switched over to my email. Mary-ela's message was at the top of my inbox. I opened it and scanned through the message, my eyes landing on Sandra's name and phone number. I stared at the information for a few moments, then turned off the phone's screen and set it down at the end of the kitchen counter. "This is crazy. What am I going to say to this woman? I noticed you scanned your sister in-law's birth certificate and posted it online. Do you wanna tell me why you did that? Oh, and I think she might not actually be your sister in-law, right? How about we talk about that, too?"

"Meow." I turned around to look at Prince.

"You got that right. This whole thing is crazy," I agreed, feeling guilty again for dragging Mary-ela into this mess. Then I yawned.

"Meow."

"You're right, it's time for bed. Tomorrow is a big day. Nathan will be here bright and early to drag me to the university. What was I thinking? Bad idea, all of this, a bad idea. Maybe some of this will make sense in the morning."

I shut the lights off and walked down the hall to my bedroom. Prince followed me and jumped up on the sofa in my room. I stopped and looked at him, "Well, this is new. Don't get too comfortable. If my allergies act up, you are out of here and back to the sofa in the front room." Just thinking about allergies made my nose prickle. I fought back a sneeze as I fell into bed. I was more tired than I realized, though. The sneeze passed and in seconds I fell into a deep sleep.

CHAPTER 14

I woke up to a cat two inches from my face. "What?" I yelled, jumping up in my bed. The big guy jumped back to the foot of the bed.

"Meow."

You are persistent when you want my attention. What are you doing? You nearly gave me a heart attack! That's no way for anyone to wake up."

"Meow."

"What is the problem? Why are you trying to wake me up? You've never done that before?" I asked, expecting an answer.

Bang, bang, bang. There was a loud knocking at my front door.

"Is this why you were being so aggressive trying to wake me up?" My nose started to prickle. I could feel a scratch in my throat. "As much as I love having you up here, buddy, you are triggering my allergies."

Bang, bang, bang, bang, bang. The loud knocking continued.

"Who on earth is knocking at this hour?" I said, exasperated. As I looked for a robe to put on to answer the door, I noticed the time. "Ah! It's five minutes to eight! How did I sleep so late? That must be Nathan at the door." I ran frantically around the room trying to find some clothes. I finally gave up. "I better just answer the door and fess up."

I ran down the hall to the door with Prince two steps behind me. I threw open the door and saw Nathan standing on the step, with his arms crossed over his chest. "Well, well, well, sleeping beauty finally got up."

"I can't believe I slept in! Nathan, I am so sorry. I just need five minutes."

Nathan laughed. "Take ten minutes. We have time. I'm early. We can get coffee on the way."

"Thank you, Nathan. Do you want to come in and wait?"

"Oh no, it's a beautiful day out here. I am going to enjoy your fabulous porch."

"Okay, I will be quick. I'm sorry again." As I closed the door, I heard Prince behind me. "I know, I won't forget you!" I ran over to the kitchen and quickly dumped some food into his dish. "Look, I won't be long. This is a morning class. I will be back by lunch, so you stay inside and chill this morning. No wandering the neighborhood without supervision this time." I am sure the big feline was scowling at me before diving into his food, but I didn't have time to make amends.

I tore off into the bathroom to wash my face, brush my teeth and do something with my hair. Then I ran down the hall to my bedroom to find anything clean and half decent to wear. I didn't have time to give much care to my attire. I threw on the first two things that matched, a solid pink t-shirt and stretchy floral skirt. Then I slid on a pair of sandals and I was ready to go. I ran into my office and grabbed my laptop, stuffed it into my backpack with a few pens and a clipboard with notepaper in it. I ran back to the kitchen to grab my keys, wallet and phone. Composing myself, I walked back across the room and opened the door to see Nathan rocking away on the swing outside.

"Okay, I'm impressed! You did that with time to spare and you look amazing!" he said, as I locked the door.

I smiled and glanced down at my watch. "How did you know I would sleep in?"

"It was just a hunch. I had a feeling last night that Ethyl and Randy might get their hooks into you after I left. Did they spark up the backyard fireplace?"

"They did indeed. You should have stuck around. It was an amazing night. I can't remember the last time I saw the sky so full of stars like that."

Nathan gave me a warm smile, "It's pretty magical back there. Maybe we can sweet-talk them into hosting another evening around the fire pit."

"I doubt it will take much convincing. I think they were happy to have an excuse to sit outside and enjoy the evening."

"Shall we make our way over to the university?"

I took a deep breath, and nodded in agreement.

"Don't be nervous. This is going to be great," Nathan responded as he extended his elbow.

I played along and linked my arm through his. "Ever the gentleman you are, Nathan Laine."

"Come fair lady, we have some higher learning ahead of us."

We laughed all the way to the street until we heard a familiar voice behind us.

"You two are in a good mood this morning!" We turned around to see Max behind us.

"Max! Come join us. We are walking to the university," I said, invitingly.

"Good to see you this fine morning. I presume you have business at the university, too?" Nathan asked.

"I do," Max replied enthusiastically. "I am teaching a course for Professor Branon. He is on sabbatical this term and asked me to fill in. There are about 250 people registered for the class. I even have teaching assistants to help me!"

"Congratulations, Max! I am so proud of you!" I responded enthusiastically.

"Well done! You deserve this, after all your dedication," Nathan added.

"Thanks for the support. I really appreciate it," Max said, as we all stepped onto the sidewalk to walk to the university. "I wish Tish was as enthusiastic as you guys," we heard Max murmur under his breath, behind us.

Nathan and I exchanged a look before he responded, "Trouble in paradise?"

I wanted to add 'again' at the end of his sentence, but I resisted the urge.

Max let out a long, troubled sigh. "I know we have been through this before. You guys don't want to hear about it again."

"Max, out with it," I responded impatiently. "Of course we want to hear what is going on with you."

"Tish and I left the party last night. We were in such a good mood. We had an amazing time at the barbecue and I was so pumped thinking about my first class today. I started talking about it as we were walking back to the side entrance. I could tell she wasn't paying attention. Finally, I asked her a question about what I had just told her, intentionally trying to expose that she was not listening to me, which of course I did. Well this led to a big fight because she accused me of being sneaky, which I guess, technically, I was, in that moment. Let me tell you, the conversation after that was not pretty and it did not end well. She stomped off and I went to bed in a huff. A great night turned upside down."

I don't know what came over me, but I started to giggle. I knew it was the most inappropriate reaction to Max's story, but I couldn't help myself. The more I tried to hold back, the more my body shook with laughter. Nathan looked at me in horror, sending me a look that told me to knock it off.

"Mona, cut it out," Nathan urged.

Then I heard a noise from behind me. My stomach sank. Was Max crying? Oh no, had I gone too far? Then I heard it more clearly and realized he was laughing, too! I whipped around to see Max doubled over with laughter. "I am sorry, Max. I don't know what has come over me. I just had this image of Tish stomping off down the driveway and I couldn't contain myself. I . . . am . . . so sorry," I sputtered through another wave of laughter, "Oh, ow, ow, my side, I've got a stitch." Tears came to my eyes as I grabbed my side.

Nathan smacked my arm. "Serves you right, laughing at a man when he's down," he said, disgusted.

"Hey, he is laughing too."

"I can laugh at my situation, Nathan. I guess it is kind of funny in a pathetic kind of way."

"The funny part is that you keep going back," I blurted out. As the words came out of my mouth, I knew I had gone too far. All the laughter stopped and we walked in dead silence. No one dared to say the next word.

"I'm sorry, Max. I shouldn't have said that. I didn't mean to hurt you," I practically whispered the words to him as we walked.

There was a long pause and then he finally spoke. "No, I'm the one who is sorry. I should never have told you what happened," he responded sharply.

A sour feeling penetrated my stomach. My mouth was dry. "Damn it, why did I have to say that?" I scolded myself.

"Now, now, Max. What Mona Lisa is trying to say . . ." Nathan gave me a sideways look, warning me not to talk so he could attempt to clean up my mess. "Mona is simply making a statement based on the track record of your relationship with Tish. History seems to be repeating itself over and over, so I have to ask, and this is me asking this time, why do you keep going back?"

There was a pause in the conversation as Nathan's question hung in the air. "Wait," Nathan continued. "I am not going to let you answer yet."

"Come on, man." Max pleaded quietly for Nathan to stop.

"Please just listen for a moment." Max complied and let Nathan continue, "We know you love her. We can see she is gorgeous, but she isn't treating you with the respect you deserve. You have given her so many chances, each time with the same result. Why are you torturing yourself in this way?"

"It's not torture," Max murmured.

"Really . . . because you were like a deflated party balloon this morning when you started talking to us about what happened last night. You are going to take that feeling into your class with your students today."

"I'll be fine. I leave my stuff at the door."

"Well, that's admirable, but also a shame. You should be able to bring your whole self through the doors of that classroom. Isn't that what you want your students to do?"

"Of course."

We finally arrived at the cafe on the edge of the university. Nathan walked up the first step, then paused and turned back to look at Max and me. "Look, I'm only going to say one more thing on this topic and I am doing this because you are my friend and I care about you. There are some great things in life, fabulous things, but they will kill you bit by bit. This is going to sound like a really bad example, but here goes. I love cigars. I would love nothing more than to enjoy a good cigar with a finely aged brandy every night. Yet, I knew that combo would kill me in the end, so I gave them up. I am tempted every day, but I know I am better off without them in my life."

"I'm not at all comparing Tish to cigars and brandy. She is

a person in your life, so your situation is way bigger. But, there could be a parallel between the two. Only you can know that for sure. I just want you to take a step back and ask what this relationship is doing to you. If you decide it is worth it, I won't say another word. I'm sure Mona won't, either," Nathan said, giving me a serious look. "I'm just asking you to think about this, Max. Can you please?"

Max stared at Nathan for a moment and ran his hand through his brown hair. Then he slowly nodded in agreement. In silence, Nathan turned and walked up the rest of the stairs toward the cafe, opened the glass door and walked in. I gave Max an apologetic look, "I'm sorry. I started all of this. The last thing I wanted to do was upset you. Can you forgive me?"

"Are you kidding? It was me who brought up my situation with Tish, again. I know our relationship is like a broken record. It must be frustrating for you and Nathan to listen to me."

"Oh Max, don't talk that way. We are just concerned, but whatever you decide, we will support you," I responded, trying to sound earnest. In reality, I hated watching Max get run over by Tish. I didn't understand why he kept going back, only to be hurt again. "Come on, let me buy you a coffee and something decadent?" I offered, giving him a big smile." He slowly smiled back and we walked up the stairs to join Nathan inside.

We all left the cafe with coffees and pastries. As we made our way onto campus, we returned to our usual jovial tone, the previous conversation set aside for the time being. Walking onto campus, I followed Nathan and Max who were now deep in a verbal jousting match of great hilarity. As we walked, I was struck by the history all around me. The cluster of old buildings, etched by years of weathering, interspersed with new construction. "I guess this is what progress looks like," I thought. I was flooded with the overwhelming urge to turn and flee, but immediately berated myself for such a thought. "I can do this. I belong here." I fixed my eyes on the path in front of me and distracted myself by listening to the two part-time jesters in front of me.

"Maybe we will run into her highness on campus today," Nathan suggested, his tone conveying no enthusiasm for such an encounter.

"Now, now, Nathan. She's not that bad," Max chided.

I bit my tongue, resisting the urge to counter Max's thought. As my gut started to churn, I reminded myself that it was a big campus and we were here for only a few hours, most of it being spent in one classroom. The odds of running into Margaritta were very low.

"Well, this is my stop," Max announced as we arrived at one of the modern buildings. "Wish me luck!" he said with a big smile.

I couldn't help but match his enthusiasm and returned the grin as we waved goodbye. As we watched him go into the building I shook my head and looked at Nathan, "Why can't Tish see how fantastic he is?"

"Perhaps the question is, why can't he see how fantastic he is?" We stood in silence, both of us lost in thought, looking at the building Max had just disappeared into.

"Do you think we overstepped this morning?" I wondered aloud.

"Well, you did!" Nathan was teasing me. Then his demeanor grew more serious and he sighed, "I don't know. I needed to say what I did. I think he heard me."

"Yes, I think he did."

Nathan turned away from the path and I fell into step with him. Then he spoke again, "I just hate seeing Max get hurt over and over. Maybe I went too far with my comments this morning, but I could not contain myself. She is poison, Mona–simply poison." I was dying to ask Nathan more, but I bit my tongue. We arrived at what I presumed was the building where our class would be held. Nathan opened a heavy brown door which contained a small window at eye height. "After you, my dear." I looked through the doorway and noticed that we were walking onto the landing of a flight of stairs. I walked in and waited for Nathan to come through and direct me where to go next. "Down this way. Follow me," Nathan said, walking down the stairs to the next level. My stomach was filled with butter-flies–part exhilaration, part dread.

After making our way through a series of hallways, doors, and tunnels, we arrived at a classroom with a double door made of solid oak. "I can do this," I told myself, trying to prevent fear from overtaking my bravery. I needed to walk through the door confidently.

"How about I go first?" Nathan asked quietly, with a wink. I smiled back, relieved. He opened the door and I grabbed the handle to hold it open while watching him walk into the lecture hall.

"Here goes nothing," I whispered with as much confidence as I could summon in the moment. I walked into the huge au-ditorium. It had seating for five hundred or more people that stretched to the top of the room. There were already students dotted throughout the theatre-style seating. No one was really paying much attention to the door, thank goodness. They were talking to each other quietly, busy on their phones or laptops, oblivious to our arrival. My nerves settled down and I searched for Nathan, who was a few steps up the stairs to the right of me. I followed him up about seven stairs to a row of seating, where we found two seats in the middle of the row.

I removed my backpack, put it down to the left of me and settled into my seat. I leaned over and pulled out my laptop, trying to awkwardly balance it on the little half desk attached to the chair. "They really need to upgrade these desks," I quietly commented to Nathan as I put away the laptop. I was glad I had brought a clipboard to use for note-taking as well. I glanced at my phone to see what time it was. There were only a few minutes remaining until the class was scheduled to start. I wondered where the professor was. "Do you know who is teaching the class?" I asked Nathan.

"No, they were reworking the schedule when we registered. The professor who usually teaches this class had a family emergency, so they were pulling in someone else," Nathan responded casually, glancing at his watch.

"Good morning," we heard, as our eyes darted toward the door. We looked at each other–stunned–as Margaritta walked into the room, up the front stairs to the front stage and walked authoritatively to a desk where she put down her bag. A wave of panic washed over me. We must be in the wrong class.

"Nathan, are we in the wrong classroom? What is she doing up there?" I whispered urgently as I reached for my bag, preparing to exit as quickly as possible. Nathan frantically pulled out the paper with the details of the class on it, scanning to determine how we ended up in the wrong room.

"Welcome to 'Financial Literacy for our Times.' I will be your professor this term. I am very excited to teach this course. Professor Russell has an unfortunate family situation that he feels must take priority over this course."

"That's it, I'm done. I can't do this, Nathan," I said, preparing to flee.

"Hold on, don't give up yet. There has to be an explanation. Margaritta is an English Literature professor. How can she be assigned to this class?" Nathan responded a bit too loudly at the exact point that a hush came over the classroom.

"Well, well, well, isn't this a coincidence," Margaritta said, laughing as she directed her attention toward Nathan and me. We stared back at her, both of us anxiously awaiting for her to say something humiliating to us. "Mona Lisa Brown, when you said you were taking a course at the university, I did not know you would be gracing one of my classes with your presence," she said, relishing the moment. "Don't look so shocked. My father was an esteemed professor of accounting here at the university for years. I didn't just study English literature. I have also been studying the language of finance for years, and consider myself to be well-versed in the subject, certainly sufficiently enough, to be more than competent to teach this first-year course."

I sat frozen in my seat. What could I do? I was surrounded by hundreds of young students, gobsmacked at the tongue lashing I was taking in the first thirty seconds of the professor walking in the door. "This can't be happening," I thought to myself. Of all the nightmare scenarios I had envisioned, this one had completely escaped my imagination.

I shivered in the air conditioning. I could feel goose bumps form on my arms, but I couldn't look away. I couldn't move. If I ran, I was a coward, fulfilling Margaritta's vision of me and surely sealing the reality that I would never set foot on that campus again. But, how could I stay in the class? I felt Nathan's hand on my arm. I knew he was trying to tell me it was going to be okay, but I was confident in that moment that it was not. This was my shot. Finally, I had set foot on this campus as a student and Margaritta was ruining it. I deserved to be there. I wanted to scream, but I couldn't. Instead, I just stared back at her, motionless.

Finally, she moved on. "Alright, let's get started. We have a lot to cover in this term. I expect you to be well-versed across all areas of this subject by the end of this class. I hear Professor

Russell was a bit of a softie. I assure you, I am nothing of the sort. I will throw you a mountain of material each class and I expect you to absorb and demonstrate competency quickly. If you can't do that, there is the door." Margaritta gestured to the large double wood doors to her right, then looked up directly at me, willing me to leave now.

Nathan leaned over and whispered, "Hang in there, kid. Do not let her get the best of you. Just get through this class. Then we will figure out what the hell is going on. Stay strong. You are doing great. Remember, you belong here, Mona."

I took a deep breath as Margaritta moved into the first part of her lecture. I leaned over and opened my bag to look for the sweater I had tucked into it. I could feel goosebumps raising on my arms, but I resisted shuddering from the cold. "Why do they keep it so cold in here? It must cost a fortune to chill this old building?" I whispered to Nathan, irritated.

"Good thing you brought that sweater. You came prepared. I'm impressed."

"I wasn't prepared for everything," I grumbled, gesturing to the front with my chin.

"Who would have thought? Don't worry, we got this."

I smiled confidently at Nathan, trying to fake the sentiment. There was no way I was going to let Margaritta take my university experience away from me. I belonged there. I looked down at her as she droned on, enjoying the sound of her own voice. As I glared at her, doing nothing to disguise my disgust, the light reflected off of Margaritta's necklace and I realized she was wearing the mysterious locket. "Perhaps Mary-ela was right, maybe I should try calling Sandra myself to find out more about our illustrious professor. The truth may tell a different story. Let's see how she handles the hot seat."

The rest of the class moved relatively quickly. We talked

through the plan for the term, reading list, assignments, and schedule for evaluations. Professor aside, the content of the class was quite intriguing to me. Even the assignments seemed well thought-out. As the class finished, I was flooded with disappointment. I couldn't possibly stay in a class taught by Margaritta. That would be setting myself up for misery. Yet, now that I was in it and had heard the course outline, I was confident that I could do well.

I put my belongings into my backpack hastily, not wanting to remain in this lecture hall any longer than we needed to be there. I looked over at Nathan, hoping my urgency was contagious.

"Don't worry, I have an escape route out of here. Follow me," he said, moving out of the row of seating in the opposite direction, toward the far side of the room. When he reached the end, he turned right and climbed up the stairs to the top of the theatre. I followed close behind him. When we reached the top of the stairs, there was a door, which Nathan pushed open. We continued through it and looked back. We watched the large wood door slowly close, leaving us in the quiet stillness of the vacant hallway.

Getting my bearings, I realized that we were on the second floor. Pausing for a second to take stock of what had just happened, I looked at Nathan, speechless. I wasn't sure whether to scream or laugh at this point. Finally, he broke the silence, "Okay, I'll admit, that was not what I had expected."

"No?" I asked sarcastically in response.

"Let's get out of here. If I recall correctly, the stairs are just down the hall this way," he said as he gestured for me to follow him. We made our way to the stairs, down and out of the building. When we walked outside, I felt the change in temperature. The warm sun on my face was glorious. I stopped to peel off my sweater and stuffed it back into my backpack.

As I lifted my bag to put it over my shoulder, a flood of emotions spilled out: disappointment, frustration, and anger, "Why does she have to be teaching the course we chose? Certainly there are other more qualified instructors than Margaritta to teach a financial literacy course. The worst part is that the course material and assignments actually sound interesting. We can't possibly stay in the class. What are we going to do, Nathan?"

"I'm starving, do you want to stop at Paul's for a sandwich? My treat."

"What?" I sputtered in frustration. "Why are you avoiding what I just said?"

"Come on, let's go get something to eat and we can talk through all of this over lunch."

"No, I am mad now, why aren't you answering me? You saw how that miserable woman treated me. Abusing her authority to cut me down. If only the administration saw how she talks to students."

Nathan looked at me with a stunned expression, but before I could ask him what was going on, I heard a voice from behind me.

"Oh, poor Mona Lisa Brown. I hate to say I told you so, but I did. You just aren't cut out for this institution. I'm sure you can get your money back, if you walk over to the registrar today to withdraw from the class. I would be happy to tell them that I concur with your decision." Margaritta walked a few steps closer to face us both. "As for your assessment of my treatment of students, I only want the best from everyone. Not everyone can cut it here. This establishment is for higher society," she said, looking down her nose at me.

"That is quite enough, Margaritta. Mona, let's go," Nathan said curtly.

I followed Nathan, not even dignifying Margaritta with a last look. The truth is that I was on the edge of tears and I couldn't bear for her to see me break down.

"The registrar's office is on your left, over there. Don't forget to drop in on your walk home," she called back to us. I could hear her laughing as we walked away. It was the sound of someone who had conquered. I held it together until we stepped off campus and turned onto the side street. Then the tears started to roll down my face. I couldn't control them. They just ran like a leaky tap. As fast as I could brush them away with the back of my hand, they kept flowing, which made me even more upset.

Nathan stopped abruptly. I did the same. I looked down, though, avoiding his eyes. I know he could see me crying, but somehow by not looking at him, I could pretend he couldn't. Finally he faced me, and gently grabbed my shoulders, forcing me to meet his gaze. No matter how hard I tried, the tears rolled down my face. My breathing was shallow and I couldn't help the stutter breaths that kept coming out. I just stared at Nathan, defeated.

"Mona, now you listen to me," he said more firmly than I expected. "What just happened back there was evil at its worst. I am so sorry. I should have been clearer that Margaritta was walking toward us. Damn it!" he said, stepping back and punching the air.

"It's fine, Nathan. It isn't your fault. I shouldn't have opened my big mouth. I was spewing my own poison when she walked up to us. I probably deserved what she said. She is right; I don't belong at the university. I should never have signed up for the class," I responded in a soft, raw voice.

Nathan faced me again. Taking a step closer to ensure my full attention, he gave me the most intense look I had ever received from him before. "Mona, now that is the biggest pile of garbage I have ever heard. You are exactly the kind of student Buckley

University needs. That raging cow has no business spewing that nasty rubbish around you. Mona, I implore you to resist believing anything she just said. Lies. That was a steaming load of lies, Mona."

"Thank you, Nathan. You are a sweet friend. It's okay. I will go withdraw from the class and put this all behind me," I replied, in barely a whisper.

"You will not!" he yelled, taking me aback with the passion in his tone.

"What do you mean?" I questioned, totally confused by his words.

"That, my dear, is exactly what she wants you to do."

Still confused, I continued to question him, "What are you suggesting, Nathan–that we stay in the class?" I laughed at the ridiculousness of his idea. "I'm sorry, Nathan. That is just crazy."

"Don't you see? That is exactly what she wants you to do! She wants you out. She wants both of us out. Can you imagine if we stay? It will drive her wild!" he said, clearly relishing this new idea.

Now I was really laughing. "I appreciate you trying to cheer me up, Nathan."

"I'm dead serious here, Mona. You said it yourself; the content of this class is great! Everything looks amazing, except for the instructor."

"But, as we plainly saw today, an instructor can destroy a class, even if the material is fantastic."

"Only if we let her," he said, with inspiring confidence. It was then that I heard Ethyl's voice in my mind, "Take back your power, Mona." A shiver ran down my back. I tried to hide my reaction from Nathan, but the memory of Ethyl's words in that moment left me speechless. Nathan was right, the best way for me to overcome this situation and 'take back my power' was to stay in the class, but to do that seemed insane. I knew Margaritta would continue to torment me, perhaps doubling down because I did not take her advice and withdraw as she had directed. It would be much easier to simply quit now and move on.

We decided to leave the matter unresolved for the moment and walked toward home. Neither of us said anything, both of us digesting all that had happened that morning. We arrived at Paul's Grocery and paused on the sidewalk. "I'm famished. How about you? Can I buy you that sandwich?" Nathan asked with a warm smile.

"That sounds amazing. Can we stay and eat outside here?" I asked, gesturing to the patio.

"I couldn't think of a better place to enjoy lunch. Well, except your front porch–that's a pretty nice place too."

"I lucked out with that spot. You might find me there with a book all afternoon today."

"A splendid idea, my dear! Let's fuel up before your literary adventure on the porch."

We walked into Paul's and headed straight to the deli counter. My stomach started to rumble as I looked at all the options. "I hadn't realized I was hungry until we walked in," I said absently as I stared at the assortment of food behind the glass.

"Food makes everything better, my dear! And great food that much more," he declared with a grin.

We took our giant sandwiches outside and picked the second table to the right of the door. All conversation was suspended as we dove into our food. Finally, we both leaned back in our chairs, basking in the afterglow of delicious food. After a moment, Nathan leaned toward me, focusing his gaze on my face. "Are you feeling better?"

I nodded slowly. "Yes, a little."

"I'm sorry about all this mess with Margaritta, Mona. I really am," he said earnestly. "I thought it would be simple. Sign up for a class. It should have been easy, but it never is as straightforward in reality, I suppose," his voice trailing off at the end of his sentence as his gaze drifted into the parking lot.

"Nathan, none of the bad things that happened today are your fault. You did a great thing. Let's hold onto that. I'll get back to my studies sometime, I promise. It's just not the right time, yet."

Nathan slammed his hand on the heavy metal table with a bang and caused everything to jump, including me. "Damn it Mona, you can't let that self-absorbed holier-than-thou twit dictate your life," he responded, on the edge of rage. He slowed his breathing and then tried again. "I am sorry. She just makes me crazy and what she did today wasn't right. But, to walk away is giving up your dream of attending Buckley University and I fear you won't return. Do you really want to let one person influence your life in such a huge way? In my opinion, she doesn't deserve that much credit."

I don't know if it was the big sandwich, the hot sun, or the adrenaline from the morning finally subsiding, but suddenly I felt exhausted. I had no more words to contribute, so I just stared back at Nathan and gave him a weak smile.

"You are tired, Mona. Let's get you home. It has been a busy morning, to say the least."

We tidied up the table and stood up with our backpacks. As we were tucking our heavy chairs under the table, I spoke up, "I know you want me to make a decision. Let me get some rest and really think about what you are proposing. I will give you an answer before the end of the day."

The next class is in two days. "Tomorrow morning is fine," he said warmly. "Come on, let's get you home."

We made our way home in the warmth of the late summer

sun. Passing by the house next door where Merl and Prince used to live, I pointed, "Hey, look," I said, surprised. "Ethyl and Randy have put the house next door up for rent again."

"Huh, well look at that. Good for them. It will be good to have some more people on the street."

"I wonder who will rent it," I added, my mind swirling with thoughts of another Margaritta . . . or worse.

Nathan and I said our goodbyes at the bottom of the stairs to my apartment. I climbed the stairs, opened the front doors and walked in. The house was quiet. "Everyone must be out right now," I thought. I looked over at the sofa. Prince was curled up at the end, near the window. He briefly lifted his head in acknowledgement, but promptly curled up and went back to sleep. I dropped my backpack, walked to the other end of the sofa and practically fell into it. Noticing my arrival, Prince padded across the sofa and curled up around my legs. His soft fur tickled my bare legs. I smiled and fell fast asleep.

CHAPTER 15

I felt a rough tongue licking my nose and drifted back to consciousness."Meow," I heard, as I opened my eyes and realized the big feline was standing on top of me. My throat was itchy, my eyes tingled and then they began to water. I slowly sat up and looked at the big cat as he stepped off of me, "Meow." It sounded urgent.

"What has gotten into you?" I asked, confused. Then I heard my phone ringing. Trying to remember where I had left my phone, I scanned the room. My eyes landed on the backpack I had dropped in front of the door. I stood up, walked over to the bag and found my ringing phone in the side pocket. "What is so important?" I muttered to myself. I looked for the button to answer the call and noticed the call was coming from the university. "It must to Mary-ela." I answered the call and lifted the phone to my ear.

"Mona, thank goodness, I thought you would never answer! Have you gotten all my messages? I have been trying to reach you."

"I'm sorry, I didn't pick up your voicemail until late last night and then this morning . . ." my voice trailed off, as I started to try to summarize my morning. "This morning, I was tied up with something. I got your message about Sandra. Don't worry, I appreciate your enthusiasm. It's okay. Maybe this is as far as we can go with this story," I said, trying to be reassuring.

"No Mona, it isn't!" she responded emphatically. "This is

why I have been trying to reach you today. Sandra called me this morning. She changed her mind. She wants to talk. I told her about you and the story you are writing. I don't know why, but she changed her mind. Mona, she wants to meet." I sat silently, still trying to wake up, but also comprehend what this meant. "Mona? Are you still there?"

"Sorry–yes, I am here. I needed a second to digest this news."

"Aren't you thrilled, Mona? This could be so good for your story!"

I was hit by a wave of guilt followed by a sick feeling in my stomach. "How could I continue to deceive Mary-ela like this? I should end this right now." My mind wandered to Margaritta and the smug look on her face this morning as she urged me to visit the registrar and I couldn't resist continuing.

"Yes, this is exciting, Mary-ela. Thank you," I replied. "When does Sandra want to talk?"

"She is really eager. She insisted on meeting today."

"Today? Why so soon?"

"I don't know, but if she is willing to talk, I think we better meet before she changes her mind. Don't you agree?"

"Yes, absolutely. What time?"

"She said she would come to the library later this afternoon. We have a private meeting room in the library that we can use."

"Okay, I will get changed and walk over. See you soon. Oh, and thank you Mary-ela.",

"You are welcome. See you soon, Mona!"

I hung up the phone as Prince jumped down from the sofa and walked over to me. "I have to go out again, Mister." He walked over to the door and looked at me insistently. "Of course, you want out. But, yesterday when I let you out, you got yourself into big, big trouble."

"Meow," he responded, not taking no for an answer.

"Fine, but you better stay away from Randy."

I begrudgingly agreed to give him his freedom and searched for a container to carry fresh water out to the bowl on the porch before I left. I placed it at the end of the counter and walked down the hall to change out of my skirt and into leggings, anticipating that the temperature in the library would be as frigid as the lecture hall this morning.

After lecturing Prince on outdoor safety one more time and ensuring he had fresh water and food outside, like a nervous parent, I set him free into the wild. "Seriously, I don't need this kind of stress. Mind you, that cat has better luck in this world than I do," I said to myself as I picked up my backpack and locked the doors. Walking down the stairs, my eyes landed on the peculiar gnome in the garden. He looked back at me with the usual quirky grin. "I bet you grin like that at all the girls, you sly dog–even Margaritta," I said with a chuckle, amusing myself.

"Stay in the class. Don't quit now," a voice whispered as clear as day. I stopped in my tracks and looked back. Nothing had changed, the gnome hadn't moved.

"I am officially losing my mind," I said in a panic. "Now the gnome is talking to me in the garden. Breathe, Mona, breathe," I told myself, trying to get a grip on reality.

Then I heard snickering. My eyes darted around the garden, trying to locate where the laughter was coming from. Finally, not being able to take it any longer, Nathan called down from his balcony, "Sorry Mona, I couldn't help myself."

"Nathan Laine! That was just mean!" I yelled at him. "You should know better than to mess with my mind after the morning I have had!"

Nathan was laughing hysterically now. He finally composed himself as I started to walk toward the street. "Sorry, Mona. I didn't know you would fall for it."

I reached the sidewalk and looked back at him, shaking my head.

"I was just trying to give you a laugh," he called down.

I gave him another look of mock disgust, then waved goodbye. I began to relax as I walked to the university. "I guess I am a little on edge right now," I thought. "This Margaritta business is messing with my mind. Not being honest with Mary-ela isn't helping, either."

My mind drifted to another thought. Why is it so important to everyone else that I stay in this class? I could easily drop by the registrar's office on my way, withdraw from the class and be done with it. Nathan's face flashed through my mind. I had told him I would talk to him first, though. I decided to skip the registrar and walked straight to the library.

I was greeted by a whoosh of cold air as I entered through the double doors of the library. I set my bag down and looked inside for my sweater. Wrapping it tightly around my shoulders again, I lifted my backpack over my right shoulder and walked to the desk to meet Mary-ela.

While I waited for Mary-ela, I looked at the students walking around the library. There was such a buzz at this time of year. A fresh new school year. Everyone was filled with excitement for the promise of what lay ahead for the year; new friends, fresh ideas. I felt envious and sad that I was not one of them. Like an outsider looking in, I watched them come and go, everyone oblivious to my gaze.

Mary-ela's voice pulled me from my thoughts, "Mona, you're here. Thank you for coming. Sandra has already arrived. We are in the private meeting room for staff. Follow me," she said eagerly as she let me into the area behind the counter.

We walked down a hallway lined with several office doors. The fluorescent lighting created an odd yellowy glow in the absence of windows. At the end of the hall to our right was a door. I followed Mary-ela into the conference room. The room was flooded with sunlight from the floor-to-ceiling windows that lined the far wall–a stark comparison to the dimly-lit hallway we had just left. An oval conference table with padded upholstered chairs around it filled most of the room. Directly across from me, sitting at the far side of the table was Sandra, I presumed.

"Mona, this is Sandra Merchante. Sandra, this is Mona. Oh, forgive me, I don't know your last name, Mona," Mary-ela said, looking a little flustered.

"Brown, an easy one to remember. Mona Lisa Brown." I smiled reassuringly at Mary-ela, then walked over to Sandra and shook her hand. I wasn't sure what I had expected Sandra to look like. I hadn't imagined her at all before I arrived, so I was struck by how pretty she was. She had long wavy auburn hair, emerald-green eyes, and a big smile. I think I expected someone a little more homely, perhaps. I don't know. "Why was that?" I wondered.

"Hi, Mona, lovely to meet you," Sandra said.

"Thank you for meeting. We have so many questions for you," I replied while setting down my bag and sliding out one of the heavy chairs near the window. I looked at the empty table and realized we didn't have any beverages or snacks to offer her. "Would you like a coffee or tea? There is a cafe only a short walk across campus," I suggested.

"It's okay," she said kindly. "I can only stay for a little while. I understand from Mary-ela that you are writing a story about Margaritta."

I looked down and fidgeted with my hands for a moment, caught in my lie. Another chance to own up to the truth, to set the record straight. "I . . . yes, that is right. I am writing a story about Professor Merchante," I responded, losing my nerve.

Sandra looked at Mary-ela, "I am sorry I reacted the way I did when you first called. To be honest, I panicked," she said with a look of concern on her face. "Let me back up and start from the beginning." Mary-Ela and I smiled at Sandra trying to make her feel comfortable while we both leaned in, eager to hear her story.

"I met my husband Peter in high school. His parents, William and Linda, are fantastic. William was a professor here at the university. They are everything all the articles written about them describe; generous, compassionate, giving people. Margaritta is several years older than Peter. When I first met her, she introduced herself as Peter's sister. We really didn't interact with her very much. She and Peter weren't close as siblings. I dismissed this as simply due to the difference in age. I knew she was a star, though, attending the university, working on her Ph.D.

"Then one day, Peter told me the truth, that Margaritta was really his cousin, not his sister. I was surprised and confused. I wanted to know more, but he quickly changed the subject and would not say any more about it. He seemed really bothered by the whole thing. I imagined a tragedy that had left Margaritta orphaned and William and Linda taking her into their home. I felt sadness and compassion for her, left alone in the world.

"This was until I met Beth," Sandra added with a harsh shift in her tone. "Peter's Uncle Barry, William's brother, passed away. His funeral was attended by many people as he was a well-known businessman. At the reception after the service, there were so many people milling about. It was too much for me. I didn't know anyone, so I left the family to talk to everyone else and found a quiet corner to sit. While I was enjoying a plate of delicious little sandwiches, a woman approached me and in the most soft-spoken voice, asked if I would mind if she joined me. I of course said yes. I was happy to have someone to talk to at the table.

"She introduced herself as Beth or 'Alyssa-Beth', my husband Peter's aunt, a younger sister to William and Uncle Barry. She was lovely, so warm and kind. She had a wicked sense of humor, too. She told me stories about people in the room and had me in stitches all afternoon. I think we ate half the table of little sandwiches ourselves. Everyone else was too busy gabbing to eat anything." Sandra paused and looked at the far wall wistfully, then continued her story.

"I enjoyed Beth's company so much that after the funeral, I stayed in touch with her. It started with tea here and there and then became a weekly event. One day, she really opened up. She told me that Margaritta was actually her daughter. I was shocked, but I didn't want to react for fear that she would stop talking. I was so confused. How had no one mentioned this before?

"Beth explained that she had given birth to Margaritta at a very young age and had raised her daughter on her own. They were very poor, but Beth was proud and would not take any handouts from anyone. She worked hard and did everything to ensure Margaritta had a better life. Scrimping on anything for herself, she spent every extra penny she had on Margaritta.

"Despite this, Margaritta resented her circumstances. She always envied the life of her aunt and uncle, longing for the prestige associated with being the daughter of a tenured Professor. Finally, being so enamored with the family, when she was in high school she left and moved in with them in Buckley Brook. She adopted William and Linda as parents who only wanted the best for their niece. Beth tried to get Margaritta to come back, but eventually, heart-broken, she gave up and let her go.

"I had noticed that Beth always wore a little gold locket around her neck. That day she opened it to show me inside, a picture of Margaritta as a child on one side and Beth on the other. They both looked so happy. On the back the inscription said, 'Always yours.' Beth told me that she saved the money to buy the locket for almost a year. It was a gift for Margaritta's thirteenth birthday.

"The day Margaritta moved away, Beth found the locket on the kitchen table. A cold farewell message. Beth told me that she sat at that table and cried until the middle of the night when there were no tears left to cry."

Sandra paused, her eyes filled with tears. I quickly leaned down to search my bag for a tissue to give to her. As I was searching, Mary-ela located a box of tissues on the small table in the corner of the room.

"Thank you," Sandra said gratefully, her voice breaking. "I'm sorry. All these years and I am still filled with sorrow at the memory of that day and what Margaritta did to her mother. It was disgusting and tragic at the same time. How could a daughter do that?" As Mary-ela consoled Sandra, I looked down at the table shaking my head. My hatred toward Margaritta was turning into rage.

Sandra took a deep breath and continued. "Beth told me so many stories about Margaritta growing up. She was so proud of her."

"I don't understand why her aunt and uncle adopted her, though. They must have realized how this would have hurt Beth. Why didn't they encourage Margaritta to return home to her mother?" I asked, confused.

"I am sure they did, but as you must know, Margaritta is very strong-willed. They knew Beth's circumstances and that they were in a position to help Margaritta achieve the life that Beth was trying to give her. Perhaps they thought taking her in as their own would help everyone," Sandra answered.

"Can you tell us about the birth certificate?" I asked tentatively.

"Yes, that," she responded, looking uncomfortable. "After Alyssa-Beth passed away, I was so sad. She had become a close friend. It was like there was a hole in my heart. I volunteered to clean out her house before the landlord rented it out again. I saw it as my last act of friendship toward Beth and thought that maybe it would bring me some level of closure.

"When I sorted through Beth's papers, I found the birth certificate. Margaritta had gone to great lengths to hide her origins, but somehow she had forgotten this last detail. My grief turned into seething contempt for a woman who selfishly abandoned her mother for her own gain. All I wanted in that moment was to get back at Margaritta. I had brought a portable scanner with me to organize any paperwork that needed to be kept. I scanned Margaritta's birth certificate with her real mother's name on it and posted it on my website, intending to expose her for what she really was. I never did anything more with it, though. I decided to forget it and just move on. I forgot about the scanned image until you called me. I didn't realize anyone would ever find it."

We sat in silence, staring at the table until I found the courage to ask a question. "Margaritta has the locket now. I saw her wearing it," I said, thinking back to the class that morning. "How did Margaritta get the locket?"

Sandra sighed, now looking tired and forlorn, "Beth left it to her in her will. Her last attempt to give it to Margaritta, I suppose."

"What a sad story," Mary-ela whispered, her eyes brimming with tears as she reached for a tissue.

"What are you going to do with this information?" Sandra asked in a serious tone, looking squarely at me.

Here was my chance. I needed to be honest with them both. I thought for a second, but all I managed to say in response was, "I don't know."

"I hope you can keep the birth certificate out of whatever you plan to do. It wasn't my finest moment," Sandra said awkwardly.

"Yes, of course. I will keep the birth certificate quiet," I assured Sandra.

"I appreciate that," Sandra said, looking relieved.

"Did you remove the image from your website?" I asked

"Yes, as soon as I found out it was public, I took it down." Sandra checked her watch. "I better get going."

"Thank you for coming to talk to us," I said, as we stood up and gathered our belongings from the room.

"You are welcome. I hope my story helped you in some way. As sad as Beth's story is, I do enjoy remembering my friendship with her. She was a lovely woman and I adored her. Thank you for giving me the opportunity to talk about her today."

We straightened up the room before walking back down the small, dimly lit hallway to the main foyer of the library. I fell in behind and listened to Mary-ela talk enthusiastically about working at the library. My mind was still caught up in the details of what Sandra had just told us. I thought about my own mother. I couldn't imagine wanting anything so much that I would have cast her aside. How does anyone do that without being tormented by guilt? The image of Margaritta's smug face came into my mind and I felt rage again. "I hope she is wracked by guilt," I thought to myself. Just as I began envisioning Margaritta afflicted in a variety of random ways, we arrived back at the library desk and I was pulled back to reality.

"Thank you again for meeting with us, Sandra," Mary-ela said as she opened the little half door for us to walk into the lobby.

Sandra smiled back at us, "It was a pleasure to meet you both." Then she looked at me nervously, "Please do let me know what you end up deciding to do with the story, just so I am prepared."

"Yes, I will. I have some thinking to do in light of what you have shared today," I responded, aware I was bending the truth at that moment. A sharp pang hit the back of my left eye. I knew full well that this was exactly the kind of dirt I had set out to discover in the first place.

We waved goodbye to Sandra and watched her walk across the library. "Wow, our research really led us to quite a story," Mary-ela said, turning to look at me. "Up until meeting with Sandra, I was caught up in the process of chasing down the facts. I didn't stop to think about the human impact. As Sandra was talking, I finally made that connection. I feel so . . . so sad right now."

I reached out and touched Mary-ela's arm. "You are quite the researcher. I'm sorry. I dragged you into this thing."

Mary-ela smiled. "It's not your fault. You didn't know what we would find." I felt another sharp jolt of pain in my eye. How was I to admit to Mary-ela now that I set out from the beginning to find information to damage Margaritta's reputation? I couldn't tell her this. Instead, I continued to play along and nodded in agreement at Mary-ela's comment. "I guess our research work is done now," she continued.

"I guess you are right," I agreed, processing the realization for the first time. We were done. "You have done an amazing job, even if what was uncovered is a little unsettling. Thank you for helping me."

"That's what I am here for; librarian at your service," she said, enthusiastically clicking her heels and giving me a little salute.

We said our farewells, both of us laughing as we parted company. I walked toward the exit and fell back into a daze, as my mind churned. I made my way through the big doorway of the library and walked outside. The wave of fresh warm air revived me a bit. I stopped to adjust my backpack to prepare for the walk home, thoughts of the day swirling around in my mind. Has all this really happened in one day–the morning class, the interaction afterward with Margaritta–the meeting at the library with Mary-ela and Sandra?

I walked absentmindedly toward home, filled with emotion from the events of the day. I was deeply disappointed about Margaritta being the professor of the class Nathan and I signed up for and that the only logical option was to drop out of it. I was still feeling hurt by Margaritta's words after the class that morning, even though I shouldn't have been surprised by her pompous arrogance. On top of that, I was shocked and disgusted by her story. How could she be revered in the academic world with this in her past? "I would love to see Margaritta squirm in front of her colleagues, exposed by this truth." As I relished this thought, a grin crossed my face. I walked in this daydream for a few minutes, feeling confident and strong. As I enjoyed thoughts of knocking Margaritta off her pedestal, I was careful to ignore any about the side effects of exposing her truth. The image of Sandra's face crossed my mind and I pushed it away urgently.

"Hey Mona, wait up," I heard from behind me.

I turned around to see Max jogging towards me. I stopped to wait for him.

"I was calling your name, but you didn't hear me," he said with a big smile. "You look lost in thought," he said, bouncing over to me with excitement.

"Yeah, it's been a bit of a day," I sighed in response.

"How did the class go?" he asked earnestly.

Not wanting to ruin his good mood, I deflected the question. "I should be asking you that! How did your first lecture go this morning?"

"Amazing! I was so nervous when I started, but I told myself, this is just like all your other classes, but with a few more people. Then I fell into my usual rhythm and I was on a roll."

Happy for the distraction, I listened to Max chatter about his class until we reached the front of the house. There was pure joy in his voice as he described the details of his experience. He clearly loved to teach and was doing it for the love of helping others learn. As we stood at the bottom of my stairs talking, I found myself envious. If only I could have landed in the class of a professor with the same outlook as Max. "I wonder what Margaritta's intentions are. Power and control, I suppose. Definitely different from Max's."

Perhaps noticing my mind wandering, Max stopped. "Hey, you didn't answer my question earlier. How was your first class?"

Feeling tired and drained now that I was steps away from my front door, I tried to deflect the question again. "Uh, a bit different than what I expected," I said, stepping onto the first step up to my door.

"Oh, I'm sorry. Well, maybe it will get better next class. Is that Wednesday?"

"Yes, perhaps you are right," I responded with a thin smile, trying to end the conversation with optimism.

"Thanks for walking partway home with me. Have a great evening, Mona."

"Thanks, Max. I really am happy that your class went well. I knew it would."

Max waved goodbye and bounced around the side of the house, still on a high. As I continued to climb the stairs up to my door, my legs felt as heavy as lead. Even with the afternoon nap, I was totally exhausted. I looked down at the bowls of food and water I had set out for Prince and noticed that he had been working at them. "Well, that's good. At least he isn't starving or stalking food in the forest. I think the only thing he is stalking these days is Randy." This thought brought a smile to my face as I imagined the big cat hiding in the garden watching Randy, waiting for just the right moment to show up.

I turned to my right and saw my cozy spot on the deck. In only a few short weeks, it would be too cold to lounge on the porch. I looked at my watch, "I should eat something. Dinner on the porch while I still can," I thought. "Maybe I could finally decide to drop out of the class." I set my bag down by the chair nearest to the door. As I stood up, and looked out to admire the late summer flowers in the garden, I saw Ethyl walking toward me. She was in running shoes and comfortable attire. In the absence of her usual leather bag slung over her shoulder or any shopping bags, I assumed she had been out for some exercise.

"Hi Ethyl. Were you out for a walk?"

"Hello, Mona. Yes, Randy and I had a very early dinner. He fell asleep on the sofa and I just couldn't waste the rest of this gorgeous day sitting around. I put on my walking shoes and hit the road. I do love a good walk. It is so invigorating!"

I couldn't help but smile at Ethyl. Despite my tired state, her energy was contagious. "Would you like to stay for a cup of tea?"

"Why, thank you. That would be perfect."

"Make yourself comfortable up here, I will be right back," I said, as I walked over to unlock the doors.

After boiling the water, I returned with two cups of mint tea. Walking out to the porch, I noticed Prince had cozied up to Ethyl on the swing. "How do you always know just when to show up,

Mister?"

"Meow."

Ethyl and I laughed. "Sometimes, I think this big guy understands us," I said, setting the tea down on the table. I dropped into my cozy spot, closing my eyes and letting out a huge sigh at the same time. "Ah, this is good," I said, still with my eyes closed. "Have I told you how much I love this porch, Ethyl?" I added, finally opening my eyes and looking at her with a smile.

"You know, Randy and I debated living in this front unit. There is something special about it. We like the privacy and the yard at the back, though. It made more sense for us to choose the back, but I agree, there is something alluring about this front porch."

I re-adjusted to lean forward and pick up my tea. As I carefully crossed my legs and settled back into my nest, I held the tea in both hands and enjoyed the warmth.

Ethyl leaned forward to pick up her mug. I saw her eyes fall onto my backpack. "I forgot to ask how your class went this morning," she said casually, as she took a sip of her tea.

I couldn't help but groan in response.

"That good?"

Shaking my head and trying not to unload on Ethyl, I paused to pick my words carefully. "It isn't a matter of the course outline. That looks amazing, actually." I paused, searching for the words. "Let's just say, it is more an issue with who is teaching the course that has me concerned. Actually, to be honest, I don't think I will be continuing with it."

"What? How bad can this professor be? Who is it?"

"She lives above me," I responded, gazing upwards.

"What? I thought you were taking a finance course?"

"I am."

"Margaritta is a professor of English literature. How can she instruct a financial literacy course?" Ethyl said, scrunching her face in confusion.

"Apparently she has also studied this subject area, enough to teach a first-year course anyway. Her father was a professor of accounting, don't you know, or so she touted to the class today."

"Did she notice you in the class?"

"Within seconds–and she wasted no time making me feel insignificant and not worthy to be in the class. She kept that going after class, too, when she ran into us as we were leaving campus."

A disappointed look passed across Ethyl's face, but she didn't say anything. She turned and looked at Prince curled up beside her and smoothed his fur a few times before looking back at me to respond. "Well, this new detail complicates your plan a bit, doesn't it?"

"That is an understatement. I think I am done. I will do as Margaritta suggested and go to the registrar to withdraw tomorrow."

"Really? Just like that?"

"Yes."

"Well, that certainly would be the easy path, wouldn't it?"

Shocked and angry at Ethyl's statement, I looked at her, confused. "How does she think dropping out of the class would be easy?"

"What are you thinking? I can see it all over your face. Go on, say it out loud."

"Why would you say withdrawing is easy for me? It is humiliating. Margaritta is going to lord this over me every chance she gets."

"Why give her that opportunity, then?"

"What other option do I have?"

"You seem to be enthusiastic about every detail, except the

professor. Have you considered continuing with your original plan and sticking with this class?"

"You sound like Nathan. That's what he is suggesting."

"What does that path look like?"

"For starters, Margaritta would have the opportunity to torment me, probably give me bad marks on my tests and assignments. She could kill my academic record before it gets started."

"Would she, though? As a tenured professor, the university holds her to high professional standards. You can only take personal agendas so far within those boundaries."

I gave Ethyl a look of disbelief. "Where there is a will, there is a way, Ethyl."

"What do you want to do, then?

"Admit defeat and move on," I said flippantly.

Ethyl locked eyes with me and gave me a really serious look, "What do you really want to do, Mona?"

I paused and pictured Margaritta's smug face. "Honestly, I want to make her feel as small as she made me feel today."

"Uh huh."

Caught up in the moment, I continued on, verbalizing my inside thoughts, "I want to banish her from my life, humiliate her like she has done to so many students. I want the truth to be known, to expose her for what she really is, a fake and a fraud." I spoke with such venom that the last words caught in my throat.

"Finally, real honesty," Ethyl said calmly.

I looked back at her, shocked at what had just come out of my mouth.

"Tell me, Mona, how do you feel right now?"

"What?" I sputtered, confused and fiercely determined to resist this line of questioning.

"I'm serious. Right now, how do you feel?" Ethyl asked smoothly again.

I took a large gulp of my tea that somehow had gone cold in my hands and looked down at my mug. Without lifting my eyes, I thought about Ethyl's question.

"Okay, so answer me this: do you feel good right now?"

"Well, it feels great to imagine taking her down," I said, smiling.

"But, now that you have said it out loud?"

I took a breath and let out a long sigh. "No, I feel terrible. Damn it! My head is pounding, I have a stabbing pain behind my left eye and my muscles ache everywhere. I feel terrible Ethyl. Why? All I am trying to do is take back my power like you suggested," I responded in defeat.

Ethyl laughed softly. "Taking back your power doesn't mean destroying difficult people. It means learning how to coexist with them."

"Even when they are imposters?"

"You mean Margaritta? Of course she is an imposter, just like you, right?"

My blood boiled at this comment. "I thought Ethyl was on my side. Why was she saying these things?"

"Mona, how did you feel walking onto that campus this morning?"

The reality of Ethyl's comment struck me. I finally whispered, "Like an imposter."

"Just like all of us, dear. Most of us feel like imposters in some setting of our lives."

"But, Margaritta is really an imposter," I stressed.

"I know."

"You know?" I whispered, shocked, looking back at her with wide eyes.

"Mona, there isn't much I don't know around here," she said coyly, giving me a wink.

I digested her comment silently for a few moments.

"There is a dark part of Margaritta's past that she has to live with every day. Why do you need to add to that burden to ease your own?" Ethyl said matter-of-factly, her tone not matching the gravity of her words.

I . . . I'm not sure how to answer that," I answered quietly.

Ethyl smiled warmly. "Do you mind if I share my observations of the situation with you?"

"Please do."

"I wonder if on some level you are seeing yourself as less than Margaritta or perhaps you think that she sees herself as better than you. If this is the case, the idea of knocking Margaritta down with the information you have discovered would be really appealing. Then you would finally gain the upper hand, a position of power over her, like you feel she has over you right now."

I sucked in a breath sharply as I registered what Ethyl had said. As much as my mind wanted to resist and deny what she said was true, Ethyl was right.

"Mona," Ethyl said gently, reaching out to touch the back of my hand. Her fingers were warm and gentle. Something about her touch brought tears to my eyes. I fought them back, blinking hard, but they wouldn't subside. Finally they spilled over and ran down my cheeks in large drops that fell onto the porch floor.

"It's okay, Mona."

"I am sorry," I said, pulling my hand away, to urgently wipe away the tears.

"Am I wrong?" Ethyl asked gently.

I sighed heavily. "No," I paused, thinking about the situation. "I'm tired of feeling like this, Ethyl. Why can't I figure out how to be happy? Actually, I would be happy just feeling content."

"Peaceful?"

"Yes! I just want some peace."

"It would be easy to expose Margaritta," Ethyl said matter-of-factly. My thoughts of revenge sparked up again and washed over me. I finally had found something big that could level the playing field between us. If only it didn't make me feel so horrible.

"Will knocking Margaritta down find you peace?"

My memory flashed back to the scene on the driveway after Randy found Margaritta's locket. The sincere expression of gratitude on Margaritta's face was unmistakably genuine. I didn't know it then, but that expression–it was relief combined with I'm not sure, maybe grief, perhaps regret. For a brief moment, Margaritta had revealed a secret part of herself. It would be easy to exploit that vulnerability for my own benefit. "Why does this have to be so hard?" I finally asked out loud.

"Doing the right thing is rarely easy."

"So, what do you think I should do?"

"That, my dear, needs to be your decision," Ethyl said, carefully shifting Prince over on the swing. "Now, I better go check on Randy and leave you to think." With this, she slowly stood up to prevent rocking the swing and throwing the big cat off. He barely noticed his swing companion leaving, though. He stretched right out onto his back and filled most of the swing.

I shook my head at him as I stood up to say farewell to Ethyl. I leaned on the railing running along the front of the porch as Ethyl descended the stairs to the garden path. "Think about what we talked about. The right decision will come to you, Mona," she said, stopping to face me at the bottom of the stairs.

"How will I know if it is the right decision?"

"This is going to sound crazy to you now, but the right decision will feel liberating."

I gave Ethyl a confused look. "Liberating?"

"Just trust me on this one. At some point, you'll know what I mean."

"Okay, I trust you," I said, laughing skeptically. "Tell Randy hello and that I hope he is behaving himself."

"I will," she said, calling over her shoulder.

I walked back to the sitting area and picked up the two mugs. "Okay, sleepy cat. Let's move your lounge act inside." The cat didn't even flinch at this comment, so I tried a different approach, "Are you hungry? Want some chow?" Still spread-eagled on his back across the swing, Prince's eyes flew open and he turned his head to look at me. "Come on, buddy, food time." With this, he flipped over and sprang to his feet, jumped down and ran to the door. I followed him and opened the door for us both.

After I took care of the big guy and he was munching away, I washed up the mugs and grazed on a few things in the kitchen. It wasn't the healthiest way to eat, but I was still lost in thought. Standing at the counter mindlessly crunching on a cluster of grapes, I stared out the front window into the garden. Evening was quickly settling in everywhere. I saw the streetlights reluctantly blink on and a warm glow illuminated the sidewalk.

As I crunched away, my mind replayed snippets of my conversation with Ethyl. Then my mind turned to Nathan, whom I knew would come knocking tomorrow looking for a decision about the class. I paused my crunching for a moment and considered remaining in the class. "How would Margaritta react to that? Ethyl might be right. Whatever beef Margaritta has with me, there are certain standards she must uphold. I can't believe I am even considering this," I muttered, as I pulled together cheese and crackers to add to the bundle of grapes.

I munched away some more, still staring out the large window into the dimly-lit yard at the front of the house. The sharp taste of the cheddar cheese took my mind to another part of my conversation with Ethyl that I hadn't properly processed before.

"She knows," I whispered out loud. "Ethyl acted so nonchalant. How does the truth about Margaritta not bother her?"

"Meow," I heard from beside me on the floor. I looked down at the big feline.

"What?" I responded in surprise, "Don't tell me you knew, too?"

"Meow." He looked over his shoulder as he walked out of the kitchen, across the room and into the hallway toward the bedrooms.

"I never get a straight answer out of you," I called out to him. I stopped as another idea passed through my mind. "I wonder if Nathan knows, too?" I asked myself. "There is no way he knows. He would have exposed Margaritta by now, for sure." The stabbing pain shot through the back of my left eye again and the crackers and cheese began to sour in my stomach. I closed my sore eye, leaned on the end of the counter with my right arm as I lifted my left arm up in the air, trying to ease the pain in my stomach with a gentle stretch.

Involuntarily, I yawned loudly. "Perhaps the big cat has the right idea. Sleep sounds like a great idea." I staggered down the hall, realizing how utterly exhausted I felt. "Maybe I will wake up tomorrow and everything will be magically sorted out," I whispered optimistically to myself, not believing my words for a second.

CHAPTER 16

I woke up with a start. My heart was racing. My body was covered in a cold sweat. I looked around, trying to get my bearings. "What time is it?" When I turned over and looked at the bright red number on the clock beside my bed, it read 12:34. "Seriously? I have barely been asleep." I listened carefully, trying to figure out what woke me up. The house was totally silent. I must have had a nightmare. I searched my memory to remember what I was dreaming about, but I couldn't recall any memories at all other than a general feeling of uneasiness. I had that same feeling when I fell asleep, though.

I got up and changed into fresh pajamas. I stared with envy at the big cat sleeping like a baby on the sofa. Now wide awake, I looked back at my bed and decided to forgo tossing and turning and trying to get back to sleep. I quietly tiptoed out of the room and down to the kitchen.

I turned the kettle on, found some chamomile tea bags and put one in a mug. The kettle clicked off and I filled my mug full of water. Looking across the room, I noticed my backpack sitting on the floor. I walked over and dragged my bag to the sofa, carefully setting my tea on the side table. I sat down on the sofa and opened up the backpack, putting the textbook and course outline we had received in class on the cushion beside me.

I flipped through the textbook and before I even realized it, I had been reading for almost 45 minutes. I scanned a few more sections of the book; the content was so fascinating. Not the late-night reading I needed right right now to get me back to sleep, though. I set the book down and read the paper course outline again. My mind was flooded with ideas for the research paper. I got lost for a moment daydreaming about being a student at the university. Then I remembered my new friends, Nathan and Max, Ethyl and Randy, and my wonderful apartment.

As I let my mind wander, I didn't notice Prince walk across the room until he jumped up on the sofa and onto my lap. "How could I forget you? Allergies and all, I am so thankful we found each other, big guy." While I petted Prince's fluffy fur coat and tried to ignore the prickling in my nose, I was flooded with joy as I continued to think about all the great things I had found in Buckley Brook.

If it were not for the miserable professor upstairs, I would be so energized right now. The spark of anger was ignited in me again. "It's not fair. How do people like Margaritta get such power? How does no one see how horrible she is to her students?" These questions circled around in my mind as I fell deeper and deeper into a space of despair, mixed with fury. Now I was wide awake, despite the time.

I shivered, the temperature noticeably cooler in the house at this hour. Picking up my mug, I carried it into the kitchen to make a fresh cup of tea. Walking back with the steaming cup, I heard a noise above me and I stopped mid-stride. The house was incredibly quiet at this hour, so any noise cut sharply through the stillness. I listened intently. "What was that sound?" It was directly above me. It must be Margaritta, I realized, making the connection. I continued to listen. The sound was faint, but unmistakable. It was the sound of someone crying.

Frozen in place, I wished I had not heard the sound and could take myself back to the moment before when I was filled with visceral hate for the woman. But in that moment, the only thing

I could feel was sympathy for someone in such deep sorrow. I lowered myself down onto the sofa. "How dare she evoke sympathy in me!" I took a big sip of my tea and slopped it all over myself. "Damn it," I yelled at the mess the tea had made as I did my best to mop it up with napkins I dug out from the bottom of my bag. "It was much easier to hate her when I wasn't listening to her cry," I continued. A lump formed in my throat at these words. I took another sip of tea, more carefully this time, but it did nothing to clear my throat. "What is wrong with me?"

I shivered again. Even the warm beverage did nothing to take the chill away. "I need to sleep," I thought, remembering that Nathan was sure to be at my door at the crack of dawn asking for my decision about the course.

"What is my decision?" I asked out loud, realizing I still didn't know what to do. I reflected on my conversation with Ethyl. "Do I take the 'easy path,' walk away from this situation, the class and possibly the university forever? Do I escape from all of this?"

"I can't let Margaritta dominate my thoughts like this any more. That is clear." "This situation with Margaritta is overshadowing all the good things I have found in Buckley Brook. It is making me miserable. I don't want to be miserable anymore," I whispered. "I have to make a choice."

I stood up, swallowed the last of my tea and set the mug on the counter top. "How do I find peace in all of this muck?" Something in that moment reminded me of Nathan trying to help me cook. The memory made me smile as I spun around and faced the sofa. With one hand on my hip and the other behind my head, I struck my best pose for Prince who stared back at me, confused. I giggled back at him. "Yes, it's true, I am officially losing my mind, kitty cat."

"Meow."

"Well, I am glad you concur, big boy." I sighed, putting both hands on my hips. "I love it in Buckley Brook. I have to find a way to be happy. The misery ends tonight. Somehow, I must figure out how to be content with everything in this place."

I yawned, sleep finally coming my way again. I turned and walked back to bed, Prince at my heels. I dropped into bed, the large cat following me. I was too tired to shoo him off to another spot. With the furry guy tucked up close to my feet, I fell into a heavy slumber.

CHAPTER 17

The next morning, I opened my eyes and stretched out. Despite being awake in the middle of the night, I felt as if I had slept well. I looked at the clock and saw that it was eight thirty. I must have managed to get some solid sleep after I finally went back to bed. I sat up and looked for Prince, but he was nowhere to be found. Then I heard the toilet flush and rolled my eyes. "Found him. Too bad he can't make the morning coffee, too," I said to myself.

I stood up and stretched again, then walked to the kitchen to put on a pot of coffee, making extra in anticipation of Nathan's arrival. While the coffee was brewing, I got dressed and ready for the day after peeking outside the window to check the weather. I could see that it was another bright and sunny day.

Like clockwork, as I was pouring my first cup of coffee, there was a knock on the door. I bounced over and opened the doors to see Nathan's smiling face. "Good morning! You are right on time. The coffee just finished brewing," I said, greeting him with a huge smile.

"What has gotten into you this morning?" he responded, giving me a suspicious smile, holding the storm door open to talk to me as I bounced back into the kitchen to pour a second cup of coffee.

"Find a spot on the porch. I'll bring the coffee and tell you all about it," I replied, giving him an uncharacteristic wink.

Nathan's smile widened, and he shook his head as he stepped

back outside, the door slowly closing after him.

I stood at the counter, closed my eyes and took a deep breath, searching for more confidence than I felt. I opened my eyes, picked up a mug of coffee in each hand and walked confidently across the room toward the door. I pulled down the latch of the storm door with my elbow and pushed the door open with my shoulder.

"So, what has you in such a good mood today, Mona?" Nathan asked, as I walked across the porch deck and placed a mug of hot coffee on the table in front of him.

I smiled as I immersed myself into my cozy spot, pulling my legs into a cross-legged position. "Before you ask, I want to tell you that I have decided to stay in the class with you," I blurted out. The words hung in the air. I felt terrified and excited at the same time. How was that possible?

"Really?" Nathan exclaimed, looking stunned. "Honestly Mona, I had prepared myself to hear the opposite this morning. You were so upset yesterday when we parted. Rightfully so, but I did not think there was a chance you would change your mind. What happened?"

"Ethyl stopped by after her walk yesterday evening. Our conversation led me to do a lot of thinking. Ultimately, Ethyl said that I have two choices, take the easy route and drop out or be brave, face my fears, and figure out how to coexist with Margaritta."

"Ethyl is quite something."

"That she is," I confirmed with a subtle nod of my head as I recalled about all the wise words of advice she had shared with me since I had moved to Buckley Brook.

"Dare I ask how you are going to 'coexist' with Margaritta?"

"I'm not exactly sure of the details yet. To be honest, that is the part that scares me the most. Ethyl talked about figuring out how to see myself as equal to Margaritta; to neutralize her power over me, if I understood her correctly."

"How do you plan to do that?"

"I have watched Ethyl with Margaritta. To be successful at this, I have to be . . ." I paused to reflect. "I think I have to be kind to Margaritta."

"What? How can you do that when she is so miserable to you?"

"But that is the thing, I don't want to be miserable. No matter how Margaritta or anyone else chooses to be, I am not going to let her or anyone get me down any longer."

"Mona, I am delighted that you have found this place. I know it has not been easy for you."

"Don't give me too much credit yet. It's still just an idea. Talking about it with you here is one thing. Putting it into practice will be another step. I know I will stumble along the way."

"And when you do, your friends will be here to help you back on your feet. That's what friends are for, right?"

I was overwhelmed by Nathan's comment. My eyes started to cloud again as tears welled up in them. I wiped them away with my hand before they could fall. "Thank you, Nathan. You are a good friend," I whispered, as I sniffled back the tears.

"You are a great person, Mona. I hope you know that."

"Thank you for believing in me." His words had touched me, and my voice wavered.

We sipped our coffees in silence for a moment, both looking out to the garden. An idea came to my mind. I wanted to ask Nathan whether he also knew about Margaritta's past, but something was telling me to let it be. It wasn't my story to dig at anymore.

"Oh, look who's back together again?" I heard Nathan say, pulling me out of my introspection.

I looked across the garden to the sidewalk to see Max and Tish walking arm in arm, sharing something amusing together. My first instinct was to say something nasty to Nathan to knock Tish down a notch, but I stopped myself. "Not mine to own. No matter what opinion Nathan and I have of how Tish treats Max, it's his life to lead."

"Mona? Are you still here?" Nathan asked.

"Yes, I'm still here," I responded with a smile.

"No snappy Tish comments today? You must have one?"

"Today, I am just admiring two people in love."

Nathan smiled as he looked back at Max and Tish on the street. Max noticed us on the porch and waved with a big grin on his face.

"Love is a funny thing. I will never understand how some people will endure so much for it," Nathan added.

"We might never understand why Max stays with Tish. Do you need to know to be his friend?"

"Nope," Nathan said matter-of-factly. "Do you?"

"No, I don't," I responded, shaking my head.

We sat in peaceful silence and smiled at the two lovebirds on the street as we witnessed them sharing a sweet moment together. I closed my eyes and took a deep breath. As I slowly let it out, I realized that at that moment everything seemed right. I wondered, "Is this what Ethyl meant about feeling liberated?" My eyes wandered into the garden for a moment, landing on the old garden gnome who stared back at me with his silly grin. As my eyes moved away, I was sure I saw him wink at me. "Clearly, my mind is taking this liberation thing to new heights, or Nathan is playing another trick on me." I pulled myself back into reality. "Nathan, how about another coffee, my friend?"

"I thought you would never ask!"

I unravelled myself and stood up. Grabbing the two mugs,

I headed back into the kitchen. "Two coffees coming right up."

"Don't forget to show that kitchen who's boss!"

"You can count on it!" I called back to Nathan over my shoulder as I struck a pose and strutted across the floor toward the kitchen.

CHAPTER 18

The next morning, Nathan and I arrived at the lecture hall a few minutes before the start of our second class. Nathan paused with his hand on the large brown door and looked at me. "Are you sure you are ready for this?"

I nodded and smiled back at him, "No, but I have to try."

About half the class had arrived by the time we took our seats. We chose two seats together farther down the same row, off to the far side of the theatre. Nathan and I bantered about the textbook as we got settled. It seemed we were both keeners and had read ahead.

The lecture hall was nearly full when Margaritta opened the door and strode in. I watched as she laid out the materials for her lecture and tried to shoo away all my evil ideas. "Breathe, Mona. Try to see her as an equal," I told myself. "Can I really do this?" I wondered doubtfully. "I have to do this," I thought, continuing to watch Margaritta. I noticed she wore the locket around her neck. "Oh, the story that locket could tell, if it could speak."

Margaritta finished getting ready and started the lecture, greeting the class with a big smile. "Good morning and welcome back! I see that I didn't scare you away after my first class." There was a light chuckle across the room. Margaritta scanned to her left and locked eyes with me. "My, isn't it Mona Lisa Brown," she said, rolling the "r" in my last name in the most obnoxious manner. "You are a tough one to scare away, I see," she said, in her syrupy sweet tone. "I will have to work harder today." She laughed at her own joke, but I caught the underlying message.

"I read your fabulous course outline and I just couldn't resist staying!" I responded in the biggest, bounciest voice I could muster, exuding far more confidence than I felt.

Margaritta looked back at me, stunned, visibly unsure of what to make of my demeanor. She gave me a sideways glance and dug deeper, testing me, "Tell me, what was it that caught your eye in the course outline?"

"It is the full exploration of the topic of financial literacy from both the personal and commercial perspective that appeals to me the most. It appears that we will be exploring finances holistically—income sources, expenses, and risk management, as well as nuances related to the field of financial services and insurance. I like that we will have a lot of freedom to choose our topic of focus for our research paper, too. I have already started thinking about my topic."

Margaritta looked back at me, gobsmacked. Silence fell over the classroom as she searched for the right response. Finally, she settled on something. "My, you have thoroughly reviewed the material. I am impressed," she conceded with a smile and walked to the other side of the room to continue the lecture.

Nathan looked at me with wide eyes and whispered, "Where did that come from?"

I shrugged with a smile and gave him a wink.

The class flew by and before we knew it, the lecture was over for the day. Nathan and I packed up our things and walked down to the front of the room to leave. We passed by Margaritta as she was packing up her belongings. I paused to face her and stated, "Great lecture today, Professor Merchante."

She looked up from the desk and locked eyes with me. Hesitating, she answered back, "Uh, thank you."

"That's a really pretty necklace you are wearing, too."

She put her hand to her chest over the necklace and took a breath. "Thank you, Mona. I got it from someone . . . someone special," she whispered, a thin sad smile crossing her lips.

"Enjoy the rest of your day," I added and waved as we walked out of the lecture hall through the same doors we had entered.

We walked through the heavy wood doors and made our way down the stairs back to street level, then outside into the fresh air. Nathan stopped outside and looked at me shocked, finally breaking the silence between us. "Okay, what the hell just happened in there?" he asked emphatically.

"I don't know," I responded sheepishly. "I tried a new approach. Do you think it went okay?" I asked.

Nathan shook his head, "I think you were a star, Mona. You never cease to surprise me, my dear."

"Thanks, Nathan. After a lot of turmoil, I have come to understand what Ethyl has been trying to tell me for some time. People are who they are. Some change over time, but most don't. The only thing we have control over is ourselves. To keep going with the class and go back today, I needed to change how I view Margaritta. I tried to respond to her from that place. When you boil it down, though, all I did was try to be nice to her."

"You are underselling what you just did in there. I could never have done that."

"Oh, sure you could have. Once I got my mind around it, the change was remarkably easy to make. I'm not saying she won't try my patience in the future or that other people like her won't do the same. For now, it's one day at a time, right?"

Nathan shook his head in agreement while his face continued to convey disbelief. "Do you mind if we stop at the library before we walk home?" he asked, shifting topics.

"Okay, as long as we can stop at the cafe, too! I have a craving for something delicious."

"I can't argue with those terms."

We walked over to the library and through the heavy glass doors. "Which floor do you need to go to?" I asked.

"I think the third."

"I need to visit the front desk for a minute. Do you want to meet back here when you are done?"

"Sounds good. I will only be a minute."

I walked across the lobby and made my way to the information desk to see if Mary-ela was working. As I got closer to the desk, I saw her organizing something on the counter along the back wall.

"Hi Mary-ela," I said enthusiastically.

She turned around to see who was calling her name and greeted me with a big smile. "Well, hello, Mona. It is so nice to see you. How are you doing?"

"I am well, thank you. I started a course this week. A finance course. I think I will need to visit you for help when I start my research paper."

"Oh, please do! We make such a good team," she said. "So, what did you decide to do with the findings from our last research project?" she asked, tentatively.

"After a lot of thinking, I have decided to let the story remain untold."

She gave me a warm smile and a nod of approval. "I am so glad this is your decision. The whole thing really got to me. It is just so sad. I think Sandra will be happy with your decision. She and I really hit it off. We have exchanged emails a few times since we met. Do you want me to call her to tell her the news?"

"Only if you don't mind."

"Of course I don't mind. I would be happy to share this news with her."

"Thank you Mary-ela, for everything. I will see you in a few weeks for some research tips for my paper."

She gave me an excited grin, "I look forward to it!" I waved goodbye and walked across the lobby, realizing that I felt good. No, not good, I felt settled with my decision to keep Margaritta's story quiet.

I spotted Nathan stepping off the elevator with a few books in his arms and walked toward him. I took a closer look at the books Nathan was holding and realized they were finance books.

"Don't tell me you are already starting on your research paper? I better step up my game!"

Nathan smiled sheepishly, "I have a topic idea that has piqued my interest. I thought I would check these out early to see if I can make this topic work. If it doesn't, I will still have a lot of time to change it."

"Makes sense. Do you need to check those out? Let's walk over to the scanning machines."

We finished up at the library and walked over to the cafe. While we walked home, I enjoyed a homemade apple fritter. As I was consuming a huge piece of the large fritter, Nathan's voice broke me out of my food daydream.

"I was thinking . . ." he started.

"About how amazing this warm apple fritter is? Because that's what I am thinking about right now."

"I wasn't thinking about fritters, although my thought was food-related," he responded, laughing.

"Good, tell me more," I said as I tossed another piece of fritter in my mouth.

"I was thinking, we should host a barbecue together. You have the beautiful front porch overlooking the garden. If you can host, I will look after the main course items."

"Okay, I can make some salads though, too."

"Oh yes, it will give you another opportunity to show that kitchen who's boss."

I smiled at Nathan and asked, "When should we have this barbecue?"

"I think we should do it within the next few weeks to take advantage of the nice weather that is still hanging around."

We were talking about dates when we arrived in front of the house.

"What happened to the 'for lease' sign?" Nathan said, pausing on the sidewalk to stare at the house next door.

"That is strange. Ethyl couldn't have rented it that fast, could she?"

"I don't know. It is a nice house on a great street. Someone might have snapped it up quickly."

This was when we noticed Randy walking around the side of the house next door, balancing a long ladder on his right shoulder.

"Uh oh, that looks like trouble for sure," Nathan said as he started walking with purpose along the sidewalk toward the house next door. I fell in step behind him. As we got closer to the house, Nathan called out, "Hey, Randy, what are you up to with that ladder? Do you need some help?"

"You two seem to show up everytime I have this ladder out."

"If I recall correctly, it was a good thing we showed up last time you had that ladder out, you old fool," Nathan said, teasing Randy.

"Where did you come from, anyway?" Randy asked, quickly changing the subject.

"We just happened to be walking along the sidewalk coming home from the university," I said casually. "What happened to the 'for lease' sign? Did you rent the house already?"

"Would you believe it? Some guy from the city called us up and offered to buy this old thing from us. Ethyl told him to make us an offer and when we heard the price he was willing to pay, we couldn't resist. I'm just out here doing a few last repairs to this place."

"You aren't thinking of going up that ladder, are you?" Nathan inquired with concern.

"I darn well am going up this ladder," Randy responded, clearly offended by our interest in his safety.

"What do you need to do on the ladder, Randy?" I asked with a softer tone than Nathan.

"One of the windows on the second floor is stuck closed. I can't get it open from the inside. I need to take a look at it from out here to see what the problem is."

"How about I go up the ladder while you look at it from the inside. We should be able to hear each other through the glass to communicate. Mona can hold the ladder steady at the bottom," Nathan suggested. I tried to hide the relief I felt at being chosen to hold the ladder on the ground.

"You two are as transparent as they come! I can see what you are doing. You don't think I can handle going up that ladder, do you?"

"No, I think you are plenty capable. I just know how Ethyl feels about it, so I thought I might help you out," Nathan countered slyly, giving me a big smile as Randy put the ladder down in place and considered our offer.

We stood in silence for a few moments, both of us hoping he would agree. Finally Randy nodded in approval, "Well, you might have a point. Even though I am entirely stable at the top of this ladder, Ethyl is not a fan and I would not want to upset her. It could avoid an unpleasant conversation if we follow your plan."

"Excellent!" Nathan responded, both of us showing our joy and relief as Randy finally agreed to our plan. "Can you give us about fifteen minutes to put our bags away? I need to change into some clothes more suitable for climbing ladders."

"Okay, I will do some other jobs while I wait."

"Ground-level jobs, I hope," Nathan said, looking suspiciously at Randy.

"Yes, yes, go, you have my word, ground-level."

We cut through the side of the property back to the front of our house and stopped at the bottom of the stairs. "Should we put a wager on whether he stays on the ground while we are gone?" I asked quietly.

"He will. He is a man of his word and I think I put some fear into him with that reminder of what Ethyl would do if she catches him back up on that ladder after last time."

"Okay, meet you over there in ten to fifteen minutes, then?" I asked, chuckling at the idea of Ethyl catching Randy back on the ladder.

"Deal."

CHAPTER 19

The next few weeks seemed to fly by between attending classes, starting the research for my paper with Mary-ela's and Nathan's guidance, and planning for our barbecue. Despite Margaritta's best attempts to rattle me, I managed to stay on a level footing with her.

The morning of our barbecue, I was on the front porch cleaning and preparing seating for everyone, with Prince lounging on the swing. As I was doing this, I watched a large moving truck reverse into the driveway next door. Curious, I stopped and watched the movers jump out to begin unloading. I saw Randy, followed by Ethyl, come out of the house to greet them as a white SUV also pulled into the driveway.

A man who looked to be somewhere between thirty and forty got out of the driver's seat. He had dark hair and was wearing jeans and a golf shirt. He walked over and shook Ethyl and Randy's hands and then the back door of the SUV opened and out came a little boy who looked like a miniature version of the man. He was wearing a red cape and holding a stuffed animal in his arms. He ran over to the man and gave his right leg a huge bear hug.

Ethyl pointed over toward where I was standing, so I quickly pretended to be sweeping the deck and not staring at them. Then the man got back into his SUV and backed out of the driveway onto the road. As I watched the SUV creep down the road toward our driveway, I heard a voice from the garden, "Spying on the new neighbors?" I looked over to see Nathan smiling up at me.

"Perhaps. Are you doing the same?"

"I heard the beep of the moving truck backing in. I walked out onto my deck to see what was going on, but I couldn't see through the trees. Thought I would assist you down here and get a better view at the same time."

"I saw a little boy about six or seven years old. I think it is a family moving in."

"Very nice, this street could use some kids to liven it up."

"Well, don't just stand there, come help so you look like you have a reason to be here when they walk around the corner."

Nathan walked up the stairs and I gave him the broom. I picked up the glass cleaner and paper towels and started cleaning the tables. We heard voices coming from the parking area. "I wonder how many people are moving in," I asked Nathan.

"Zoom zoom!" we heard, as the little boy emerged in front of the porch, running along the path. He ran past us through the garden path, holding his cape with one hand to make it look like he was flying as he held his stuffed animal in the other. After a few laps, he stopped in front of the stairs and looked up at us right at the same time as the man caught up to his lead.

"Let's be polite. This is someone's house. We need to be respectful," the man said, looking embarrassed.

"Not to worry at all," Nathan responded, leaning on the porch railing with one arm as he held the broom in place with the other.

"I'm Nathan. What is your name?" he asked, looking at the little boy with a big smile.

"I'm Spencer. We are moving in next door. This is my dog. His name is dog. He isn't real, though. I want a real dog, but my parents said no. Dogs are certainly too much work. We used to live in the city, but now we are going to move here. But sometimes I still have to go to the city because we left my Mom there in her shoebox. It's not really a shoebox. She lives in a condo, but my Grandma said it is like a shoebox and anyone who chooses a big job in the city over their family has got to be a f . . ."

"That's quite enough, Spencer," the man interrupted, looking at his son. "Do you mind if he runs through the garden? He has a lot of energy to burn after the drive," he asked sheepishly.

"Not at all," I added, walking to the top of the stairs to join the conversation. Prince jumped off the swing across the porch and stopped to sit beside me, also joining the group.

"Whoa, that's a big kitty," Spencer said, with wide eyes. "I've never seen a kitty that big before."

"His name is Prince. He used to live in the house you are moving into over there. He lives with me right now."

"Very nice to meet you, Prince," Spencer said, using a serious tone to address the cat.

"Meow."

"He talks," Spencer said, amazed.

"Yes, he is a very good listener, too. If you ever need someone to talk to, just come over here. But, ask your Dad first, of course," I quickly added, imagining the adventurous boy disappearing on his poor father.

"I'm sorry, I didn't introduce myself. My name is Jack."

"Great to meet you, Jack, I'm Mona; this is my apartment here."

"And I am Nathan. I live upstairs."

"Look, Grandma is here!" Spencer said excitedly, pointing at the driveway next door.

"Without missing a beat, Spencer ran between the houses to greet his Grandmother.

"Wait, Spence!" Jack yelled. "Sorry, I better go tell my mother that she can park over here to give the movers room in the driveway. "That was so kind of Ethyl and Randy. Are they really as nice as they seem?"

"Yes, they really are," Nathan and I answered in unison, which prompted us all to laugh.

"We are having a barbecue tonight. We would love for all of you to join us. You can meet your other neighbors," Nathan offered.

Jack hesitated. "I am not sure the kitchen will be in any shape today for me to cook anything to bring over."

"Don't worry about that!" I responded quickly. "Nathan is cooking! There will be plenty of food. Please just come. Everyone will arrive between five thirty and six."

"Okay, that would be really nice. Thank you. I better catch up with Spencer and make sure his energy doesn't get him into trouble. Nice to meet you, Nathan and Mona. I will see you this evening," he said, walking across the path in front of the porch toward the property next door.

After he was out of earshot, Nathan started in, "Well, well, well, Mona," he said coyly.

"What?" I asked, playing dumb.

"Could he be your type?"

My face turned hot bright red, "Nathan!"

"Just saying, you know. Sounds like he's available, from what Spencer said." We both laughed at Spencer's oversharing, ignoring what sounded like sad circumstances.

"I don't know, life feels right at this time. Adding a relationship could mess things up."

"Or make life more exciting."

"Perhaps."

Nathan looked at his watch. "Oh, I need to get the sauce ready for the meat. You need to prepare yourself for this meal. In fact, you better go warn Jack. This might be the most fantastic thing you have eaten, ever."

I shook my head, "I think there is something to the element of surprise."

"Shock and awe! That is good. I like it. Until later, my dear."

"Until later."

CHAPTER 20

Nathan arrived at my door shortly before five thirty with the most heavenly-smelling food. He was holding a large, deep circular dish tightly covered with layers of tinfoil, so I couldn't peek to see what he had created. "If this tastes as good as it smells, we are truly in for a treat," I offered, hoping he would reveal his creation to me.

Nathan smiled. "Top secret until it hits your plate! If you put your oven on its lowest setting, this dish will stay warm and will be perfect to serve in about an hour."

I diligently complied and lifted the big dish into the oven. I had managed to pull together three different salads without setting anything on fire, so I was feeling quite pleased with myself. I casually looked across the room and saw Prince sleeping on the sofa. I beamed at the creature that had brought me such joy, admiring how serene he looked in his slumber, then it hit me like a cold water balloon in the face, "Nathan! Prince!" I pointed frantically like a mad woman.

Nathan looked at me, confused. "What?"

"I have to hide Prince before Randy arrives and sees him in here!" I exclaimed in total panic.

"Oh! Prince!" Nathan responded, his eyes as big as saucers as he caught up to my train of thought.

"Go, take him into the other room. I will finish up here. Don't worry."

I quickly ran over to Prince and tried to cajole him into getting off his warm sofa, but it was to no avail. "Prince!" I said urgently to the big cat, "Randy is coming! If he sees you in here, there is going to be trouble. I need you to move to the other room. Please, Please!" I pleaded.

Finally, he stood up slowly, stretched his legs, looked at me nonchalantly and jumped off the sofa. I watched him pad slowly across the room and down the hall. I followed him down the hall, urging him to move faster until he turned the corner into my room and settled onto my pillow.

"Seriously, my pillow? You know I have allergies!" I said in dismay, with my hands on my hips.

"Meow."

"Fine, you win this time. Please stay here. I will leave the door open in case you need the, err . . . the washroom. Am I seriously having this conversation with a cat?!"

"Meow."

I walked back down the hall, relieved to have sorted that problem out, I hoped.

Nathan gave me a thumbs-up from the kitchen. "All set in here, Mona. Do you think he will stay put?"

"One never knows with that big guy, but I can say I tried," I answered, throwing my hands up in the air in exasperation.

We left the kitchen and walked outside to make the final touches to the seating before our friends and neighbors arrived. Randy had brought over some extra chairs earlier and we put them down in two groups on the path in front of the porch on either side of the stairs. All the food would be set up inside on the front counter in my kitchen, buffet style. We decided that this was the easiest way, given our expanded group.

First to arrive were Jack, his mother and Spencer from next door. We watched the trio walk across the lawn toward us. Jack was holding Spencer's hand and his mother was carrying a tray of some sort. As they got closer to us, I could clearly see the family resemblance.

Spencer noticed us on the porch and waved., "Miss Mona, Mr. Nathan, I'm here!" he called to us. He pulled free from Jack's hand and broke into a run until he reached the bottom of the stairs. Jack and his mother closed the gap and smiled up at us.

"Hi, Mona and Nathan. I would like you to meet my mother, Roberta," Jack said, in a rich, warm voice. Roberta had smooth straight, thick silver hair just brushing her shoulders. Her ice-blue eyes were piercing against her beautiful skin. It looked like she had never spent any time in the sun.

"I would shake your hands, but they are busy right now," she said with a coy smile.

Nathan didn't miss a beat and floated down the stairs toward Roberta, "I can take that for you, Roberta."

"Hey, you weren't supposed to bring anything," I said, mock-scolding Jack.

"Where I come from, we don't come to a party empty-hand-ed," Roberta said, with charm to spare.

"It is just a cheese tray. Nothing fancy," Jack added. "We discovered the grocery around the corner. It is something else."

"We love it. Best grocery in town and it's steps from our door. You have to try their deli sandwiches!" I said eagerly to them.

"Roberta, I can see where Jack and Spencer get their good looks from," Nathan said boldly.

"Who is this smooth-talker, Mona? I might have to visit your porch more often. You are good for an old gal's ego, Nathan."

"Nathan is good for every girl's ego!" I assured her. "Are you here to help Jack and Spencer move in and get settled, Roberta?" I asked.

"Actually, I have decided to sell my house and move in, too. It has been so lonely the last few years, living in my house by myself. I think it will be good for all of us."

Jack smiled warmly at his mother. Wrapping his arm around her shoulder, he gave her a hug. I was touched by the affection between mother and son. I felt a pang of sadness, longing for the same companionship.

"Wonderful," Nathan responded, a new spring in his step. "Welcome to the neighborhood! I will put this lovely cheese tray in the kitchen with all the food." Nathan was all smiles as he turned to go in the house with the cheese tray.

"May I get you something to drink?" I asked, trying not to giggle at Nathan.

I took everyone's drink requests and followed Nathan into the house. "Aren't you a smooth talker," I said, teasing Nathan in the kitchen.

"What?"

"Oh, don't you play dumb with me. I saw your reaction when you heard Roberta say that she is also moving in next door." Nathan gave me an innocent look. He was saved by another voice at the door, interrupting me as I attempted to give him a hard time.

"Hello, Mona! We are here," Tish called to us in her sing-song voice.

"Welcome!" Nathan said, giving me a quick wink before he walked toward the door to greet Tish and Max. "Oh my, what have you brought?" Nathan exclaimed.

"I made it myself," Tish admitted nervously. "I hope it is okay."

I walked over to the group and noticed what Tish was holding. I couldn't help but gape, my mouth hanging wide open. "Tish, that is the most beautiful creation I have ever seen!" I uttered in astonishment. Sitting on the crystal platter in Tish's hands was a tall layer cake covered in tiny little leaves in fall colors. It must have taken hours just to decorate.

"You like it, Mona?" Tish asked, still unsure.

"Tish, I knew you were an artist, but I haven't seen any of your creations. It is too pretty to eat!" I responded earnestly.

"Thank you. I had fun with this one. The cake is banana cream. There are five layers."

"Amazing!" Nathan said. "Well, I won't hesitate to dive into your dessert! My mouth is watering already."

Tish giggled and Max grinned at her. I carefully took the tray from Tish and brought it into the kitchen to store her beautiful creation in the fridge until we were ready for dessert. I slowly closed the fridge door to admire her culinary work of art for a moment longer.

The group moved outside with their drinks and I was left in the kitchen until Ethyl poked her head in the door. "Hi, how are you doing? What a great day for a party! Thank you for organizing this. It worked out so well with Jack, Roberta, and Spencer moving in today. I am glad you invited them to join us."

On the counter, Ethyl placed a fresh loaf of bread, a large basket of dinner rolls, and what looked like whipped butter with bits of chives in it. I presumed Randy was outside talking to everyone.

As I set out all the cutlery and plates, Ethyl whispered to me in a concerned tone, "Where is our friend?"

"Safely stowed away in my room, on my pillow, no less. It was a fair trade, I suppose."

Ethyl gave me a relieved look. Before she could say anything more, we heard Margaritta's distinctive voice from the doorway.

"Mona Lisa Brown," she announced. I bristled. "Sorry I am late, I was grading the quiz from last class. Tsk, tsk, tsk," she said.

My stomach clenched, my mouth went dry. "Stop, resist, don't fall for the trap. She is just trying to get a rise out of you, Mona." I put my hands on the back counter, drew myself up tall and turned on my heel to face Margaritta with a giant smile on my face. I looked down at the tray Margaritta was holding and exclaimed, "Deviled eggs! I love deviled eggs! Did you make them yourself?"

"Of course I made them myself," she said defensively. "What? Do you think that I can't cook?" I fought the urge to utter the myriad of smart replies running through my mind, none of which would have been fruitful in that moment.

"Not at all," I offered in response, laying it on thick. "A woman like yourself with so many talents, I would expect nothing less than homemade deviled eggs!" I continued, doubling down on my gushing.

A huge grin crossed Margaritta's face, "Why, thank you, Mona," she said, sounding mildly modest in tone.

"Do you want a peek at Tish's masterpiece?" I asked Margaritta and Ethyl.

They nodded conspiratorially. I looked to see if the coast was clear, for dramatic effect, then waved them over to the fridge and opened it so they could see the cake.

"Wow, she really is talented," Ethyl whispered in astonishment.

"Stunning," Margaritta added. "How can we eat that?"

"That's what I said!" I responded enthusiastically.

After a bit more chit-chat, Margaritta decided to go outside to tell Tish what a fantastic job she had done on the cake.

Ethyl turned and gave me a scrutinizing look. "What just happened there?" she said, suspiciously.

"Ugh, that was exhausting," I said, mock collapsing on the

counter.

"Oh stop, you handled that marvelously, Mona. I am so impressed."

"After a lot of thinking, I took your advice. When she gets under my skin, even when she irritates me, rather than following my instinct to push her down, I try to see Margaritta as an equal. I try to find a common ground and be kind, but let me tell you, today that was hard! Sheesh!"

Ethyl chuckled. "It was fantastic to watch. You found all the right things to say to neutralize her barbs. Every one of them. Well done."

"Thank you."

"Don't thank me. That was all you, today."

"No, I am serious, thank you. Your counsel has changed everything. Well, not everything. That sounds like I am exaggerating. I really mean it, my life is different because of our conversations, no exaggeration. Thank you."

Ethyl gave me a warm smile and said with sincerity, "I am happy to help, anytime."

Out of the corner of my eye, I noticed the time on the microwave, "Looks like it is time to eat." I surveyed the food laid out along the counter. Reaching for some oven mitts, I announced to Ethyl, "I will get Nathan's creation from the oven. He has promised this will be sensational."

I carefully lifted it from the oven and set the warm dish on the cutting board sitting on the counter. Peeling the tinfoil back from the top, I could see what he had made. My mouth watered and I was struck by the most amazing aroma of pulled pork. "I cannot wait to taste this!"

Ethyl moved the large basket of dinner rolls and a pair of tongs next to Nathan's creation. "Here, these go with the pork dish."

"Seriously! You knew what he was making?"

Ethyl smiled knowingly and giggled.

"Okay, let's go tell everyone that we are ready to eat!"

It was a bit of a production shuffling everyone through the kitchen to fill their plates, but we finally managed to get everyone settled in a place to eat outside. After dinner, everyone sat and basked in the afterglow of the delicious meal. While there was a lull in the conversation, Spencer asked in a huge voice that everyone could hear, "Miss Mona, where is your big kitty today?"

I tried to hide the look of horror, but despite my efforts, it crept onto my face. This was a disaster. Randy caught me looking desperately at Ethyl. Then he looked back and forth from Ethyl to me suspiciously. "I knew it! You two have been in cahoots the whole time!"

Not wanting to cause a scene in front of our new friends and neighbors, Ethyl touched Randy on the arm, "Now, now, dear, the poor cat had to live somewhere. Don't forget, you are his legal guardian. If it wasn't for Mona, the big guy would have moved in with us," she explained, giving me a wink.

With this comment, Randy stopped protesting, and grumbled incoherently for a few seconds until the subject changed.

"Well, since the secret is out, I might as well let the big guy out of hiding." I walked into the house and down the hall to my bedroom. When I looked into the room, Prince jumped down and walked over to greet me. I bent down, ruffled his fur and scratched him behind the ears. I held his soft face with both of my hands and told him the good news, "Okay big guy, our secret is out. But go easy on Randy. He is just getting used to the idea of you living in his house."

With a meow, he slid between the outside of my leg and the door jamb, then bolted to the front door.

I walked down the hall and opened the storm door to let him out.

"Kitty!" I heard Spencer call out as he ran up the stairs to greet Prince, who was surprisingly good-natured about the gregarious greeting.

"Be gentle," Jack said firmly to Spencer. "If you sit on the step and let him come to you, maybe he will let you pet him." Jack looked at me quickly, "Is that okay? Do you mind?"

I smiled back, "He is his own cat. Put your hand out and let him decide if he would like you to pet him."

Luckily, Prince accommodated Spencer's enthusiasm. I walked down into the garden and stood beside Jack. We smiled as we watched the interaction between the two. Then we both noticed a vehicle pull into Jack's driveway next door.

"Do you mind watching Spence for a few minutes? I need to go next door. I have a surprise for him," he said excitedly.

"Of course. He is in good hands here."

"I'll only be a few minutes. Be right back," he replied, already walking toward the house next door.

Curious, I watched as a woman exited the vehicle. Jack gave her a big hug, at which I felt my stomach knot with disappointment. "Get it together, Mona." I chastised myself and turned my focus to Spencer and Prince. I walked up the stairs and took a seat on the top step on the other side of the large feline.

Prince had settled onto the step and was purring now, as Spencer petted his fur gently. He was surprisingly gentle for his age. I smiled at the fickle feline who looked to be enjoying the extra attention.

Suddenly, I heard Jack yelling from across the lawn. "Wait, wait, Buddy!"

We looked up and saw the fluffiest white dog galloping toward us. His leash was trailing behind him as he ran. His tongue was flopping to the side of his mouth which looked like it was turned up into a smile.

Spencer jumped up with a screech of joy, "Puppy! It's a puppy!" This alerted Prince, who jumped up and sought higher ground. He ran along the porch behind us and leapt up onto the back railing for safety.

As Jack finally caught up, Spencer ran down to greet the fluffy dog at the bottom of the stairs. The puppy climbed onto Spencer and and licked his face.

"I am so sorry we crashed your party," Jack said, winded– picking up the leash and wrapping it around his hand. "I don't know what happened. I thought I had a firm grip on the leash. This guy is strong."

"What's his name?" Spencer asked Jack.

Jack bent down onto one knee, "His name is Buddy. My friend helps to find new homes for dogs who need them. She knew how much you wanted a dog and that we were moving to a new house with a big yard, so she called and asked me if he could live with us. Spencer, can you help take care of Buddy?"

Spencer gave his Dad an emphatic nod, and then gave the dog a bear hug. Happy tears came to my eyes. Feeling foolish, I tried to quickly wipe them away. Ethyl stepped closer, put her arm around my shoulder and I leaned my head against hers.

"Meow," we heard from behind us. I turned and looked back at Prince, who had tiptoed closer to us along the porch railing. I reached up behind me and ruffled his fur.

"It's okay. He is fluffy like you. He looks like a big teddy bear," I whispered to Prince.

"Maybe the fluffy puppy and the big kitty can play together," Spencer suggested innocently.

We each made a skeptical face as we looked at him. "Sometimes animals take a bit of time to get to know each other," Jack said to Spencer, as he stood up.

"There is a little man in your garden, Miss Ethyl," Spencer said, changing the subject matter-of-factly like only a child can do. "He is giving me a funny look," he continued, scrunching up his face as he stared back at the garden gnome.

"Oh yes," Ethyl replied warmly. "Some say he has magical powers."

I listened more intently as Ethyl continued.

"Really? What kind of magic?" Spencer asked, looking skeptical.

"Whatever kind of magic you need when you see him. If you catch him at just the right time, he might give you a little wink."

My stomach clenched. "Maybe it wasn't all in my head after all. How could it be real, though? Come on, Mona."

Ethyl turned to me and gave me a knowing smile. I couldn't tell if she was pulling Spencer's leg or sending me a message.

Spencer's eyes opened wide and he looked at the gnome suspiciously. "I don't know. He looks a little silly."

Ethyl laughed. "How about we take a closer look together?"

I turned and watched the two walk up to the garden gnome and grinned. The sun had disappeared behind the trees, leaving us in the glow of early evening. I smiled as I looked across the garden, watching everyone as they enjoyed each other's company. Prince held his position on the railing, still pondering the new furry addition to the neighborhood. At this moment, I was flooded with warmth and gratitude to have found such a fantastic place to call home.

Surrounded by friends, human and furry, who cared about

me like family, I was learning from them how to live life in new ways: with courage and kindness. This life in Buckley Brook was certainly extraordinary. Maybe this was ordinary for many people, but for me, what I had found was beyond anything I could have imagined.

As for the magic of the little gnome in the garden, I never did get a straight answer from Ethyl. It's simply one of the many things that makes life in Buckley Brook truly extraordinary.

Thank you for reading **The Peacemaker's Patch**!

Amazon reviews are incredibly helpful to me as an author. To **leave a review**, follow the QR code below or search for the book title on Amazon.

Please **share this book** with a friend or family member. Thank you for your support!

Acknowledgements

Dave, my Muse, thank you for more than 20 years of joy, laughter, frustration, and brilliance. You are a remarkable human being; my ally and supporter. Thank you for seeing the world in different ways than I do. I am better for it.

Xavier, when I embarked on this adventure, I couldn't have imagined the role you would play. Our little chats about characters and events over the year it took to write this book were not only helpful to the process, they made it fun. Thank you for your insight, feedback and encouragement. You have so many gifts; I can't wait to see what you do with them next!

David, your resilience and determination inspire me every day. Keep challenging the world, landing on your feet, and don't ever lose that smile. You have a bright future!

Catherine, thank you for keeping me on track with our weekly chats, especially in the dark winter days of the second COVID-19 lockdown. Your feedback and our discussions helped keep me going until the end.

Gloria, thank you for diving in with your careful attention to detail during the editing process and finding things none of us noticed. Your watchful feedback helped move this novel into its final form. Dad and Gloria, thank you for sharing your advice and experience in navigating the world of business. I have and will continue to draw heavily on this knowledge as a self-publisher.

Louise, your gentle, kind, and astute approach to the editing process transformed the first draft into something stronger. Thank you for shepherding the creation of the final product. Your knowledge allows little fish like me to play in the big pond of publishing. I am so grateful to you.

Jill, I am amazed at how you brought the text to life with your gorgeous painting used in the cover artwork. Thank you for diving into this adventure with us and helping to shape the final product.

And to my wonderful Mother, thank you for exposing us to the arts and for fostering an environment for our creativity to blossom. You have taught me to be bold and courageous. Your sage advice I carry always–There are no mistakes, only design elements.

About the author

Shauna lives in Kitchener, Ontario (Canada) with her husband and their two boys who each supply abundant amounts of inspiration and encouragement for Shauna's creative pursuits. Fascinated by the dynamics of human relationships, Shauna's writing draws from life experiences wearing many hats–Wife, Mother, Daughter, Business Leader, Landlord, Home Renovator, Minor Hockey enthusiast, and lover of the Arts. Shauna has always enjoyed writing. The pandemic lockdowns provided space to finally create her first work of fiction. A bright spot in a time of adversity.